LYN HAMILTON

THE MAGYAR VENUS

AN · ARCHAEOLOGICAL · MYSTERY

BERKLEY
PRIME
CRIME

$6.99 U.S.
$9.99 CAN

11/26/019 2nd Good
A Little sad @ end.

ISBN 0-425-20154-6

9 780425 201541

5 0 6 9 9 >

S EAN

Praise for Lyn Hamilton's Archaeological Mysteries

THE MAGYAR VENUS: A suspicious suicide and a twenty-five-thousand-year-old artifact draw Lara to the fascinating city of Budapest . . .

"Lyn Hamilton's archaeological mysteries follow a formula sure to have armchair travelers on the edge of their settees."

—*The New York Times Book Review*

THE THAI AMULET: Broken terracotta amulets lead Lara on a search for a missing antiques dealer in Bangkok—where the sights and sounds cloud her judgment . . .

"A fascinating addition to the series."   —*Library Journal*

THE ETRUSCAN CHIMERA: An ancient mythical creature rears three of its ugly heads in the form of deception, dishonor, and murderous greed . . .

"A journey that is as every bit as magical as the elusive chimera."

—*The New York Times Book Review*

THE AFRICAN QUEST: The sea and shopping take a backseat to murder when Lara leads a tour group to Tunisia . . .

"The exotic world of Northern Africa comes vividly alive."

—*Midwest Book Review*

THE CELTIC RIDDLE: Lara joins a wealthy Irishman's heirs in a quest to solve a riddle leading to a mysterious treasure, but the price of success could be *death* . . .

"The well-drawn characters' foray through Irish countryside and Celtic myth will delight readers."   —*Library Journal*

Basis for *Murder She Wrote: The Celtic Riddle* starring Angela Lansbury on CBS

continued . . .

THE
MAGYAR VENUS

LYN HAMILTON

BERKLEY PRIME CRIME, NEW YORK

THE BERKLEY PUBLISHING GROUP
Published by the Penguin Group
Penguin Group (USA) Inc.
375 Hudson Street, New York, New York 10014, USA
Penguin Group (Canada), 10 Alcorn Avenue, Toronto, Ontario M4V 3B2, Canada
(a division of Pearson Penguin Canada Inc.)
Penguin Books Ltd., 80 Strand, London WC2R 0RL, England
Penguin Group Ireland, 25 St. Stephen's Green, Dublin 2, Ireland (a division of Penguin Books Ltd.)
Penguin Group (Australia), 250 Camberwell Road, Camberwell, Victoria 3124, Australia
(a division of Pearson Australia Group Pty. Ltd.)
Penguin Books India Pvt. Ltd., 11 Community Centre, Panchsheel Park, New Delhi—110 017, India
Penguin Group (NZ), Cnr. Airborne and Rosedale Roads, Albany, Auckland 1310, New Zealand
(a division of Pearson New Zealand Ltd.)
Penguin Books (South Africa) (Pty.) Ltd., 24 Sturdee Avenue, Rosebank, Johannesburg 2196,
South Africa

Penguin Books Ltd., Registered Offices: 80 Strand, London WC2R 0RL, England

This is a work of fiction. Names, characters, places, and incidents either are the product of the author's
imagination or are used fictitiously, and any resemblance to actual persons, living or dead, business
establishments, events, or locales is entirely coincidental.

THE MAGYAR VENUS

A Berkley Prime Crime Book / published by arrangement with the author

PRINTING HISTORY
Berkley Prime Crime hardcover edition / April 2004
Berkley Prime Crime mass-market edition / March 2005

Berkley Prime Crime Books are published by The Berkley Publishing Group,
a division of Penguin Group (USA) Inc.,
375 Hudson Street, New York, New York 10014.
The name BERKLEY PRIME CRIME and the BERKLEY PRIME CRIME design
are trademarks belonging to Penguin Group (USA) Inc.

PRINTED IN THE UNITED STATES OF AMERICA

10 9 8 7 6 5 4 3 2 1

For Cher and Michael

ACKNOWLEDGMENTS

As always, many people helped me with this book, including Bella Pomer, Natalee Rosenstein, and my favorite critic, my sister, Cheryl. I am particularly indebted to Agota Gabor Cunningham who took me along on her recent visit to Hungary. Agi not only shared stories of her experiences growing up in Hungary, and of her flight from the country in 1956, but she even allowed me to use some of them.

PROLOGUE

March 3, 1900—

I am quite decided that I will travel. Indeed I feel quite giddy at the prospect. Given my change of circumstances, I can see no real impediment. Of those attributes which Mr. Galton considers prerequisites to travel—health, craving for adventure, a moderate fortune, and a definite objective which would not be thought impracticable by experienced travellers—I enjoy the first two in abundance. As to the last, I am convinced that while many of my acquaintance will think me mad, those who have already experienced travel would not find what I propose to be without merit. It is true that I lack even a moderate fortune, but I have a modest income, and, as Mr. Galton advises, some men are known to support themselves by travel. It may well be that, as is my goal, I will find objects of natural history that will be of sufficient interest on my return that I may recover some part of my expenses.

In preparation, I have read Mr. Galton's most excellent book, and indeed attended one of his lectures three years ago. His subject that evening unfortunately was not advice to travellers but rather his theories on what he calls eugenics, with which I simply cannot agree. One cannot doubt the passion he brings to his beliefs, but for my part, I find his ideas on the restriction of marriage to only the most physically and mentally fit a perversion of the scholarship of Mr. Darwin and Sir Charles, both of whom I have made the subjects of personal study. Indeed it is my careful perusal of Mr. Darwin's writings that encourages me in my objective, which is to find evidence that would support his theories. Mr. Galton's views on marriage do not seem to me to hold up to the rigour of even the most rudimentary observation. I myself have observed that some of the most unfortunate amongst us where the complexion is concerned have comely children, and madness does not always pass from generation to generation. But perhaps I am guilty in that latter statement of what I accuse Mr. Galton. I must believe that madness is not an inevitable result of procreation of those who are stricken by it.

Be that as it may, Mr. Galton's advice on travel seems to me to be worthy of some attention. He has, has he not, travelled extensively in some of the most inhospitable places. Having booked passage for a little less than a month hence, I have visited the shops of High Street and selected my travel attire with care, mindful of his instructions on the efficacy of flannel. As to what else I should take with me, I am quite unsure. Tea and biscuits, of course, and a pistol, a penknife, stationery, a few powders to treat mild affliction, sturdy boots and some instruments for my studies, a macintosh for inclement weather, and some sketching books. How I wish I knew more of the terrain I will visit.

As to what I will find I am even less certain. I will go down to London within the month, and thence to the continent. I take comfort in Mr. Galton's advice that savages rarely murder newcomers.

CHAPTER ONE

September 5

I'M NEVER QUITE CERTAIN WHAT PEOPLE MEAN WHEN THEY tell me to stay out of trouble. What I do know is that no matter what they intend by it, being caught with one of Europe's oldest men hidden under the bed would hardly be considered staying out of it, even if, given he'd been dead for about twenty-five thousand years, I could hardly be accused of the blow that killed him.

I was, however, immeshed in the demise of a more contemporary soul, and, not to put too fine a point on it, almost got myself killed. When, in the harsh light of hindsight, I subject my actions to rigorous self-examination, something I by and large try not to do too often or for too long, it is clear a rather unfortunate chain of events might have been avoided had I paid attention to signs, obvious to everyone but me, that disaster was nigh. Instead, I was swamped with a sort of psychic lassitude, my normal instinct for survival dulled by a fuzziness of thinking, a lack of will. In short, I was in something of a funk.

My friends certainly thought so, even if I wasn't prepared to acknowledge my state of mind, at least not while I was in it, and certainly not out loud.

"I expect you're feeling a little glum about your breakup with Rob," my best friend Moira Meller offered rather tentatively.

"I don't think so," I said. "It was for the best, you know, and really very amicable."

"That's good," she said. "He seems a little depressed. I was worried you might be, too."

"I don't know why," I said. "Neither of us was really getting what we wanted out of the relationship. It may be that I am one of those people who are happier on their own. You haven't been talking to him, have you?" I said suspiciously.

"He did call," she said. "And I did talk to him, but only for a minute, you understand. I think he wanted me to try to talk to you about getting back together. I told him I wouldn't presume to do anything like that."

"Thank you," I said. I looked at her warily. Was there more to this than she was saying? The expression on her face was studiously bland.

"Any time you want to talk about it," she said, "I'm here."

"Thanks, but I'm fine," I said.

"Okay," she said. "Whatever. By the way, if you have some time one evening this week, I could use your advice. I'm thinking of giving the salon a bit of a makeover. I have some color swatches and I'd be grateful if you'd have a look at them. Maybe you and I could go out for a drink and dinner after."

"Didn't you just completely redecorate the place six months ago? It's gorgeous!"

"Um, yes. But there is one spot I've never been entirely happy about. You know me, obsessive personality that I am. It would be great if you'd come over."

"Okay," I said. Her motives were entirely transparent, and I suppose it was nice of her to try to cheer me up, but I wished she wouldn't bother.

"You'll miss Jennifer, I expect, won't you, Lara?" my neighbor Alex Stewart said.

"I'm sure I'll see her almost as much as I did when her father and I were together," I replied.

"Will you?" he said. "I'm glad to hear that. I was wondering, might there be any chance you could give me a hand with my garden on Sunday? I could use your help moving one of the rose bushes."

"Sure," I said. "I'd be glad to." *Not another one!* I thought.

When I wasn't doing favors for my friends, I tried to throw myself into my work. That usually does the trick when I'm feeling a little down. Even at the antique shop I co-own with my ex-husband Clive Swain, though, it was not business as usual. Diesel, the Official Shop Cat, who normally ignores me, had taken to leaping into my lap whenever and wherever I was sitting, and doing figure eights between my legs when I wasn't.

The one person I can always count on to show me no sympathy is Clive. "This business with Rob is making you a little crabby, Lara," he said.

"Thank you, Clive," I said, feeling much cheered by this lack of solicitude. "You, of course, are all sweetness and light."

"I rest my case," he said. "You need a holiday. Now that you're unattached, you could go out to one of those swinging singles places in the Caribbean. Sun, sand, sex with no commitment. Very therapeutic. I remember those times with fondness."

"And those intensive therapy sessions would have been while you were still married to me, would they?" I said.

"Worse than crabby. Downright testy," he said. "Isn't there somewhere else you need to be right now?"

"I suppose I should go to that auction preview at Molesworth & Cox. I probably won't find anything interesting, though, and even if I do, it will be too pricey."

"Have I mentioned your less than positive outlook on life?" Clive said. "Get going. And by the way," he called to my departing back. "I didn't have nearly as many affairs as you thought I did, and not until it was basically over."

"You sound like Prince Charles," I said. "Trying to justify Camilla whats-her-name."

"The auction?" he said, treating my comment with the contempt it no doubt deserved.

I hesitated in the doorway, waiting for the parting shot, something along the lines of "by the way, you were no Princess Diana." It didn't come. Instead he said, "Moira and I are attending the gallery opening at the Cottingham. If you're going, we'll see you there." *Even Clive,* I thought glumly, *was being nice to me.* At least he had stopped short of asking me for help with an imaginary project. I'd moved three rosebushes before Alex decided they had looked better where they were, and we moved them all back—which couldn't have done the roses much good, regardless of what it did for me. In a related activity, Moira, ostensibly with my help, picked a color for the walls of the changing rooms at her salon that only a creature with a preternatural sensitivity to color could possibly have noticed was any different from the one that was already there.

And anyway, I was fine. I managed to park my car without scraping the curb or hitting the parking meter, something I seemed to have had a propensity to do ever since I'd parted company with Rob—that and slamming file drawers on my fingers and cutting myself on every sharp object within miles—and made my way into Molesworth & Cox, Auctioneers. Just as I predicted, it didn't look very exciting. One of the rooms contained a display table that, intentionally or not, was entirely covered in pairs: silver candlesticks, twin Staffordshire china dogs, matching table lamps, salt and pepper shakers, gold cufflinks, pearl and garnet earrings, two of everything. It made me think of my bathroom at home, with its identical bottles of shampoo, tubes of conditioner, packets of mint-flavored dental floss, waxed, two tubes of toothpaste to brighten your teeth and avert gum disease simultaneously, and even two hairbrushes. Only one of each pair belonged there, the other having until recently rested on a shelf in Rob's bathroom before I'd packed up and moved out.

Staring at those identical twins, I realized that if someone actually asked me why I'd done what I had—and my friends were assiduously avoiding doing that, for all their concern—I wasn't sure what I would say. On the surface, Rob Luczka and I were very compatible. We hardly ever argued, I adored his daughter, and we liked so many of the same things. Forced to explain it from my perspective, I would have said something to the effect that we fundamentally saw the world differently. In the end I'd simply told him that the relationship just wasn't working for me. His hurt and baffled expression was now engraved on my brain.

There was nothing at the auction house that even remotely interested me. In fact there was nothing at all at the moment that engaged me. I just didn't care that a shipment had gone missing somewhere between Denpasar and Los Angeles, or even that we'd been selected as one of only two antique dealers to exhibit at a posh design show. As recently as the day before I had been thinking I should sell my half of the business to Clive, and move to the south of France or something, and indeed, had even suggested it to him. He told me to go have a massage.

It was a muggy day, summer's last gasp, the air thick enough to cut, and as I left the auction house, a light drizzle began to fall. A drifter was sitting on the sidewalk, water dripping off his filthy baseball cap, a scruffy dog at his side. It was all so unspeakably dreary. It was five o'clock and another depressing evening alone at home loomed. I had the invitation to the gallery opening Clive had talked about, but I couldn't summon the energy to go. I wanted to do something, something fun, with somebody who didn't know anything about Rob and me, and who would therefore not try to engage me in conversation about how I felt, or invent some completely unnecessary activity to keep me busy. I just didn't know what that something would be.

And then, there it was!

"Lara? It is you, isn't it? Lara McClintoch?" I turned to a woman who looked vaguely familiar. "Diana MacPherson," she said. "Remember me? From Vic? The place on Dovercourt?"

"Vic" was Victoria College at the University of Toronto. Dovercourt was the street we'd both lived on. It was also a long time ago. "Diana!" I exclaimed. "Of course I remember. How are you?"

"I knew it had to be you," she said. "The strawberry hair.

You still look nineteen!" she exclaimed. It was a lie, of course, but a nice one. "I would have known you anywhere. How long has it been? Twenty years?"

"At least. You look exactly the same, too." She didn't, any more than I did. Her hair, once dark, was gray now, and her face bore the mark of experience, some of it, judging by the lines around her mouth, bitter.

"Do you ever see any of the old gang?" she asked.

"Not for ages," I said. "I don't know why, really. We've just lost touch."

"Are you married?" she said. "Kids?"

"I was married," I replied. "Once. But, no, no kids."

"Me, neither. This is so great," she said. "I can't believe I've run into you after all these years! Do you have time for a drink?" she asked. "I'm meeting a couple of our former classmates, maybe three. You remember Cybil, don't you? Cybil Harris. It's Cybil Rowanwood now. And Grace? Grace Young? You have to remember her. And Anna Belmont? There's a chance she'll be there, too."

"Of course, I remember," I said.

"So will you? Come for a drink right now, I mean?" she said. "It would be such fun, a mini college reunion."

I hesitated.

"What am I thinking?" she said. "This is so last-minute. I'm sure you already have something planned for this evening."

Normally I would rather chew glass than attend any event with the word *reunion* associated with it. The only activity I could think of for myself that evening, however, was watching my toiletries doing the Noah's ark thing in the bathroom, two by two. "I'd love to come," I said.

"That's great!" she said. "We're meeting up at the bar on the top of the Park Hyatt, for a quick one. Some of us are off to another event after. I can't believe I've just run into you like this. This is so great. Do you want to take the subway, or share a cab?"

"I have my car," I said. "I'll give you a lift."

"Great!" she said again. "This is just so much fun! The others will be so surprised!"

The hotel was only a block or so from the shop, so I parked in my usual spot off the lane way behind it. The store was already closed up tight.

"Oh my goodness!" Diana exclaimed, putting her hand up to her mouth. "Is this yours? The shop I mean? Are you the owner? I've walked past this place at least once a week for years, and I've never run into you. I've even been in it. I don't know why it never occurred to me that the McClintoch of McClintoch & Swain would be you."

"There's no reason why you should have," I said.

"We always knew you would be a success," she said.

"I don't know that I would actually call this business a success," I protested. In truth, Clive and I are happy when we turn the smallest of profits.

"You're in Yorkville," Diana said. "Don't be so modest. It's one of the fanciest places in town."

"You see it as fancy. I see it as high rent," I said.

"You say tom-ay-to, I say tom-ah-to," she laughed. "Well, I'm a freelance bookkeeper for a small agency. Right now I'm working at a museum."

"That sounds interesting," I said.

"You see it as interesting. I see it as a position in danger of being replaced by a new software spreadsheet program."

"Oh," I said.

"Here we are," she added rather unnecessarily, as we stepped off the elevator at the eighteenth floor and turned left into the bar.

"Over here, Diana," a woman's voice called from the alcove on the far side of the room.

"Hi, girls. Look who I found just walking along the street," Diana said. "You remember Lara."

"Oh my gawd," a rather large and seriously middle-aged woman shrieked. "I don't believe it!"

"Hello, Cybil," I said. I didn't believe it either. "And Grace! How are you?" I said to a slim dark-haired woman who in truth did look much the way she had in college. And . . ." For a moment the name escaped me. "Anna," I said. Even though Diana had already mentioned Anna, I had trouble identifying the rather shy and retiring woman of indeterminate age in front of me with the dynamo called Anna I'd known in college. "It's great to see all of you."

"We have a surprise for you, too," Grace said, gesturing toward an empty chair and a lipstick-smudged drink glass. "She's just gone to the ladies room."

"Who is it?" Diana asked.

"Guess," Cybil said. "You never will."

"Hello, Diana," a voice said behind us. "And Lara! I didn't know you were coming. What a nice surprise."

"Hello, Vesta," I said. "I didn't know I was coming either."

"You have to call her Morgan now," Cybil said. "It's her professional name. Doesn't it suit her?" It did, rather. Morgan was tall, very slim in a smashing scarlet silk suit, beautifully made-up, with matching fingernails and red silk shoes. I immediately felt like a middle-aged frump.

"One could hardly have a modeling career with a name like Vesta Stubbs," Morgan said.

An extra chair was found and squeezed in around the circle, another glass of wine fetched. "I can't believe my eyes," Diana said. "The Dovercourt Divas together again. After all these years!"

"Wasn't that the most awful place?" Morgan said. "The way the bugs in the kitchens scurried about if you turned on the light without making a lot of noise first. The smell from that restaurant below. The whole place should have been condemned as a fire trap. We did have fun, though, didn't we?"

We did, indeed: six University of Toronto students who lived in a little warren of tiny bachelor apartments over a Chinese restaurant on Dovercourt Road. You got up to the apartments through what the landlord rather optimistically called a courtyard at the back. We named ourselves the Dovercourt Divas, and for a year or two we'd been inseparable.

But that had been a long time ago, and at first it was rather heavy going with none of us quite knowing what to say, other than "it's been years," or "you haven't changed a bit." By the time the second round of drinks had been ordered however, we were all talking at once.

"Stop," Diana said. "I think we should each summarize our lives since we left Vic. Let's make it twenty words or less. I'll start. Graduate school, master's degree, doctorate, taught for awhile but failed to get tenure. Took up bookkeeping. Never married. I think that's too many words."

"It is, but I'll make mine shorter to compensate," Cybil said. "Got knocked up, shotgun wedding. Never graduated. Had four kids. Gained forty pounds. Divorced the creep. How many's that?"

"Sixteen," Diana said. "Unless shotgun is two words, or knocked up is one. I never was so hot at spelling as you may recall. Lara?"

"Traveled. Brought back stuff. Opened store to get rid of it," I said. "Got married. Got divorced. Lost store in divorce. Started another one. Got back in business with ex-husband. Not sure why. No kids. Live alone."

"You and I always were the talkers," Diana said. "That's way too many words. You'll have to buy the next round. Morgan?"

"Traveled. Modeled. Got too old," Morgan said, counting on bejeweled fingers. "Married well. Big house. Husband screws around. No kids. Starve to keep thin. Love botox. I believe that is exactly twenty."

"What's botox?" Cybil said.

"It's a poison you inject into your forehead to get rid of your wrinkles," Morgan replied.

"You're kidding," Cybil said.

"I'm afraid not," Morgan said.

"A poison?" Cybil repeated.

"It's related in some way I do not understand to botulism."

"Yikes," Cybil said.

"I tell everyone I have it done because it helps my migraines," Morgan said. "Which maybe it does. But since you know me all too well, I'll confess that's a lie. I do it to look younger. I've also had my eyes done, twice, in fact."

"All I can say is that you're gorgeous, and you would be even with wrinkles," Cybil said loyally. "And you don't need to be a toothpick, either. Not that I'm suggesting you let yourself go the way I have. I said forty pounds, but it's closer to fifty. Okay, sixty."

"I envy you. I put on three pounds and my charming husband tells me I'm getting fat," Morgan said.

"You envy me?" Cybil snorted. "Not. Why don't you just leave him if he's so picky?"

"Given I have no marketable skills to speak of, the modeling thing being a young person's game, I have to hold on to him. Did I mention that I have to walk on my toes when I'm in my bare feet because I've been wearing very high heels for too long?"

"A rather pathetic attempt to gain our sympathy, Vesta. I mean, Morgan," Cybil said. "It won't work."

"You're also cheating on the number of words, Morgan," Diana said. "With all these additional comments. And we have yet to hear from Anna and Grace. Anna, you're next in the circle."

"No, please," Anna said, blushing. "I couldn't."

"Have another sip of wine, " Morgan said. "I've been candid. We all have."

"Anna doesn't have to if she doesn't want to," Cybil said in a protective tone.

"Why not? How bad could it be?" Morgan asked. Cybil shot her a warning look.

"I want to," Anna said. "It's just . . . Give me a minute."

"Okay," Diana said. "Grace, your turn."

"Hmm. Medical school in the States. Family practice five years. More medical school. Surgeon at Toronto General. Married ten years to a really wonderful man. Widowed now, and haven't found wonderful man number two. I would say no time to find man number two, but I've run out of words."

"You're cheating too," Diana said. "Sneaking in extra words under the guise of an aside."

"A surgeon!" Cybil said.

"Very impressive," Morgan said. "What kind of surgeon? Plastic, I hope, so I can get a discount for old times' sake." We all laughed, even Anna.

"Heart," Grace replied. "Sorry."

"Boy, two doctors here, Diana the PhD, and Grace the surgeon. I always knew you two were smart. All of you were smarter than I was. Yes, you were," Cybil added as we all demurred. "Grace, you make me think of that riddle we used to tell each other while we were in college," she went on. "You know, the one about the man and his son who are in a car crash. The man is killed and the kid is seriously injured, and when he's brought to the hospital, the surgeon says "I can't operate on this boy because he's my son,' and you're supposed to guess how that might be."

"The surgeon is a woman," Diana said. "I remember that. Some people actually couldn't guess the answer. I suppose we've come a long way. I'll bet you have lots of stories to tell about what it was like for you along the way, though, Grace."

"I do, but it would take a lot more than twenty words."

"Would it be way too awful to ask about your husband's death?" Cybil asked.

"Heart attack, wouldn't you know?" Grace said.

"Oh dear," Cybil said.

"Yes. The way I see it, he died because I wasn't there. One could argue whether I should have been at the time or not, or if I had been whether it would have made any difference or not, but there you are."

"Oh dear," Cybil said again.

"Got married. Had three beautiful children," Anna suddenly blurted out. We all looked at her. She was twirling a lock of dirty blond hair around her finger and her face was red. "The little boy died. I had a nervous breakdown. Daughters live with their father. I live with my mother." There was an audible gasp from the rest of us.

"My God," Morgan said. "I had no idea. What happened?"

"An accident," Cybil said, patting Anna's hand.

"How awful," I said. "Anna, I'm so sorry."

"It is awful," Morgan said. "And of course, here I am complaining about dieting. Well, as I'm sure you all remember, I am nothing if not extremely shallow."

"You mustn't blame yourself, Anna," Grace said.

"Please," Anna said. "There's nothing you can say. It's nice to be here with you again. It makes me feel as if I could start over. I want to hear more about what everybody has been doing. Do any of you travel to faraway places? I'd love to hear about that."

"We have all kinds of catching up to do," Cybil said. "I want to hear all about Lara's antique business, too."

"Love to, some other time," Morgan said, looking at her watch, a Cartier, I believe. "Command performance. Exclusive event. People there my husband wants to impress. I wish I could take you all with me. Which," she said, digging about in her purse, a lovely embroidered silk evening bag, "perhaps I can. Here," she said, pulling out an engraved card. "It's for me and a guest. I wonder if they'd allow me to have five guests."

"Maybe we don't want to come," Diana said. "What is it?"

"The Cottingham Museum. They're opening a new gallery of prehistoric art. I could take one of you."

"Doesn't your husband count as your date?" Cybil said.

"Believe me, darling, Woodward does not need an invitation. Now who would like to come with me?"

"Would that be Woodward *Watson* by any chance?" I said.

"Of course," Morgan said. "Did I not mention that?"

"I don't believe you did. I, too, have an invitation to the opening," I said, pulling an identical card out of my bag. "I wasn't sure whether I wanted to go or not, but I'm game if someone else wants to come, too."

"I'm actually a member of the museum," Grace said. "I have an invitation as well, but I'm afraid I already have a date."

"A date!" Cybil said. "That's rather nice."

"He's gay," Grace said. "And you all know him. Remember Frank Kalman?"

"Frankie! I didn't know he was gay," Morgan said. "Didn't I date him?"

"We all did, I think," Diana said. "You dated everybody, Morgan," she added. That was true. Morgan as Vesta drank, smoked, skipped classes, and, if the stories were true, slept with just about any guy who asked. A lot of guys asked.

"I liked him because he was the only guy I dated who didn't paw me," Morgan said. "I guess I now know why. Speaking of dating, I want you to know, Lara, that I've forgiven you for stealing Charles Miller away from me," she said.

"Who? What?" I said.

"You've forgotten," Morgan said.

"What?" I repeated.

"That you stole Charlie away from me."

"I did?"

"The graduation ball? You and Charlie?"

"Yes. So . . ."

"He and I were dating."

"You were?"

"You didn't know?"

"No," I said. "Since when would anyone date me if they could date you?"

"Don't be ridiculous. Did you really not know?"

"No, honest," I said. "As a matter of fact, I thought he'd been dating Grace."

"So you stole him from me," Grace said.

"Did I? No, that's not fair. It's coming back to me. You and I went for a coffee and I asked you and you said it was all over between the two of you, and you didn't care if I went to the dance with him."

"And you believed her?" Cybil said. "Silly you."

"Perhaps I did say that," Grace said. "And I may or may not have meant it at the time. A lot of water under the bridge, either way."

"I thought Charlie was the most beautiful man I'd ever seen," Anna said. "I still do."

"Charlie was adorable, wasn't he?" Cybil said. "Smart, funny, very good-looking. We were all jealous when you went to the dance with him, Lara. Pea green with envy. Did you date him too, Diana?"

"I did not," Diana said in a rather tart tone that suggested further questions on that subject would not be welcome.

Cybil did not appear to notice. "You did, too, Diana. I saw the two of you together smooching by Hart House."

"I am sure you are mistaken," Diana said. "If you want to know, I loathed him. I thought he was a pompous, self-centered, egotistical pig."

"I'm not sure I would go that far," Grace said. "But he was always rather more interested in people who could help him get ahead. Given I was there on a bursary because my parents couldn't afford the tuition, I was of no interest. The truth is, Lara, he dumped me. I was just too proud to tell you."

"Perhaps I should have known that," I said. "But I didn't. I suppose that's the reason you froze me out the last semester, is it? I always wondered what I'd done to offend you."

"I wish you hadn't brought that up, but yes, that's why. Ridiculous when you think about it."

"You really didn't know?" Morgan repeated. "About Charlie and me?"

"I really didn't know that either," I said. "I swear."

"Too bad. There's twenty years of bitterness and recrimination totally wasted."

"You're kidding," I said.

"No, I'm not," she said, but she couldn't keep a straight face, and soon we were all laughing, even Anna, just like the good old days.

"I was rather enamored," I said. "I have to admit it."

"Me, too," Morgan said.

"Me three," Cybil piped in. "He was a dish."

"My husband was a truly wonderful man, but he wasn't Charlie," Grace said almost wistfully. "Maybe that's a good thing," she added.

"Did we all date him?" I said.

"If we didn't, we wanted to," Anna said.

"So how many of us slept with him, I wonder," Morgan said.

"Oooh, Vesta. Morgan, I mean. You always were—what's the word I'm looking for here?—daring? Bold?" Cybil said.

"I expect the word you are looking for is shameless," Morgan replied. "Or maybe it's just plain tacky. I can see we will have to wait for another time before the confessions really start. Maybe we'll have a nightcap after the museum thing."

"I don't think shameless is the right word," Cybil said. "I always admired the way you said what you thought."

"It has gotten me into a lot more trouble than I dare tell you," Morgan said.

It had been a very long time since I'd thought about Charles, but the mere mention of his name transported me back to spring of my final year—walks in the park, notes passed back and forth in lectures, stolen kisses in the back row of the movies—all terribly prosaic, of course, but at the time Charles Miller had been the man with whom I wanted to spend the rest of my life. It had ended when we'd both gone on to do other things. For awhile we'd written. I'd penned notes I thought were touching and profound, but which were probably just banal, if not downright silly. I couldn't even remember which one of us had made the decision final, but I do recall I cried for days when I realized it was over.

"I wonder what happened to him," I said. It seemed a bit odd to me that I'd so completely lost track of him. He'd been the first real love of my life, a divine dancer, handsome, debonair, and charming when he wanted to be. Sort of like Clive, when it came right down to it. Maybe I had a weakness for suave and handsome but shallow men. Except for Rob, of course. Maybe that was the problem. Rob hadn't been nearly shallow enough for me. It was a depressing idea.

"You really don't know where he is now?" Grace said.

"No," I said. There seemed to have been rather a lot I'd missed both at the time and in the intervening years.

"I'd say you were in for a little surprise," Cybil said. "Isn't she, girls?"

"She is, indeed," Morgan said. "Speaking of which, who is coming to this gallery thing?" The rest of them tittered. "Obviously Lara has to go. I think we all should. I'd hate any of us to miss it now."

"What do you mean obviously I should go, and what's so funny?" I said. "I'd be happy to give my invitation to someone else."

"No, Morgan's right. You have to go," Grace said. "But we're short one invitation. Do you think they'll keep that close track?"

"I'm not dressed properly," Cybil said. "I'm never dressed properly. Anna, you go."

"I don't think I could stand to see . . ." Anna said.

"I also have an invitation," Diana said. "I work there, part-time. We all go."

"I thought you said this was exclusive," Cybil laughed.

"Waiter, the bill, please," Morgan said, smoothing her skirt, tugging at her jacket, and with a certain air of resolution, pulling the straps of her bag over her shoulder. "My treat, girls. The evening might even be bearable if you all come along."

"You look as if you're girding yourself for battle, Morgan," Cybil said.

Morgan looked at her for a moment before she replied. "Maybe I am," she said.

CHAPTER TWO

September 5

GIVEN HOW THE EVENING WAS TO END, IT'S STRANGE HOW clear some of it is. I recall it not so much as a sequence of events, one flowing into the next, but rather as a series of quite distinct vignettes, each a still photograph that I can study time and time again. And that I have done, feeling perhaps that if I stare at them long enough and carefully enough I will see what I missed, I will understand what was to come.

But perhaps a photograph is not quite the right analogy. A play, I think, might do it, the players frozen for a moment as the curtain rises before they begin to say their lines. I am both actor and spectator. Act one, scene one, then, takes place outside the Cottingham Museum. Perched on a prime piece of real estate at the corner of a busy intersection it reminds one of nothing so much as a big bird. Both the museum and the building it is housed in are, it is clear, monuments to self-indulgence.

The product of an international design competition, won by one of those architects noted for buildings that make a statement but do not necessarily work very well, the building is not large, four stories, on a relatively small lot, but it dominates the corner. Clad in undulating sheet metal with various protrusions that resemble beaks and wings, in a neighborhood heretofore noted for its gracious Edwardian elegance, the Cottingham has set itself apart.

But it is not the building that is important in this scene, it is the figure in the foreground: Woodward Watson looking impatiently at his watch as the wind ruffles his beautiful gray hair and clutches at his cashmere suit and the white silk scarf draped casually, but of course elegantly, around his neck.

"Hello, darling," Morgan says, taking his arm. "Sorry I'm a bit late. You should have gone in without me. I met some old school chums. Is there something you want me to do here tonight? Someone in particular you would like me to meet?"

Woodward draws her aside for a moment, leaving the rest of us to look awkwardly about, not sure whether to wait or go on.

"Of course, darling," she says, and we all move inside. It is clear now we are not to be introduced.

ACT ONE, SCENE two: the atrium of the museum, all glass and marble, and at this moment packed with people. Jackets are whipped away as soon as one enters, and a glass of champagne is immediately to hand.

A receiving line of sorts has been set up. In it are Major

Cottingham himself, looking much older than I recall, and his wife of five years, the spectacular Courtney, former actress and party girl, now the partner of an exceptionally wealthy man thirty years her senior. Of Courtney it is often said rather unkindly, quoting Dorothy Parker, that you can take a whore to culture but you can't make her think. It is clear from her every utterance that she left school long before she should, that she knows nothing about the art that is such an important part of her husband's life. Despite all the money her marriage to Major has brought, she still dresses in short skirts, high boots, and low-cut tops, usually in either a fuzzy or a metallic fabric. Tonight she is decked out in way too much jewelry, and a gold sparkly suit. Still, she is a very attractive woman, and one who knows very well the power she has over men.

The Cottinghams are Old Money. Major Cottingham— for the longest time I thought this was his rank when in fact it's his name—has collected art for many years, as did his father before him, and when for some reason he found the need for a significant tax receipt, and was unable to negotiate a big enough one from any of the existing art museums in the country to which he tried to donate his collection, he first built, then opened, his own.

While critics of the museum's architecture are many, few dare to sneer at the collection. Cottingham has a passion for art, and the wherewithal to support it. He also has strong opinions on it, and went through a string of curators in the first few years, most of whom only stayed as long as they could stand Cottingham's bullying. The museum has been set up as a not-for-profit corporation with a board of directors as legally required, and indeed, Woodward Watson, Morgan's philandering husband, is on that board, but there is no question who runs the show. It was an interesting boondoggle, really. Cottingham gets to treat the collection as if it is still his own, has the benefit of the tax receipt, estimated to be in the many millions, and now has a staff of flunkies to do his bidding. According to the rumors, curatorial responsibilities include taking care of Major's dry cleaning, providing several parking spaces day and night, and covering most of his entertainment expenses. Over the few years they've been together, Major and Courtney have held many lavish dinner parties at the museum with some of the finest caterers in the city, or they have until recently. The society pages have not seen much of the Cottinghams of late.

Still all cannot be entirely rosy. The cost of running the museum is considerable, and without regular infusions of cash from Cottingham it would probably have closed. While the collection is first-rate, it hasn't quite captured the public's imagination. It is perhaps not a sufficiently large collection to make it a destination for travelers, and it does not really have a focus. There are all kinds of art, from all time periods, but it just isn't very exciting to any but the most enthusiastic student. A year before the action in this scene begins, in an effort to develop the collection in a way that would have more appeal, Cottingham hired what might very well be the last curator he will ever be able to harass, a man I have yet to meet, but have heard much about, one Károly Molnár.

The Hungarian-born Molnár has worked in England, at a small but prestigious institution called the Bramley Museum, and apparently it was something of a coup for Cottingham to have snagged him. Molnár is known for his innovative exhibit design and for having a real sense of what the public wants to see. There has been much speculation about how long the new fellow will last, but a few months after Molnár's arrival, Cottingham surprised everyone by announcing he would step down, and Molnár consequently was offered the position of executive director as well as curator. Tonight, we are told, Molnár will unveil an extraordinary discovery, an artifact that will set the Cottingham firmly on the list of top cultural attractions anywhere in the world. It is called the Magyar Venus, and we are all there, breathless in anticipation, to see it for ourselves.

Morgan and Courtney air-kiss, and then Morgan is off to chat up someone, a bank president by the look of him, on behalf of her husband. Courtney smiles enthusiastically at everyone who speaks to her, but Major is uncharacteristically quiet. Up close he is thinner than I remember, and pale. I see a number of people I know, including Clive and Moira, who wave at me. I can tell from their smiles that they're glad their rather morose friend Lara is making an effort.

I turn at the sound of a voice behind me. "Frank?" I exclaim to the tall, handsome man who has tapped my shoulder. "After all these years. You look terrific."

"Hello, Lara," Frank says. "You, too. You can call me Ferenc, now, by the way. A little in-joke," he adds.

I am perplexed. "She doesn't know yet," Cybil says.

"What don't I know?" I ask, but the others just laugh.

"You'll have to wait a little longer to get in on the joke, I suppose," Frank says. "But not to worry, it will happen soon."

"Anna!" Frank exclaims when he sees her. "My goodness. You're here."

"Hello, Frankie," Anna says. "Yes, I'm here."

"Why that's . . . that's wonderful!" Frank says. "And so unexpected." I wonder what that means, too.

At that very moment Courtney goes to a microphone near the bottom of the escalator that leads to the second floor. "Ladies and gentlemen," she says. "The official part of this reception, the unveiling, is about to take place. I would ask you to leave your drinks here—I can promise there will be more later—because food and beverages are not allowed in the galleries."

"The suspense is too much," Diana says as we reluctantly set down our champagne, and the curtain comes down on the cast ascending to the second floor.

ACT TWO, SCENE one takes place in the gallery of prehistoric art. A small platform with three chairs and a podium has been set up at one end, and a spotlight shines on a museum case that, as the scene opens, is covered in dark blue silk. The Cottinghams take their seats on the platform, beside a woman in a rather unpleasant dress and overly coifed hair. The action begins as Woodward Watson takes the stage.

"My name is Woodward Watson," he begins. "And I am chair of the board of directors of this museum. It is my pleasure to welcome you here tonight on behalf of Major and Courtney Cottingham. This is a truly historic occasion," he says. "Or perhaps I should say this is a truly prehistoric occasion." There are titters and groans from the audience.

"This is going to be a long evening," Frank, behind me, whispers.

"That was terrible, wasn't it? I couldn't resist," Woodward says, with a self-deprecating smile, and the audience laughs with him. Morgan blows him a kiss. "There are a number of very distinguished people here this evening," he goes on. "The Cottinghams you know, of course. Take a bow, Major and Courtney." They do, to polite applause.

"The Cottinghams have made a real difference to the cultural life of this city, so generously donating their collection and building this very fine museum, and we thank them for it." Another smattering of applause.

"Someone else who is making a real difference to the cultural sector is our next speaker," Woodward says, introducing the woman with the terrible hair, the minister of museums and something or other, and soon she is at the microphone, congratulating herself for promising to give the Cottingham a loan with which to advertise the Magyar Venus internationally. She has an unpleasant voice, the sort that gets harsher the more excited she is, and she is clearly very excited now.

"If I had to wake up to that voice every morning," Frank whispers again, "I would have to kill myself."

"Thank you, Minister," Woodward says. The minister smiles and waves. "The Minister is only one of the extraordinary ladies you will meet tonight, and I know that there is a very special one you all want to be introduced to soon," he says, gesturing toward the shrouded display case. "So without further ado . . ."

Behind me, Frank says, "How sad. Here I was counting on a lot more ado."

"Without further ado," Woodward repeats. "I'm pleased to present our brilliant new executive director, the man we managed to lure away from the Bramley Museum in London, England, no less, ladies and gentlemen, Dr. Károly Molnár." A handsome man in a dark suit, white shirt, and red tie bounds up the steps onto the stage to considerable applause.

"What?" I say, and the others put their hands over their mouths to stifle their snickers. "What's he doing here?"

"Surprise!" Frank says.

"Thank you, Woodward," the man says. The others, by now, are almost doubled over with laughter.

Károly Molnár, I think. Charles Miller. Károly is Charles in Hungarian, I suppose. Miller, Molnár. They sound somewhat similar. That's what Frank had meant when he'd referred to himself by his Hungarian name. I raise my eyebrows at the rest of them.

"She's got it," Cybil whispers. "His real name is Károly Molnár. Apparently he just made up an English version for himself when he went to university."

"Why didn't I know this?" I said.

"I don't think he's been looking up his old classmates," Diana whispers. "He's created a new persona, and he's sticking with it. Frank knew, for reasons that will soon become apparent, and he told Grace. That's how I got the job here."

The woman standing to one side of us looks on disapprovingly, and we all fall silent. I, however, am feeling quite school-girlish about seeing my old love.

"I'm afraid I am going to make you wait a little longer before I unveil the lady you have all come to see," he says, gesturing to the display shrouded in blue, "the lady of the hour, the Magyar Venus, because I want to tell you something about her.

"Let me begin by saying that some women reveal their charms all at once," he says. "Rather like a harlot," he adds, and the men in the audience laugh. "Others reveal themselves more slowly, and they are all the more alluring for it. This lady belongs to the latter category. Like so many women, she was loathe to reveal her age." The audience laughs again, but I find myself uncomfortable with this analogy, and try to recall if Károly was something of a male chauvinist when we dated.

"But with a little encouragement from science, her secret

has been revealed," he goes on. "She is about twenty-five thousand years old." The audience gasps.

"This places her squarely in a period called the Upper Paleolithic, the most recent stage of what some people call the Old Stone Age. This was a lengthy period which included the last great Ice Age, when, for part of it at least, both Neanderthals and *Homo sapiens,* our ancestors, coexisted. Earlier theories to the contrary, we are not descended from Neanderthals. We are the creatures that were first able to think creatively, had some concept of the other, I suppose you might call it, whether that might be magic, or a higher power, perhaps even life after death. It is in this context perhaps that our little lady was carved, from mammoth ivory, the inner part of the tusks of the now extinct great mammoth. She was placed deep in a cave, in what may well have been a shrine, near the grave of someone undoubtedly special. We know that because the skeleton was adorned with necklaces and many, many bracelets made up of thousands of shell beads. Only a person of some stature in the community would be buried that way. On her we have found traces of red ochre, which was, we think, a substance both significant and precious to Paleolithic man. We cannot, of course, know exactly what her creator was thinking, but we cannot help but feel she had some magical power. You'll understand what I mean when you see her.

"She is extraordinarily beautiful, and she will now take her position in the group of what have come to be called Venus figures, *art mobilier* or portable art, that date from very ancient times—the Venus of Willendorf, the Venus of Lespugue, the Venus of Vestonice, extraordinary goddesses all, who were created in Europe during the Upper Paleolithic. These Venus figures were found in a band stretching from Siberia to France. This is not to say there are many of them today. They are exceedingly rare, of course. But there are a precious few, and some believe that they represent a cult, common to ancient people in those areas over a significant period of time, that worshipped goddesses. These Venuses are now all named for the places they were found, Willendorf in Austria, Lespugue in France, Dolni Vestonice in what is now the Czech Republic, for example, and our lovely lady will be no exception. I will return to that in a minute.

"We owe her presence here to two very special people over a century apart. One is a lady you will meet in a few minutes. The other is an intrepid Englishman by the name of C. J. Piper."

I hear a gasp nearby and turn to see Anna looking white as a sheet. Indeed, I think she's going to faint. Cybil grabs her and tries to comfort her, but Anna stands there, staring first at the podium and then in my direction, opening and closing her mouth as if gasping for air.

"I guess she can't stand the crowds," Diana whispers. "Poor thing." I have no idea what she's talking about, but right now my attention is riveted on the man at the podium. I notice only that in a moment or two the crowd parts to let Anna and Cybil through.

"It is Piper," Károly goes on, oblivious it seems, to the little drama in the crowd, "who in 1900 set off from his comfortable existence in England to travel and to study in Europe, eventually stopping in Hungary, what was then the Austro-Hungarian empire. It is he who found our lady in the cave in the Bükk Mountains, a fact he duly recorded in both his diaries and in a paper he presented to a learned society in London on his return in 1901. That paper came with illustrative material that clearly places our Venus with a grave in a cave in that region. We cannot know for certain which cave, but we do know the country, and it is the country and its people for which she is named. Henceforth, she will be known as the Magyar Venus. To have her here at this museum is an extraordinary happening. Think about it. This lady lay hidden for about twenty-five thousand years! That she should be here now is a most happy event." The crowd murmurs its approval.

"You can probably tell from my description that I am rather enamored of the Magyar Venus," Károly says as the crowd settles down. "She will draw visitors to the Cottingham and to this great city from all over the world. But in truth, I am in love with a much, much younger woman. While we owe C. J. Piper for her initial discovery, the Venus would not be here without her. Ladies and gentlemen, it is my great honor to introduce the love of my life, the little lady who donated the Venus to us: Lillian Larrington. Come up please, Lily, and be recognized."

To a roar of approval and huge applause, a tiny lady of about eighty in a pale pink pantsuit, comes up to the stage. She wears a corsage of pink and white carnations, her hair carefully coifed, and she blushes at all the attention, as Molnár kisses her hand.

"Oh dear," she says. "Can you hear me?" The microphone squeals in an unpleasant way. "Is it on?" she asks. Károly assures her it is. "I just want to say how happy I am to be able to bring the Venus to this museum," she says. "I don't think I deserve all this attention. Károly is the person who should be thanked. He is very persuasive," she adds, and everyone laughs. "I can't imagine anyone else talking me into this. Anyway, it is my pleasure. I'm glad I could do something. I wish my dear husband could be here tonight. He died a year ago." The audience murmurs. Károly puts his arm around her shoulders.

"Don't forget the book," Frank calls out from behind. Károly looks startled, and Courtney rushes to the microphone.

"Lily is right. Károly is being much too modest," she says. "He has neglected to mention his role in the rediscovery of the Venus. It is the Cottingham's own executive director who found not only the scientific presentation of Piper's findings, but Piper's diaries themselves. He has edited the diaries with a commentary on the Venus and her discovery. The book is just out, and we have it for sale in the shop downstairs. I'm sure he'll sign your copy, won't you, Károly?"

Károly looks suitably embarrassed. "I must protest," he says. "Despite the fact that my publisher, Frank Kalman is here," he adds, gesturing in Frank's general direction. "I have to tell you that the book tells the story of Piper's finding of the Venus in his own words. *The Traveler and the Cave* contains Piper's diaries. My input really is minimal. But I'd be thrilled if you'd all buy a copy because part of the proceeds are going to support the Cottingham." The crowd applauds again.

"Are you a publisher?" I say to Frank.

"Sure," he said. "Kalman and Horst. That's me."

"No kidding!" I said. "Kalman and Horst. I thought . . . Didn't I read?" I stop myself from saying anything else.

"You thought Kalman and Horst had gone bankrupt?" Frank says. "Or was about to be bought up by one of the giants? It was that close. Fortunately I got some more financing."

"Where's my wife?" Major Cottingham says suddenly from the stage.

"I'm right here, dear," Courtney says.

"Not you," Major says. "My real wife."

The audience shuffles uncomfortably. Morgan catches my eye. "Alzheimer's," she mouths.

Károly takes things in hand. "And now, Lily," he says, leading her off the platform to the display case, as Major is hustled off the other way. "The moment everyone has been waiting for. Will you do the honors, please."

Lily tugs at the cover, and in a second, the Venus is revealed. "Ladies and gentlemen," Károly says. "The Magyar Venus!"

She rests in the spotlight, a figure maybe three inches high. It is a head and elongated neck and part of the torso only, large, pendulous breasts carved into the ivory, now darkened with age. Another crescent shape, a horn perhaps, or a crescent moon has been carved into the shoulders at the back. She is, indeed, beautiful. Her face has few features, just the eyes and a line for the nose but no mouth, and her hair looks to be in braids. One side of the torso, such as it is, has been eaten away by time. But there is something so expressive about the carving, something that speaks across millennia. I am as enchanted as everyone else. The crowd files past the case, oohing and ahhing, before going back downstairs for another drink.

ACT TWO, SCENE two: Back in the lobby. I grab a proffered glass of champagne and look for the others. I can't find Anna, nor Cybil, and the Cottinghams have vanished from their own party. I head for the powder room, and there I hear, in one of the cubicles, the sound of someone sobbing.

"Are you all right?" I call out, and in a second or two Anna replies. "Leave me alone," she says.

"Anna," I say, "please, come out. Talk to me."

"Leave me alone," she says again, this time almost a howl. "Please go away." Reluctantly I do, but set out to find Cybil in hopes she can reason with her friend. I realize I've left my glass of champagne in the bathroom.

ACT TWO, SCENE three: As I walk down the hall toward the party, I pass what is obviously Károly's office, and turn down a little hallway toward the sound of his voice. As I approach the door, I realize that Morgan is in the office, and she is holding what looks to be a check, half extended toward Molnár. "I suppose you think I am one of those harlots who reveal all their charms at once," she says.

"Morgan, please don't make a scene," Károly says. "I thank you for your donation. Let's leave it at that."

Morgan turns on her heels and heads for the door. "Bastard," she hisses. I don't want her to see me there, so I quickly pull at a door at the end of the hall, and when it mercifully opens, I go in. I find that I've taken another door into the offices of the executive director. I'm standing in what is probably the reception area, now dark, and I don't know what to do. I have a feeling that despite my efforts, Morgan may know I was there and wonder what I've heard. Should I just go in? I hesitate for a second, and hear footsteps coming down the hall, Morgan returning perhaps. But it isn't.

"Why won't my key work in my office door?" Diana says.

"Because you're fired," Károly replies.

"What do you mean, fired?" she says.

"Dismissed, sacked, let go," Károly says. "Fired. Effective immediately."

"I want to know why," she says.

"You know perfectly well why," he says. "A bookkeeper is in a position of trust. You are lucky I haven't called the police. Now get out of here before I change my mind and call them in."

"You have to let me into my office," she says. "I have personal belongings in there."

"You are most welcome to make an appointment to come back to clear out your office," Károly said. "When our security staff are available to escort you."

"You can't do this to me," she says.

"I not only can, I have," he says. "Get out. If you ever come back, I'll see to it that you're put in jail."

"I will get you for this," she says. "If it's the last thing I do."

"How very dramatic," he said. "If you're still here when I go back to the party three minutes from now, you will be very publicly led out of here in handcuffs."

I hear her footsteps retreat down the hall and Károly shuffling papers on his desk. I feel a sneeze coming on, and as I put my hand over my nose to stop it, I dislodge something on the desk. The paper shuffling stops. I hold my breath. I can picture Károly standing there listening intently. I think that if this play I'm in were Hamlet, I'd be skewered through the arras for a rat. As it is, I stand shifting my weight from one foot to the other in acute embarrassment. But nothing happens, and after a minute or two, Károly turns out the light in his office and I hear his steps receding down the hall. I count to fifty very slowly, then quietly open the door and head out into the crowd.

ACT TWO, SCENE four: I've purchased at great personal expense, seventy-five dollars and change, although I expect it is worth it, the book called *The Traveler and the Cave: The Mystery of the Magyar Venus,* and I'm standing in line to get my copy signed. It's a very long line—Frank will have to be pleased—and I've lost my glass of champagne, the third one I've taken and haven't finished. But I'm curious to see what Károly's reaction will be, and I wonder how I'm going to feel about it too. I reach the head of the line, book in hand, and he gives me a dazzling smile. "Hi," I say, handing him the book. "It's great to see you."

He takes it, and opens it to the title page. "Would you like it just signed?" he asks. "Or personalized?"

"Oh, make it to me," I say. There is a pause, and he looks at me expectantly.

"And your name is?" he says at last.

I am stung, although part of me knows this is ridiculous. It is just that for a brief period in my life, Charles Miller was everything to me. How can one forget such a time, even twenty years later? Obviously he has. Even standing there I am aware that had it not been for the fact that Rob and I have just split, I wouldn't really care.

"I've changed my mind," I say. "Just sign it for me, please."

"You look familiar," he says, handing me back the book. "Have we met?"

"I don't think so," I say, and turn and walk away.

ACT THREE, SCENE one: Back in the bar at the hotel. Frank, Diana, Grace, and Cybil are with me.

"Where's Anna?" someone asks. Frank, I think.

"I put her in a cab and sent her home," Cybil says. "Poor thing."

"What happened?" Grace says.

"I guess the crowds were too much for her," Cybil says. "She wasn't very coherent. She just kept saying 'I don't believe it, I don't believe it' over and over again. I hope she's okay. Perhaps it was a bad idea to bring her to something so crowded and public so soon after she's gotten out of the house."

"What does that mean, 'so soon after she's gotten out of the house'?" I ask.

"It is such a sad story," Cybil says. "You heard her say her little boy was killed in an accident. It was a terrible thing to happen, and Anna just couldn't handle it. She got that condition where you can't leave the house. What's it called? Something phobia."

"Agoraphobia," Grace says. "That's not the technical term. It means fear of the marketplace, the public place."

"Right," Cybil says. "The thing was, she wouldn't let her other children go out either, not to school or anywhere. Her husband left her, social workers moved in, and the kids were taken away from her. She was in therapy for ages, and it's only recently that she has been able to go out in a crowd like this. But she wanted to come and see everybody. Obviously, it was a bad idea."

"Dreadful thing," Grace says, and we all agree.

"Is Morgan coming?" I ask. I'm wondering how she is faring after that unpleasant little set to with Károly.

"Don't know," Cybil says. "Off to some swank society 'do' no doubt. I told her we were coming here. She could come if she wanted to. She seemed to be in a rather strange mood, though."

"The next round's on me," Frank says. "A book launch as it were."

"You published Károly? Do I have that right?" Cybil says.

"You do indeed," Frank replies. "He looked me up when he was ready to have the book published and we were able to reach a deal. I didn't know who this Károly Molnár person was, but I recognized him the minute I saw him, and he me. I'm sure in the bidding war that ensued, the fact that we went back so many years worked in my favor. It's hard for me to compete with the big guys. I'm thrilled, of course. I think, what with the international media on the Magyar Venus, this one is going to be a best seller. The advance sales are, shall we say, gratifying. The diaries themselves are interesting, and Károly's commentary is a hoot. Scholarly, of course, but in a really accessible way. Well, you saw him tonight. People were standing in rapt attention while he went on and on about the Upper Paleolithic, for God's sake. You have to admit that's some feat."

"So why didn't you invite him to join us?" Cybil says.

"I did," Frank says. "He told me he had a better offer. Not in so many words, of course. He's still got all that charm."

"Pig," Diana says suddenly. It's the first word I've heard her utter since that unfortunate confrontation overheard in Károly's office.

"Who?" Frank says.

"Károly Molnár," she replies.

"Why would you say that?" Frank says.

"Because" is her only reply.

Frank has signaled the waiter. "What was that drink we used to have in college?" Frank asks us. "The one with the strange name."

"B52s," Grace says. "Not a good idea. Lethal, if I remember correctly."

"Don't be such a killjoy, Grace. A round of B52s, on my tab." he says to the waiter.

"Where's the bathroom," I say, realizing that while I had intended to go earlier, I'd forgotten when I'd come across Anna. When I return, the party has spread out. Several people have come over from the Cottingham, some I know, others I don't. Frank gestures toward a lethal-looking concoction on the table.

"Yours," he mouths at me. "Be careful."

"What's in this, anyway?" I say, sipping it.

"Just about everything, " Cybil says. "Chambord, creme de cacao, heaven knows what else. Brings back old memories, doesn't it?"

"Brings a tear to your eye, more like it," Grace says. "It's awful, really. Watch yourselves."

I think she's right. It really is awful, so I only take a sip or two, and order another glass of wine.

"I see he came anyway, " Diana says, gesturing toward a group at the bar which now includes Károly, Woodward Watson, and Courtney Cottingham. "In more important company."

"Do you think he's screwing her?" Cybil asks, gesturing in the general direction of Courtney.

"Isn't everybody?" Morgan says, sliding into the seat beside me.

"I'm not," Frank says, leaning over Morgan from behind her.

She stretches and plants a big kiss on his cheek. "I adore you, Frankie. I always have." Frank smiles and heads for the bar.

"He fired me," Diana says.

"Yes," I say.

"How did you know that?" she says, suspiciously.

Oops, I think. "He didn't even recognize me," I say morosely.

"You're not going to start crying in your cups, are you?" Grace says.

"You said yes when I told you I'd been fired," Diana says. "How did you know?"

I cast about for an answer, but am saved a reply because trouble has arrived in the person of Anna. She walks directly up to where Károly and the others are standing, and says in a voice loud enough to carry across to where we're sitting, "How could you?"

Károly looks first at her, and then at the crowd around him and shrugs. "Excuse me?" he says.

"Who are you?" Courtney says.

"Have we met?" Woodward says.

"Now, Anna," Frank says.

"You know," she shouts. "You all know."

Cybil rushes over and tries to pull Anna away. "You got it wrong. You'll see," Anna shouts. The bartender signals one of the waiters, and the two of them start to escort Anna out of the bar. Cybil attempts to go with her, but she is angrily brushed aside. "Are you part of this, too?" she says, and Cybil backs off.

"What was that about?" I say. "Are you part of what?"

"I don't know," Cybil says. "She just isn't well, is she?"

"Maybe we should go and see that she gets home," I say. "I'll come with you, Cybil."

"I don't think she wants me to," Cybil replies. "She seems to think I'm part of whatever this is. I think we should just let her calm down."

"I agree," Frank says, coming over to the table. "Just let her be for tonight, and give her a call tomorrow. Here, I've ordered you all another drink."

"Why don't you give me Anna's address, Cybil," I say. "I am going to have to take a taxi after that B52 anyway, so I'll swing by her place and make sure she's okay. She can't blame me for whatever this thing is. She hasn't seen me in years."

"Your drinks are here," Frank says. "Lara, yours is the white wine?"

"I think you should just leave her be," Diana says. "I

don't think she was in the mood to be talked to, or she would have let Cybil go with her."

"Something must have set her off," I say. "What could it be?"

"I expect it's about Károly being a first-class jerk," Diana says as Frank leaves us to join the group at the bar.

"I agree," Morgan says.

"At least he recognized you," I said. "He didn't even know me."

"You've mentioned that," Diana said.

"What are you doing, sitting there like a bump on a log?" I ask her, at least that's what I try to say, but the words don't seem to be coming out of my mouth exactly right all of a sudden.

"I'm plotting my revenge," she says, gesturing toward a group at the bar.

By now I am feeling really peculiar, a little light-headed, and wonder if I'm coming down with the flu or something. Frank, who has left us temporarily to go and chat up a cute young man at the bar, comes and sits beside me, and I think how attractive he is. I remind myself he's gay, but I find myself looking at all the guys in the bar rather lasciviously. A couple of them come over and chat me up, and I remind myself I'm unattached and can do whatever I want. I may be dirt to Charles Miller, but I can still attract a man.

But I'm really feeling strange by this time, and even stumble a little. "Whoa," Frank says. "You gotta watch those B52s." I think to myself that I only had a sip or two.

"Do you really only like men?" I say to Frank. He looks startled.

"I'm afraid so," he says.

"I couldn't change your mind, could I?" I say.

"Not likely," he says, "I have my eye on a divine young man at the bar, but if I ever do change my mind on that subject, you'll be the first to know."

"Oh, good," I say.

"I think maybe you've had enough," he says, taking the glass of wine out of my hand and carefully but firmly pushing me down into a chair beside Diana, who has pretty much sat out the party.

"Give that back," I say, rather too loudly. Grace looks askance.

"I don't think so," Frank says. "Gotta go join my author at the bar."

"Here, have mine," Diana says. "I haven't touched it."

"I think it's time we all went home," Grace says. "Some of us do not seem to know when to stop drinking."

"Charlie's going to be really famous," I say, but even to me, my voice sounds funny. "Whether we like it or not. That Venus is going to make him famous, and Frank thinks the book will be a best seller."

"Lovely thought, that," Morgan says. "I'd better go, too. I feel a migraine coming on. I blame it on seeing Károly."

"You have given me an idea," Diana says to me.

"I have? What did I say?" I am having trouble following the conversation.

"You said that the Venus was going to make his reputation. So you know what?"

"No," I slur. The room is starting to spin.

"I'm going to steal the Magyar Venus right out from under Károly Molnár's nose. And you," she says, turning back to me, "are going to help me."

And that is the very last thing I remember.

CHAPTER THREE

September 6

I AWOKE TO A PAINFUL THROBBING AT MY TEMPLES, AN unpleasant queasiness in my gut, and an annoying ringing sound in my ears. Apparently my reunion with my college buddies had resulted in a college kind of drinking spree. It was clear to me why I had given it up the moment I left college. I felt positively vile.

I was in my underwear in my own bed, but how I'd managed to get there, I had no idea. My clothes were scattered in a line from the doorway, and my bag was by the bed, contents spread over a wide area. The car keys were on a chair. *Oh my,* I thought, looking at them.

The noise stopped for a moment or two, to my great relief, but then started again. I realized it was the phone. I had recently purchased a new one with all the bells and whistles available to anyone silly enough to buy them, and it seemed to take an immense effort to make it work. "Hello," I croaked.

"Are you all right?" Clive demanded.

"Why would you think I wouldn't be?" I snapped. If he thought I'd been crabby yesterday, today was going to be quite a trial for him.

"A couple of reasons," he replied. "One is that it is 11:00 in the morning, and as you may recall, we open at 9:30. The second is that your car is here at the office and you're not."

That's good, I thought. It was a relief to know that apparently the part of my brain that knew enough not to drive had still been operating when all other higher brain functions had ceased. "I didn't feel like driving," I said.

"You got a parking ticket," he said. "A rather large one."

"I did?" I said. Our parking places off the lane behind the store were perfectly legal day and night. "How come?"

"You left your car on the street," he said.

Not good, I thought. I had no recollection whatsoever of moving it.

"I also have a rather large parking ticket," he said.

"Why?" I said.

"Because you left your car blocking the lane so I had to park on the street this morning, too."

Not good at all, I thought again. "There's a spare set of car keys in the desk in the office," I said. "You can move my car."

"Where?" he said. I could hear him rummaging around in a most annoying way. "Okay, found them. How did you manage to make that rather large dent in your bumper?"

Very bad, I thought. "I'm not sure," I said.

"I'm getting worried about you, Lara. Are you coming in today?"

"Maybe later," I said.

"Did you hear the news, by the way?"

"I hate it when you ask questions like that," I said.

"Then I won't tell you," he said.

I waited. Clive could not hold on to a good story for long.

"There was a break-in at the Cottingham," he said. "Somebody probably trying to steal the Venus. Didn't get it, but I gather the place is something of a mess. Somebody just drove a car into the glass windows at the back, if you can believe it. Of course it made a terrible racket, the alarms all went off, and whoever it was just backed the car up, according to police, and made their getaway. Unbelievable!"

Very, very bad, I thought. How much did I have to drink anyway?

"Good grief!" he exclaimed. "Now we're going to get towed. I've got to go. I'm worried about you, Lara. This is not like you."

"I'm fine," I said.

"You'd better pull yourself together," he said. "We need to talk."

"Did you not say you were about to get towed?" I said.

"I'm going to call you back to discuss this," he said.

"Please don't. I'm fine," I repeated. I wasn't though. The minute I stood up, I realized I was going to be sick, which I was. I couldn't believe it. What had I been thinking? Did I actually believe I could drown my sorrows? And more important, what had I done?"

The phone rang again. "I'm fine," I snarled into the mouthpiece.

"Well, I'm not," a man's voice said.

"Rob?" I said. "Sorry, I thought you were someone else." Was Rob calling because he'd seen on the wire that a nation-wide manhunt for me was underway?

"I'm trying to understand this thing," he said.

"What thing?" I said. Yes, the police were almost certainly looking for me.

"Why you left me, of course," he said irritably. "Or have you forgotten that already?"

"I'm hanging up," I said. Praise be it was only about that.

"No, please," he said. "I'm sorry."

"Rob, we've been over this," I said.

"I know, but I still don't get it," he said. "I feel as if—I don't know—I guess I was missing all the signs or something, but it just came out of the blue. I don't understand what 'you and I just don't see the world the same way' means, in real terms."

I thought back over the last year, the things I'd done, the decisions I'd made that I had never felt I could talk to him about. "Maybe you don't really know me," I said.

"I think I know you pretty well," he said. "You are loyal to a fault, generous to your friends, you have a strong moral and ethical sense, you are a fine stepmother to Jennifer. She feels terrible about this, you know."

"Please don't play that card," I said. "That's not fair."

"Sorry," he said.

"Believe me, Rob, you don't know me. I have done things you would never approve of."

"Oh, please, Lara," he said. "Like what? Are we talking about your love for what we affectionately call French parking?"

"French parking?" I said.

"You know, that thing you do when you see a parking place on the other side of the road and zip into it, so you're parked facing the wrong way? That's a no-no here in Toronto the Good."

"It is?" I said. "They do it all the time in Europe, especially Paris."

"I believe that's why we call it French parking," he said.

"Oh," I said. "Well, we probably shouldn't. I'm sure it's politically incorrect."

He chuckled. "I do love you, Lara, for many reasons, not the least of which is that you make me laugh. What I'm trying to say here is that I can't imagine you doing anything that I wouldn't approve of. You didn't even ask me to call one of my esteemed colleagues at the Ontario Provincial Police when you got that speeding ticket. I loved you for that, too."

"I wouldn't dream of asking you to do anything like that," I said.

"My point exactly. Look, give me something I understand here. I'm a guy. 'You don't really know me' doesn't work for me. Do I bore you, in bed or otherwise?"

"No," I said.

"Do I have annoying habits you can no longer tolerate?"

"No."

"Do I watch too much baseball on TV?"

"No," I said. "Okay, maybe, but that's not the point."

He laughed again. "What if I promised never to watch another baseball game, not even the World Series?"

It was my turn to laugh. I shouldn't have. It made my head throb even worse. "You know that is a promise you would never be able to keep, and if you tried you wouldn't be fit to live with."

"Is . . ." he hesitated for a second or two. "Is there somebody else?"

"No," I said. "Let me ask you a question. Let's take your speeding ticket example. What would you have done if I asked you to make a call for me?"

"I wouldn't have done it," he said. "It would not have been right. You were speeding. You got caught."

"Exactly what I would expect you to say and do. Now what if our situations were reversed. I'm the cop, you're the driver. You ask me to make a call. What do you think I would do."

"I have no idea," he said.

"There you are," I said. "I'm going now."

"I can't decide whether to put my energy into getting over you or into trying to convince you to come back," he said.

"I think you should choose the former," I said.

"I know. But it's going to be the latter."

"Goodbye, Rob."

"Till next time," he said.

Two minutes later the phone rang again. "No, Rob," I said.

"Hello," a woman's voice said. "Is that Lara?"

"Sorry," I said. "I thought you were someone else." Why I was paying for call display on a fancy new phone I didn't bother looking at was a mystery to me. "Is that Diana?"

"Yes," she said. She sounded funny, as if she was talking underwater or something. "Have you heard the news?"

"I certainly have," I said.

"Isn't it dreadful?"

"It certainly is." Which one of us had been driving, I wondered, when we decided to take on the glass wall of the Cottingham.

"I just don't understand it," she said.

"What do you mean you don't understand it? It was your idea, surely."

"What did you say?" she gasped. "How could you!"

"You did suggest it, did you not?"

"I can't believe you are saying something so awful. What could I have done to make this my fault? You were always one to speak your mind, but I didn't realize you could be so cruel. You're nothing but a mean drunk," she said. "Poor Anna." The line went dead.

I stared at the phone for a minute, then started flailing around in the bedside table drawer to find the manual for the stupid thing. In a minute or two I was calling the last number that had called me. I got an answering machine.

"Diana, please pick up the phone. I think maybe we were talking about different things."

In a few seconds, she came on the line. "What were you talking about?" she said. She had obviously been crying.

"The break-in at the Cottingham," I said.

"Was there a break-in at the Cottingham?" she said. "I didn't know that."

"You did say we were going to steal the Venus right out from under Charlie's nose, did you not?"

"I didn't mean that literally," she said.

"Then what were you talking about?" I said.

She took a deep breath. "Anna's dead. She killed herself," she said.

"What!" I exclaimed. "No! What happened?"

"She threw herself off a bridge over Rosedale Valley Road," she said. "She landed on the hood of a car that was unfortunate enough to be passing under the bridge at that moment. Poor guy."

"Is the driver all right?"

"Not really," she said. "He's alive. His car was destroyed. I guess even someone as small as Anna would make quite an impact falling from that height. He's in serious condition but expected to recover. No doubt he'll be in psychotherapy for the rest of his life, but at least Anna didn't take him with her. I suppose that's something. It's on the news channel. You get to see the car every fifteen minutes or so."

"This is horrible," I said.

"It is. I thought she was getting better, you know. I really did. So did Cybil, who is, I have to say, absolutely devastated. She thought Anna was way better too. She was getting out of the house. She seemed to enjoy herself last night, at least part of it. Maybe we should have known this sort of thing could happen, but we didn't."

"Last night," I said. "What happened?"

"To you, you mean? You passed out."

"I know that. What happened then?"

"I'll pay for the damage to your car, okay? It will take me awhile but I'll do it."

"That wasn't the question," I said.

"I steered you back to your car, realized you couldn't drive, and decided I would drive you home and take a taxi from your place. I wasn't used to your car, and that lane is very narrow, and I really shouldn't have been driving anyway. I scraped the fender, I know. There was a post at the end of the lane way where you turn into the street, and I didn't notice it. I just kind of freaked, and left the car where it was because I didn't think I could get it back in its place without hitting something again. Did you get towed?"

"No," I said.

"That's good. I got us both into a taxi, dropped you off at your home, and went home myself. I was going to phone you first thing to tell you about the car, but then this business with Anna . . ." Her voice trailed off.

"You don't know where I live," I said. "Do you?"

"It's on your driver's license, and you did confirm it was your place when we got there. I watched you stagger in the door."

"I can't remember any of this," I said.

"Obviously, you have a problem with alcohol. But right now, I have to say it's just not that important to me," she said. "Anna's dead. The funeral's Friday. Let me know the damage on your car." She hung up abruptly.

No doubt she thought I was a selfish sod, worried about my car when an old friend had thrown herself off a bridge. How could I explain that I was filled with a sense of dread, an unshakable feeling that I had been involved in something terrible the night before?

I turned on the television. The car Anna had landed on was there, all right, flashing on the screen every few minutes as the bland commentator droned on about it, including constant mention of the fact that the jumper had suffered from mental disorders and was known to have been depressed. The car was hopelessly crushed, and it was a miracle the driver was still alive. I made myself some tea and toast and tried to pull myself together. I just didn't know what to do. I felt I should probably just turn myself into police and go to jail for whatever it was I'd done, but given I didn't know what it was, I would certainly look like an idiot at the police station. I could call Rob back, but what would I say to him?

By midafternoon I was in sufficiently decent shape to venture forth. I went to the shop first, and endured Clive telling me how nice it was of me to drop by, and went to look at my car, the lane way and the post. The car had sustained a fair amount of damage: no doubt it would be an expensive repair, which obviously I was not going to charge to Diana. As for the post, the truth was just about everybody hit that post at some point, and there were so many marks on it, I really couldn't say whether my car had hit it or not. What I did decide was that it had not sustained enough damage to have gone through the glass at the Cottingham, so I told myself to relax.

Then I drove to Rosedale, parked my car on a side street, and walked on to the Glen Road pedestrian bridge over the Rosedale ravine. It was a beautiful fall day and the colors were splendid, the sun warm but the air with a touch of a chill. I found it hard to believe that something so terrible had happened in such a lovely place. I went and looked over the railing. It was a very, very long way down. A few yards away a tiny piece of pale blue cloth had caught in one of the uprights. Anna had been wearing a blue dress, and that was almost certainly a piece of it. This must have been the spot where she'd gone over the side.

"You're not going to jump or anything, are you?" an anxious voice behind me said.

I turned to see an elf-like man in plaid pants, a green jacket, and a rather jaunty tan cap.

"Don't worry," I said. "I have no such plans."

"Woman jumped last night," he said.

"I know. She's an old college classmate of mine. I just came here to . . ." To what, really?

"Saw the whole thing," the little man said.

"What?"

"Live there," he said, pointing to a yellow brick apartment building on the edge of the ravine. "My window is the one at the end."

"You saw it?" I said.

"Don't sleep much anymore. Retired, you know. Don't have enough to do during the day. Sit at my bedroom window for hours. It's interesting at night—the trees and the city lights, the fire hall across the way. The city never sleeps, just like they say."

"So what did you see last night?"

"Young woman runs out on to the bridge."

"What do you mean by young?" I said.

"Born in 1922," he said. "Looks young to me. She keeps looking over her shoulder like she's being followed. Then there's this bang, and she's up and over the side. Took her two or three tries, and all the while she's looking over her shoulder. Figure she was running away from somebody she's pretty scared of."

"This bang?" I said.

"Sounded like a car hitting something, like maybe the barricade at the end of the bridge. Can't see that from my window. But there was something. Told the police, but they think they're dealing with a crazy old coot. What do you think, being her friend and all?"

"I don't know," I said. "Let's go look at the barricade."

The truth of the matter was that it would be difficult, but not impossible, to get a car past the flower beds and up to the barricade, but no way to get up enough speed to actually knock down it down. The barricade was metal and showed many signs of wear, but nothing that I could see that looked particularly fresh. The stone wall around the flower beds was a different matter. A large stone had been dislodged and there was dirt on the sidewalk around it. The last geranium of summer lay on its side, roots exposed.

"There," the man said. "That's where it must have been."

I kicked the stone to roll it over, and sure enough there was a streak of color on it, a scrape really, in silver, and while silver was an extremely popular color for cars, it just happened to be the color of mine. I had eliminated one possibility, I'd thought, for the dent in the bumper, and had just been presented with a truly dreadful alternative. My stomach churned.

"You know who'd have been chasing the poor thing?" he asked me.

"I have no idea," I said.

"You believe old Alfred, don't you?"

"I think it's possible," I said.

"Then, maybe you'll tell the police," he said. "Hearing it from somebody like you might make them believe it."

"I'll try," I said. But I didn't. I got the man's name—Alfred Nabb—and phone number, and after commiserating with him for a few minutes about shoddy police work, made my escape. I picked up the phone to make the call several times that afternoon, but I didn't really know what to say. They had the same information I did, and if they chose to do something with it, then surely that was up to them. For myself, I was going to have to wait until I felt better to figure out what I was going to do.

September 9

Anna's funeral was a dismal affair, but perhaps that says more about me than the event, having spent the two days in the interim expecting the police to arrive at my door at any second. I kept pulling at the threads of my memory, but still there was nothing. The service was held in one of the huge downtown churches, way too big for the dozen or so of us who turned out. Our footsteps echoed on the stone floors, and we huddled together in the first row. Cybil sobbed through the whole thing. They'd already cremated the body, and a rather plain urn sat where otherwise a coffin might be. All of those who had been at the reunion were there, including Frank, as well as Anna's mother, a sad little creature by the name of Doris, and quite remarkably, Alfred Nabb.

"Thought old Alfred should pay his respects," he said,

continuing what was obviously a habit of avoiding the word "I" at any cost. "Under the circumstances. You call the police yet?"

I had to confess I hadn't, but promised I would.

"Too late," he said. "The city's already been around to fix the stone wall and the garden. If you wanted them to do it, it'd take them years to get around to it."

"I'm sorry," I said.

"Won't bring her back anyways, will it?" he said as he toddled off to take his seat.

Just before the service was to begin, a nice-looking man appeared with two sweet little girls in tow. They took their places in the front row across the aisle from the rest of us. The older of the two girls was about nine, I'd say, the other only four. They were in their very best dresses, pink for the elder girl, blue for the young one, with lacy collars and big skirts. They wore white tights and black patent Mary Janes, their blond hair was pulled back with matching barrettes, and they were two of the prettiest little girls I had ever seen. The younger one was the spitting image of Anna, the older looked more like her father.

We were about ten minutes into the service when the clear bell-like tones of the little girl filled a momentary pause in the proceedings. "Where's Mummy gone?" she said. The sound seemed to rise to the very top of the cathedral, echoing from every corner of the church. We all started, and some of us gasped. The man leaned down and murmured something to her. I think he said something about heaven. "When is she coming back?" the little girl demanded in a plaintive tone. The older child put her arms around the shoulders of the little one, and gave her a hug. The man, Anna's husband, looked terrible. Cybil burst into tears, and it was all I could do, not to do the same.

I sat through the rest of the service in a little puddle of misery, going back over that evening for the thousandth time, and wondering if I'd been responsible in any way for the little girl's pain. How many drinks had I consumed? I had a glass and a half at the bar before we went to the museum. The wine was lovely, but you would never call the glasses large, and I hadn't had time to finish the second one. I'd taken three glasses of champagne at the Cottingham, but I'd not got more than a sip or two out of any of them. Indeed I felt I'd spent the whole evening looking for my stray champagne glass. I'd barely sipped the first glass when we'd been asked to set them down to go upstairs. I'd been served another afterward, but only had a couple of sips before leaving it in the bathroom. I got a third, but then I'd had to set it down to go into the shop to buy Károly's book. When I came out there were several half-drunk glasses where I'd left mine, so I'd just given up on champagne. That meant that by the time I returned to the bar, I couldn't have had much more than two drinks in me, two and a half at most. There was the B52, or course, which had been a bad idea. They didn't name those things after military aircraft for nothing. But still, I'd only had a couple of sips, certainly not enough not only to pass out, but not to remember a thing. I'd started drinking at five, and recalled seeing the clock over the bar at midnight, awhile before it all went black. That meant I'd had seven hours for the stuff to work its way out of my system. Maybe, I thought, I had a peculiar virus or a brain tumor. Or maybe, more likely, I'd just had a helluva lot more to drink than I recalled.

There was no interment ceremony, although Cybil told us that her mother had chosen a plot for Anna's ashes in the cemetery that led down into the ravine where Anna had died. After the service we all went back to Anna's mother's apartment. It was in a yellow apartment building very similar to Alfred Nabb's and only a block or two away from the bridge. Mrs. Belmont served tea and those sandwiches we used to get at children's birthday parties, pinwheels of peanut butter and banana, cucumber and cream cheese, and impossibly constructed squares of pink and brown bread that look like a chessboard. Cybil, who was quite obviously dealing with this by stuffing her face, ate most of them. There were cakes, tiny petits fours, with pink icing, and for those who needed something a little stronger, in this case Alfred Nabb, there was some truly awful sherry.

"Didn't know she was a neighbor of mine," he said, looking at the picture of Anna, taken in happier times, that rested prominently on a table beside the small urn of Anna's ashes. "Been living in that building for over twenty years, and saw everybody who'd walked across the bridge. Never remember seeing her. That lady," he added, indicating Doris. "Her mother. Seen her many times, but not that poor girl."

"I didn't know she was a neighbor, either," I said. "I live just across the bridge in Cabbagetown, and she was a classmate of mine at college, and I didn't know she lived just a few blocks away from me. She didn't get out much."

I looked at the many photos Doris had on display. The most poignant of them all was Anna with her family: her husband, smiling, a boy of about three in his lap, the older daughter about six standing beside her mother and smiling at the baby in Anna's arms. Many of the photos dated to our college days. Anna had been the clown of the group, always sneaking into our apartments to short-sheet our beds, or to dream up some prank we all had to participate in. In the photos, she was the one holding up her fingers behind someone else's head, or mugging outrageously. That she should come to such a sad end, after years of anguish, seemed impossible. I'd thought of going after her that night in the bar, to get her address from Cybil, to just sit with her to see what was bothering her, but instead, I'd just hung around the bar drinking myself into a coma.

"This is so sad," Morgan said, looking about the apartment. "I can't even imagine what it would be like being afraid to go out. Did she just sit here, day after day, staring out the window?"

"I think she had visitors. Cybil certainly came over. And Diana told me that even though she lost custody of her children, they came over to see her once a week."

"I hope she at least went out on the balcony or something," Morgan murmured. "Being stuck in this little apartment would have the opposite effect on me. I'd be clawing at the walls trying to get out."

The apartment was tidy, but, as Morgan had pointed out, rather small. There was a bedroom that obviously belonged to Doris, one bathroom, and a second, much smaller room with a single bed that doubled as a couch, a small chest of drawers, and, the dominant feature of the room, a rather large desk. "Anna's room," Cybil said, joining me. "Tiny isn't it? I guess she really did close herself in. She had virtually nothing, you know. The cupboard's small, but it was big enough for her stuff. She had lots of books, that's about all. She read everything. Frank and I cleaned out the room yesterday. I didn't think Doris could manage it, and I thought I'd need a guy to do the heavy lifting. Frank volunteered, which was nice of him. He came to visit Anna a few times while she was shut in, or whatever we want to call what she was doing. I didn't really need his help, as it turned out, but it was nice to have his company. We got everything into three small cartons. We took pretty well everything to a women's shelter. Frank said he'd take her books to a library, if Doris didn't want them, which she didn't.

"It was her shoes that really got to me," Cybil went on. "She had three pairs. When you looked at them on the floor of the closet they looked perfectly normal, but when we put them in the box, on the bottom they looked like new. The apartment has broadloom as you can see, and the soles never got worn. The tops had some spots on them, of course, what you'd expect—spaghetti sauce or something, on one of them. But the soles . . . It hit me then. She really never went out."

"We can't imagine that, can we?" I said. "You hear about people like that, but you can't understand it."

"No, you can't. Could I ask a favor, though, while you're here? Would you mind having a look at the desk? Doris was going to give it away, but I think it's rather nice, and I thought she should save it for one of the little girls. I had the idea it might even be worth something. What do you think? Is is an antique or anything?"

I took a closer look, opening the drawers, and pulling it out from the wall to look at the back. "It's not terribly old," I said. "Maybe fifty or sixty years. But it is a lovely desk, solid wood. They don't often make them like this any more. Notice it has a pocket shelf over the bank of drawers on either side. It's a nice feature. If you need a bigger work surface, you just pull out the shelf and work away, and then slide it back in when you're done," I said, demonstrating. A small piece of paper came out with the shelf. I glanced at it before handing it to Cybil, to see that it contained only two words: Calvaria Club.

"Find anything interesting?" Frank said, joining us in the room. In that place, three was definitely a crowd.

Cybil handed him the slip of paper. "What's Calvaria mean?"

"Beats me," Frank said.

"I'm trying to remember," I said. "It sounds familiar. Isn't Calvaria Latin for something?"

"Latin?" Cybil said. "How would I know?"

"Skull," I said. "Calvaria is Latin for skull."

"The skull club?" Cybil said. "Weird."

"She was a very strange woman, I'm afraid," Frank said, crumpling the paper and looking about for a wastebasket. "Very strange. Nice desk, though," he added, opening the drawers.

"See the little shelves," Cybil said. "Aren't they neat?"

"They are," I said, as Frank wandered off. "In any event, yes, I think it would be a very nice idea to save the desk for the girls."

"I'll talk to Brad, that's Anna's ex—did you see him in the church?—about coming to get it."

"It's nice of you to take such an interest," I said.

"Nice? Anna was a good friend, you know. She maybe didn't go out of the apartment, but she wasn't, like, bonkers, or anything. Raving, I mean, or incoherent. She just wouldn't go outside, that's all. She read, she took Internet courses, she watched TV. She didn't turn into a vegetable. She was even working on her master's thesis from home. She did the course work, but got married and had kids before she got around to doing the thesis. She was really trying to get better, maybe get her husband and kids back."

"What happened to the little boy, do you know?" I said.

"He fell off an apartment balcony. Several floors. He was visiting his other grandmother with his sisters. I guess the three of them were too much for her. The baby was crying and the grandmother went to look after her, and the little guy just went up and over. It shouldn't have happened, but it did.

"I keep thinking about her being out on that bridge. All that open space. Maybe she just couldn't stand it, or maybe because the little guy fell, she just sort of fell, too. I don't know. What I do know is that I should have gone home with her instead of letting her go off by herself like that. She said she didn't want me to come with her, but I should have insisted. She might still be alive now, wouldn't she?"

It was a good question, of course, but a futile one. "Don't think about that. She wasn't bonkers, as you say, but she wasn't well, either. It is tragic, but not your fault."

"I'm trying for my own sanity to believe that," Cybil said. "I really am." *Me too,* I thought. *Me too.*

We stood around a few minutes outside the apartment building until Grace suggested we all go for a drink. Frank declined, and after some debate it was determined we'd go back to the bar where we'd last seen Anna. Everybody ordered a Scotch except me. I was still on a mineral water regimen.

"Good idea," Grace said as I ordered.

"Look, I know I behaved badly the other night," I said to the group. "But I don't usually drink that much. In fact, I don't actually remember drinking too much."

"You always had a drink in your hand when I saw you," Grace said.

"We're not here to talk about that," Diana said. "We have to put our plan into operation. We're counting on you, Lara."

"What plan?" I said.

"This from the woman who doesn't actually remember drinking too much," Grace said, rather sarcastically.

"Our plan to bring down the high and mighty Károly Molnár, of course," Diana said.

"By stealing the Venus. I thought someone had tried that already."

"We'll need a little more time to put the material together, now that I'm no longer employed there," she said, ignoring my comment.

"You're not?" Cybil said.

"No, I'm not. As Lara apparently knows, I got sacked at the party."

"No!" Morgan said. "Why?"

"I was fired on an entirely trumped-up charge of stealing from the till. Please be assured I did no such thing. Now to get back to the plan."

"You must have done something," Grace said.

"I believe Dr. Molnár has figured out what I was up to, which will make our plan more difficult, but not impossible, to carry out."

"You mean he knew what you were researching," Cybil said.

"That's the only explanation I can come up with," Diana said.

"The worm," Morgan said. "Is everybody thinking what I'm thinking?"

"Pretty much," Grace said. The others nodded.

"What are we thinking?" I said.

"That Anna killed herself because of something Károly said to her at the party, of course," Cybil said.

"Isn't that a bit of a stretch?" I said, but in my mind I was back to the bridge and the overturned stone.

"You were there. You saw how she went right up to him at the bar."

"You can't actually say that," I said. "She went up to a large group of people at the bar, and I for one couldn't tell which of them she was shouting at."

"Don't tell me you're still infatuated with him," Grace said.

"Hardly," I said. "And even if I had been, that night would have cured me. He didn't even know me."

"I'm afraid you told us that already—several times in fact—in the bar afterwards," Diana said.

"I did?"

Diana made a face at the others. "The plan?" she said. She'd pulled a copy of the previous day's newspaper and was tapping the front page of the arts section, which prominently featured Károly and his Magyar Venus. As Frank had pointed out the evening of the unveiling, Károly could charm the birds out of the trees, and the interviewer, a woman, was obviously besotted. She made it sound as if Toronto were singularly blessed to have such a dynamic individual in our midst. There was, of course, a great deal about how he'd tracked down the Venus and how extraordinarily perceptive the Cottinghams had been in snaring both Károly and by extension the artifact.

"Would somebody please tell me what this plan is?" I said. Were they going to make me beg?

"Okay, let's take it from the top, as they say," Diana said. "Several of us have reasons to dislike, dare I say loathe, dear old Charlie. I have already mentioned mine."

"That scum," Cybil said. "I just know he said something awful to Anna. I just know he did."

"If it makes you feel any better, Lara, he didn't seem to remember much about me when I got the assignment at the museum, either," Diana said. "I reminded him, though. I suppose that's what put him on his guard. I was responsible for his expense accounts, and I found something there that would probably get him fired. That's why I got sacked. I leave it to the others to decide whether they want to talk about their reasons for disliking the man enough to take part in this endeavor, but in a nutshell, the plan is as follows: we, with your help, Lara, are going to prove that the Magyar Venus is a fake."

"How are we going to do that?" I said.

"I don't know. That's what you're going to tell us. We'll have to check the whatever you call that thing, you know, who owned it when, who sold it to whom."

"Provenance?"

"Provenance, right. We'll need to establish that the Venus's provenance is a fabrication. Dr. Molnár's reputation will be in tatters, something I for one will enjoy."

"Hold it!" I said. "I don't much like Charlie these days either, but what makes you think it's a fake?"

"The Piper diaries, of course. Have you read them?"

"Not yet," I said.

"Read them," Diana said. "There is something patently wrong there. I can't put my finger on it, not yet anyway, but they do not ring true to me," she said. "This C. J. Piper is not what he's supposed to be, I'm sure of it."

"By 'not what he's supposed to be' do you mean he didn't have the academic qualifications?"

"Just read the diaries," she said. "You'll see what I mean. It would hardly be the first time a lot of people were fooled. There was that Piltdown business, wasn't there? That was a complete hoax and we still don't know who did it."

"We have a lot better testing methods now, and would perhaps not so easily be fooled, although I grant you there are a number of prized exhibits in museums all over the world that are being quietly put in storage because the centerpiece has been proven to be at best suspect."

"What's a Piltdown?" Cybil said.

"Piltdown man was a skull found in Sussex, England, in the 1920s that purportedly was the missing link between ape and man. People believed it for years. I think there's even a plaque where the skull was found. But it was proven to be a complete hoax, and Diana is right, while there have been several theories posited about who did it, no one is entirely sure."

"So, Diana, you are convinced the Magyar Venus is a similar hoax? Are you saying Charles manufactured it in his garage or something?" Grace asked.

"I'm not necessarily saying he manufactured it, no. I am saying that there is something the matter with the diaries, and Charles is either pulling the wool over everybody's eyes, or he is guilty of faulty scholarship. Either way, the Venus has to be a fake."

"Were people faking art a hundred years ago?" Morgan asked. "I mean, could it have been faked then, rather than now?"

"Sure," I said. "But a hundred years ago, most of the fakes of objects that were supposed to be as old as the Venus were found in North America, not Europe. They were attempts to prove—I use the term loosely—that man was on this continent tens of thousands of years ago."

"I'm telling you it's a fake," Diana repeated. "We need you, Lara. It was a godsend that I ran into you on the street the other day. Given what's happened, we need you more than ever. Now, if we want to prove the Venus is a fake, where should we start?"

"I'm really busy right now," I said.

"No, you're not," Diana said. "You told us the other night that you were thinking of taking a leave from the shop for a month or two. How long could it take to prove this thing is a fake? A month, give or take a week or two?"

"Have I mentioned that this thing, as you call it, is about twenty-four thousand years older than anything I know anything about? Give or take a millennium or two," I said.

"Where do we start?" Diana repeated.

I looked at their expectant faces, and in an instant I knew that I was going to have to follow this thread wherever it took me, because I had to know what happened the night Anna died. Somehow this group had to be part of it. One of them had to know.

"We'd start with Lillian Larrington," I sighed.

CHAPTER FOUR

September 10

"HELLO, LILY," MORGAN SAID, AS THE DOOR OPENED. "I hope we haven't caught you at a bad time. We were just driving by, and I thought I'd see if you were in. This is my friend Lara McClintoch. She and I were at college together, and she's an antique dealer. We're on our way to lunch."

"Morgan! How nice," Lily said. "Come in. We'll have a drink. You aren't supposed to drink alone. At least that's what they tell you. I'm always glad when someone comes to call. A gin and tonic, perhaps? Or a nice glass of sherry? The sun is over the yard arm, isn't it? Come and sit down."

She led us into the living room of her home, a rather unprepossessing ranch-style bungalow in one of the wealthier Toronto suburbs. I looked around the room. It did not look like a collector's home to me. The art, by which I mean one painting over the fireplace, was traditional and not particularly good. There were a couple of Royal Doulton figurines, and that's about it. Not that that necessarily meant anything, but I had a pretty good idea which way this was going to go.

"What will you have to drink?" she said, turning to me. "What did you say your name was again, dear?"

"It's Lara," I said, as Morgan and I sat side by side on the pink sofa. "But no drink, thank you." Lily looked very sad. Morgan nudged me.

"Okay, perhaps just a little sherry," I said. Lily's eyes brightened.

"We'll all just have a drop," she said, pouring an enormous amount of sherry and handing it to me.

"I just wanted to stop by and personally say thank you for donating the Venus," Morgan said, taking a tiny sip from an equally large container. "We are all so thrilled. This really will put the museum on the map. It was just so generous of you, and I wanted to tell you that in person. I felt badly that I didn't get a chance the other night, what with the crowds."

"Wasn't that a marvelous evening?" Lily said. "I had seen the Venus before everyone else, of course. Károly saw to it that I had a special private showing, but still, I wanted to see what the reaction would be."

"You mean Károly let you see how it was going to be displayed," Morgan said.

"That too," she said.

Morgan glanced over at me. She looked rather perplexed. From my perspective it was playing out pretty much the way I'd expected when I first entered the room. Sometimes in this business checking provenance is a slam dunk. Sometimes it isn't.

"When did you get to see it for the first time?" I said. "That must have been exciting."

"Oh, it was!" she said. "It was just that afternoon. It was supposed to come back from the restorer, or whatever you call those people, a week before it was displayed, but it didn't get there until that day. Károly was so nervous it wouldn't be ready, it was quite funny. He is such a dear. He looks so confident and everything, but underneath, he's really quite sweet and rather shy. Intelligent, too—he has his PhD, you know—and so polite. If I had a son, I would have wanted him to be just like Károly. I was sure the Venus would get there in time, but the suspense was quite something."

"Are you saying . . . ?" Morgan said, then hesitated. "How long have you owned it. Was it in your family for some years?"

"You are not listening, dear," she said, taking a large gulp of her sherry. "I never saw the Venus before the day it was unveiled." Morgan's jaw dropped. "That's an interesting question about my family, though," Lily said. "Károly thought I might be related to the man that found it in the first place—C. J. Piper. My maiden name is Piper. I've made a stab at tracing it back, but no luck so far. I'm told you can do that kind of thing on the Internet, but I don't like computers. People have such bad handwriting nowadays. They've lost the skill. I used to be complimented on my handwriting. When I was young people wrote the loveliest letters, and diaries, of course. You sent off a letter and waited for the reply with such anticipation. Now it's all instantaneous, and with complete strangers, too. Károly agrees with me, you know. He said when he had a minute he'd help me trace my ancestors, give me some addresses I could write to."

"I'm sure that was a very generous donation that you made so that Károly could acquire the Venus," I said.

She hooted. "Reg would turn over in his grave if he knew I'd spent all that money on that little thing. He'd have a fit if he were alive. I gave Károly a million dollars of Reg's money," she giggled. "I still have lots," she added. "Enough, anyway. Auto parts."

"Auto parts?" Morgan said.

"That's how Reg made his money. Pots of it. I wasn't quite sure what to do with it all when he died. We didn't have children. Then I met Károly, and he had such a good idea. I like the Cottingham. After Reg died I decided to do some volunteer work, and that was the place I chose. The people there are lovely—I rather like your Woodward, Morgan—and it's nice when people like you come to visit. Károly comes to visit quite often."

"Where did Károly find the Venus?" I said.

"I don't know," she said. "Wherever people like him find things like that. Have some more sherry, will you?"

"No, thanks," we said in unison.

"Don't mind if I do," she said, refilling her glass. "I'm not sure I was supposed to tell anybody about the money," she said.

"Oh, we won't tell anybody," Morgan said. "Will we, Lara?"

"No," I said. "Not if you don't want us to. But why wouldn't you tell people? It's a very generous donation, and it might encourage others to do the same."

"I don't think Károly wanted me to," she said. "That's why."

Morgan looked a little like the Cheshire cat. "Well, Lily, we'd better get on our way," she said. "We don't want to take up too much of your time."

"Oh, it's no bother," she said. "I don't suppose you'd come again?"

"Of course I will," Morgan said.

"You come too, Lara," she said. "Soon."

"Isn't that something?" Morgan said as we reached her car. "The woman saw the Venus practically the same time we did. And that creep Károly lied about it. I can't wait to tell the Divas."

"Hold on a minute," I said. "I can't remember Károly's exact words, but she did donate the Venus in a way. She gave him the money to acquire it, and the Cottingham would never have managed to acquire it without her. I think he simply said that she had made a very generous donation. He may have been a little vague on the form that donation took, that's all. We could fault him on sins of omission, I suppose, in that he didn't actually mention the check. But this proves nothing."

"Whose side are you on?" she said.

"I'm on the side of intellectual honesty," I said. "You and the others have decided the Venus is a fake and Károly is a fraud, but we have proved no such thing, nor have we proved otherwise. All we've done is confirm that the Venus was never in her possession. Given her maiden name, it would have been interesting if the Venus had been in her family for some time. This just makes it a little harder, that's all."

"Intellectual honesty? You are beginning to sound almost as pompous as he does. I suppose you're still in love with him," she said. "Admit it."

"Don't be ridiculous. It was twenty years ago, and he doesn't even remember me."

"So you've mentioned," she said. "I'm not sure I believe you, but," she said, her voice softening, "I can understand it in a way. But you know what I'm thinking? I'm thinking maybe he's the one behind the attempted break-in. He knows the Venus won't stand up to the intense scrutiny of the scientific establishment, so unveils it, gets all the credit, then tries to steal it so no one who knows anything can get a close look at it."

"I would have thought that if that was his intention, to steal the Venus, I mean, he'd have done a better job of it, knowing all he does about the security systems."

"Hmm," she said. "I suppose you're right. What next, then?"

"I'll have to think about that. I should just ask Charles, but given I didn't use the opportunity the other night at the Cottingham to get reacquainted, I'll have to figure out how to approach him," I said. "Would you . . .?"

"Don't look at me," she said. "Charles and I do not get along."

So much for that idea. I suppose I could have predicted it based on the conversation I'd overheard at the Cottingham. "Then I'll have to think about how to approach this," I said.

As it turned out, I didn't have to work at it at all. Within a few hours, my telephone rang.

"Lara McClintoch, please," a man said, and my heart leapt. I would have known that voice anywhere.

"Speaking," I said, a little breathlessly.

"Will you forgive me for not recognizing you the other night?" the voice said.

"I'm not sure," I said. I should have said "Who is speaking, please?"

"Will you have dinner with me so I can persuade you?"

"I don't know," I said. My conversational skills, such as they were, seemed to have deserted me.

"Browne's Bistro in an hour?" the voice said.

"Browne's in an hour," I replied.

"Please don't stand me up, even if I deserve it," the voice said.

Thereupon followed an incredible forty-five minutes of trying on various outfits and almost screaming with frustration when my favorite suit had a mark on the lapel. I finally settled for what I thought was a sophisticated black light wool crepe pant suit, black silk pumps, and a silk shirt in what I hoped was a flattering shade, seafoam green, a color that Rob used to tell me matched my eyes. Did I care the suit was a little too warm for these early autumn days? No, I did not. It made me look thinner, didn't it? Needless to say, I was late.

He stood up the minute I walked through the door. He was dressed in an expensive gray suit that matched the touch of gray at his temples—and a pair of tortoiseshell glasses.

He took my hand and kissed it. It should have been a nice gesture, but it reminded me of his speech the other evening and his rather patronizing comments, I thought, about women, or rather ladies, to use his term, and his harsh tone with one or two of our fellow classmates. "So now I see what I missed by being too vain to wear my glasses," he said. "It serves me right. You look absolutely wonderful." He pulled out my chair, still holding my hand. Indeed he didn't let go of it for some time.

"I was afraid you wouldn't come," he said. "I've been sitting here in agony." In an instant, I forgave him everything.

"How could I resist seeing the fabulous Charles Miller again?" I said. "Also known as Károly Molnár, the man of the hour in the Toronto arts scene."

"You're teasing me," he said. "Here, please sit down. I have ordered a bottle of champagne. May I?" he said, lifting the bottle and a flute.

"Just a little," I said. "It's good to see you, but in order to be forgiven, you are going to have to explain this Charles/ Károly business right away. And then I want the whole scoop on the Magyar Venus. How you got her. Everything. But start with the name." I didn't want him to get the impression I was only there for the Venus. And maybe I wasn't.

"I was born in Hungary," he said, as we clinked glasses. "I expect I never told you that. Károly Molnár is my real name. My parents, Imre and Magdolna, fled the country during the 1956 uprising, when I was three years old. I believe I have just revealed my age. I'm older than you are."

"I know that," I replied. "That was part of your appeal in college."

"Was it?" he smiled. "The sophisticated older man. I wasn't really very sophisticated, now was I?"

"I thought you were," I said.

"No, you didn't. I'm sure a whiff of my humble beginnings must have crept through, no matter how hard I tried."

"I remember nothing of the sort. I can't recall meeting your family, though, now that you mention it. You told me they were in Europe, didn't you? Was it London?"

"It was London, all right. London, Ontario, actually, but I didn't specify. I was too embarrassed to introduce them to you. You were so worldly. Father in diplomatic corps, lived all over the world. I remember you invited me to your home for dinner. Such charming parents, fabulous conversation, lovely food! I came from a decidedly working-class family. If you'd come to my place, you'd have eaten *paprikás csirke*, chicken paprika, at the kitchen table. I didn't speak English until I went to school, and never at home. My mother never learned enough English that she would speak it at home. My father was a factory worker, and my mother worked in a bakery. She made Hungarian cakes—*dobos torte* and and the like, and they served her *gulyás* at lunch time. It was a hard life for both of them, and frankly at some point they just embarrassed me, I regret to say."

"You would hardly be the only or even the first kid to be embarrassed by his or her parents," I said.

"Perhaps, but not all of them deluded themselves that their parents didn't exist. I don't know if you remember, but I didn't attend our graduation ceremony, because I didn't want to have my name—my real name—read out."

"I remember you weren't there. It was a big disappointment for me, but I thought you had a job interview in Paris, or something like that."

"I know. As for your recollection I was in Paris, that's probably what I said. When I went to university, I created this whole new persona—I changed my name, although not legally, and just pretended I was someone else. Part of me just got tired of always having to correct the pronunciation of my name everywhere I went. I always got Carol-lee. That sounds like a line of frozen cakes, if you ask me. 'Kar-roy,' I was always saying. 'It's pronounced Kar-roy Mole-nar, emphasis almost always on the first syllable in Hungarian.' I got really tired of saying that."

"I can understand that. I don't much like Lera, either. It sounds like a video game. It's Lah-ra. I'm named for the character in *Dr. Zhivago,* the one played by Julie Christie in the movie. My mother was reading the book while she waited for my arrival. I never did understand why I don't look like Julie Christie, with a name like that."

"You have just proved my point," he said. "Your parents read Boris Pasternak. Mine didn't. I wanted parents who read things like that. I'd have settled for parents who knew who Boris Pasternak was!"

"I don't know what you're going on about," I said. "My parents claim to this day that it was the Hungarians that made Toronto the cosmopolitan city it is. There wasn't a coffee house in Toronto before 1956 when so many Hungarians fled the country during the revolution. They brought the first whiff of European sophistication the city had ever seen. Budapest was one of the most cultured cities in Europe at one time, maybe it still is, for all I know. My father was there, in Austria, I mean. It was his first foreign posting. He was there in 1956. He told me often how some time in 1956 the people rose up to throw off their Communist oppressors, and—"

"October twenty-third," Charles said.

"October twenty-third, then. He said that for several days the country was united against the Communists, and for a few wonderful days, it seemed as if the country would be free. But then the Communists came back."

"The night of November third," he said. "The Communist tanks which had circled the city of Budapest moved in. I can remember my mother telling me there was a tank in Pannónia utca, Pannónia Street, at Szent István körút, which was very close to where we lived, and how frightened she was."

"Yes. And then people found whatever transport they could—buses, trucks, cars, and they headed for the border. And when they couldn't get any further, they got out and walked, streamed across the border into Austria. My dad was there. Maybe he met your parents! Western countries had set up kind of mini-consulates in tents just across the border in Austria, and my father was a low-level cultural attaché working in the Canadian tent. They worked day and night to process the applications. He was very proud that so many Hungarians—tens of thousands of them!—chose Canada."

"They emptied the jails you know, in those heady days

when they rather naively thought the Communists would allow them their freedom. There were lots of political prisoners, certainly, but there were also common criminals who went free. No doubt some of those streamed across the border, to use your term, and hence to Canada too."

"I'm sure some of them did. You could say the same thing about Castro letting people leave Cuba. The criminal element came with them. But, on balance we have been enriched by the people who came, their art, their culture, their food."

"Maybe," he said. "You are obviously the kind of person who sees the cup as half-full."

"I think that's probably true. I tend to be optimistic more often that not." Not that I was feeling particularly optimistic these days, but why bother to mention it?

"I, I'm afraid, am a cup-half-empty kind of guy. All I'm saying is that people had many reasons for leaving Hungary in 1956, not all of them positive. I must tell you, though, that I owe my life here to a goose. Don't laugh. It's true. The way my mother told the story, they had a wonderful apartment in Budapest. You'll understand that was an accomplishment during that time. Still, when the revolution came, my mother and father wanted to leave Budapest while they could, while my grandmother, who was living with them, didn't. They were very hungry. The Soviet forces had surrounded the city and cut off the supply of food. My grandmother, according to my parents, was a wizard at finding stuff on the black market. She said she knew where to find a goose. My father said he was going to get a truck to carry us to the border. It was agreed that if my grandmother got the goose, they'd stay. If not, they'd take the truck and make a run for it. My grandmother lined up for the goose, but they ran out of them just two people ahead of her in

line. So here I am. I have always thought of that as a meta-
phor for my life, the role that fate seems to play in it from
time to time, but also there's something about it all hinging
on a goose, a certain farcical element that dogs my steps."

I laughed. "So why go back now, then, to your real name?"
I asked. "My mother thought you were absolutely divine, by
the way, when she met you."

"Thank your mother for me. She's well, is she? Yes?
Good. I guess I just acquired enough credentials—I got my
doctorate in fine arts as you may know, and a fancy wife and
job, enough polish, maybe, that it didn't matter anymore.
Or maybe I just couldn't go on the way I was. It catches up
to you. You can't maintain the façade, at least I couldn't.
And, to be perfectly honest, there was some advantage in it.
I was only one of hundreds, thousands of curators in Britain,
but after the fall of Communism, there was a great deal of
interest in seeing what kind of art exhibits one might put
together with the new regimes in Eastern Europe. I volunteered that I could speak Hungarian, so they sent me off to
Budapest. I made contacts reasonably easily, given I could
speak the language, although Hungarians do say I speak it
very well for someone who wasn't born there—I remained
silent on the fact that I *was* born there—and I got to curate
a very popular exhibit on the hidden treasures of Eastern
Europe. Moved right up the hierarchy with that one."

"And the fancy wife?" I wasn't going to ask that question, but somehow it just popped out of my mouth.

"Still in England. We are legally separated, and not particularly amicably, I'm afraid. I'm sure that even as we speak
she is telling her lawyer what he has to do to make my life a
misery."

"Perhaps not right this minute," I smiled. "It's the middle of the night in England."

"If I told you that she now sleeps with her lawyer, would you believe me? I gather that relationship was going on a lot longer than I knew," he said ruefully. "But never mind. I have recreated myself anew, as the suave, debonair eligible bachelor. Lady's man, even," he laughed. "I'm thinking about having laser surgery on my eyes, so what happened that night at the museum won't happen again. What do you think? Foolish to be a lady's man who can't see the beautiful ladies, isn't it?"

"I suppose," I said. "But speaking about being a lady's man, what was all that garbage the other night about being in love with a much younger woman, and the little Venus who wouldn't reveal her age and everything," I said. "That was a bit over the top." My tone was light, but I was really interested to hear what he'd say.

"Wasn't that awful?" he said. "The things I have to do."

"It was rather . . ."

"Sexist? Insincere? I hate to think of the impression I must have made on you, but I am required to look at it a different way. My job is to flatter. Do you know how many people that evening wrote a check to the museum, how many people became members? Forty-five. We got almost $60,000 in pledges that one evening alone, and a well-known art collector told me he wants to come and talk to me about donating his collection of Shang bronzes. A rather fabulous collection it is, too. Look at the audience. They were, by and large, older and rich. My job is to help them part with a tiny bit of their money. God knows we need it. Cottingham donated his collection and built the place, but like so many people who build these monuments to ego, he didn't give anything to keep it operating. Lillian is a real dear, a very generous woman, and she loved it. For me, that is what counted. I adore her. Have you met her, by the way?" He looked right at me as he said that, and I had the distinct feeling he knew the answer. I was lobbing questions at him that I hoped would reveal something I needed to know about him, and he was doing exactly the same thing to me.

"I just met her today," I said. "Morgan, you know, Vesta, and I were planning to meet for lunch and she suggested I come along with her when she went to visit to thank her for the donation."

"Ah," he said. "That was nice of her. Did our Lily offer you a drink?"

"Oh yes," I said. "It was a little early in the day, and it was the largest glass of sherry I have ever seen. I believe I could have arranged a large bunch of flowers in the container she handed to me. But like you, I know what is required. I sipped it very carefully."

"She does tipple a bit," he smiled. "Speaking of which, have some more champagne. You've hardly had any."

"I'm cutting back. It's a New Year's resolution."

"It's September," he said. "You're either too early or too late. Drink up. So what did our Lily have to say?" He was studiously casual. It was another of those questions.

"To tell you the truth," I said—always beware of statements that begin with "to tell you the truth"—"It was a little confusing. The sherry perhaps. It was hard to tell if she had donated the Venus or if she'd donated cash toward the purchase."

The ball was now back in his court. "Cash," he said. "A great deal of it. As I believe I mentioned, I adore her."

"That's nice. She said you come to visit her quite often."

"I do, perhaps to make up for the disgraceful way I treated my mother."

"Where are your parents now?" I said.

"Dead," he said. "And I never got to say I'm sorry."

"Oh, Charles!" I said. "That's . . . I don't know what to say."

"There is nothing you can say," he said. "But will you call me Károly? I know it will be awkward at first, but it would mean a lot to me. I suppose it's my way of trying to make it up to them."

"Of course I will," I said.

"Thank you. And now, please, enough about my sordid past. It's your turn. I want to know everything you've done since we last saw each other. You aren't married, are you? You aren't wearing a ring."

"I was once, to a guy by the name of Clive Swain. I'm divorced."

"Do you ever see him?"

"Every day. We're in business together. We own an antique shop called McClintoch & Swain."

"How, er, modern," he said. "What kind of relationship is it, if I may ask?"

"You may. It's business," I said. "Although I do see him socially as well, because he lives with my best friend, Moira. How modern is that?"

"Too much for me," he laughed. "I feel like a dinosaur. It's probably why I like antiquities. I can't even contemplate being in business with my soon-to-be ex. For that matter, I can't contemplate being in the same room with her ever again. But might there be someone else in your life? Given I've been so frank about my marital status, and given our common past, you'll notice I feel quite comfortable asking. Tell me if you'd prefer I just shut up."

"I don't mind answering. I too have just recently joined the ranks of the unattached. I was in a relationship for a few years, but it's over."

"You're not thinking of starting a business with him, are you?"

"Not a chance," I said. "He's a policeman."

"I see," he said. "Are you hurting, or anything?"

"Hurting?"

"I get the impression the breakup is very recent."

"I'm fine," I said for the thousandth time on that subject. "But let's not talk about our past love lives. Tell me about the Venus. Where you found her? What she cost? How you know she's authentic."

"I suppose you really are interested," he said. "Given you are in the antique business. I had an antique shop once, very briefly, a few years back. I didn't last long. I'll be interested to hear how you manage it. But how nice to talk to someone who would not only be interested, but would understand what I'm talking about!"

"Same here," I said, and he reached across the table and took my hand.

"Are you hungry?" he said.

"Starving," I said.

"Me too," he said, as we both looked at the menu. "Shall I order for us both?"

"No," I said. "I'll order for myself. You really are a dinosaur," I added.

He laughed. "Okay," he said. "Decide what you want, but don't tell me, and I'll tell you what I would have ordered for you."

"Okay," I said in a minute or two. "I'm ready."

"Green salad to start," he said. "Followed by the grilled salmon. And, for the middle of the table—you wouldn't have ordered this for yourself, which is why I'm doing it for you, because you really want it—a bowl of *frites*. How did I do?"

"You were just exactly right," I said. "Even about the French fries. Especially about the French fries."

"Ah ha!" he said. "I knew it! You'll be having that molten chocolate thing for dessert if you let me order." He turned to the waiter. "Did you get that?" he asked. "I'll have the same. And we'll have a bottle of the—"

"Oregon pinot noir," I said. "Did I get it right?"

He threw back his head and laughed. "You did. Have I mentioned how absolutely wonderful it is to see you again? Why didn't we stay in touch? Why did we both marry other people?"

"Oh, I don't know," I said. "But here we are. Now about the Venus. What a coup! You must have been just thrilled to get her. She is exquisite, by the way. I didn't quite know what to expect, and I suppose being in the business I might be a little jaded, but she almost took my breath away. Others thought so too, obviously. Didn't I hear someone broke into the Cottingham that night?"

"You are dodging my question. No doubt I am going too fast. So, as to your question: the police think it was a break-in. I think it was a drunk who just didn't notice he was off the road and that there was a glass wall in front of him. In fact there was very little damage, just one of the large glass panels. It could have been accomplished with a hammer, I think. But there are car tracks. I don't mind the break-in story though. The Cottingham can use the publicity, and the idea that someone would make a grab for it the night it is unveiled can't hurt the mystique."

"So where did you get her?" I said. "I confess I haven't had a chance to start your book about Piper, but I will soon. I'm looking forward to it."

"That's nice of you. But as to how I found the Venus, I found the diaries first. As I think I mentioned, I had an antique store. It was in Budapest. I rather glossed over my stay in Budapest. My parents died within six months of each other. I suffered a little crisis at the time. That's a nice way of putting it. I completely fell apart. I took a leave from the Bramley Museum and went to Hungary to—what?—try to find my roots? Atone for my sins? I don't know. But it was 1990, and these were very interesting times in Budapest. A lot of Hungarian émigrés went back. People thought there were unusual and attractive business opportunities, and there were. After the Communists were tossed out, people were given the opportunity to buy back businesses that had been confiscated by the regime. I found a man by the name of Béla Szilágyi whose family had owned an antique business, and I got the capital for him to repurchase it. I ran it for him. At least that's what we said, because he was supposed to be the one that owned it. What I did was pay him a small share of the proceeds. For awhile we both did reasonably well.

"There were fabulous things to be found. A lot of art was confiscated during those terrible years and redistributed—I suppose that's the word—to people deemed worthy by the regime. With the Communists gone, and capitalism restored, there were suddenly a lot of people rather badly off, and selling their art was one way of getting cash. Budapest was, at the turn of the last century, a very cosmopolitan city, certainly the equal of Vienna, for example, and it may even have put London to shame. People were well educated, and cultured. So yes, there was a lot of art to stock my shop, but it was perhaps best not to ask too much about where it came from. People simply walked in with it. There are government-controlled antique shops, but also private ones. I was on Falk Miksa. Do you know Budapest at all?"

"No. I've never been there."

"Falk Miksa is a relatively short street at the Pest side of the Margit Bridge. You know that Pest is on one side of the Danube, and Buda on the other? Yes? The street is very near the Parliament Buildings. And it is just lined with antique stores. So it was a good place for the shop, and it was where Szilágyi's family had theirs before it was taken over by the state. My wife hated Budapest. She couldn't speak the language. It was the beginning of the end of our marriage. I suspect now that she took up with a Hungarian. Women find Hungarian men very attractive."

"You are a Hungarian man," I said.

He laughed. "You're right. I never thought of it that way. I loved being in Budapest. The cafés, the opera, the theater. It was ridiculous of me to think, though, that my wife, sitting in our apartment just off Andrássy út, nice as it was, would be having a good time all by herself."

"But the diaries?"

"Right. The diaries. An elderly Hungarian woman walked in one day with a box of stuff that she said had belonged to her father. I took a look through it. There were letters and, as it turned out, several pages from a diary, as well as some sketches that were obviously part of it. It was in English. I felt sorry for the woman, and bought the whole box of stuff, although there was nothing, I thought, of interest. Shortly after that, my wife put her foot down and demanded we go back to England. I finished up my other freelance work, which was the touring exhibit I mentioned, sold my interest in the shop, and we moved back to England. I took the box with me. I have no idea why. Fate, I guess. There seemed no reason to leave it in the shop because there was nothing of value there.

"One day—I was back at the Bramley Museum, forgiven, and in fact promoted to chief curator, because I'd done that exhibit—I was going through a collection of papers belonging to C. J. Piper. He'd held the same position I did, and all his documents came to the Bramley when he died. In any event, as I was going through the papers, I found a record of a presentation he had made to a group of men that apparently met monthly in a private room in a pub just off Piccadilly. Some of these men were doctors, several worked at the Bramley, including Piper, and others were just some interested citizens. They all apparently had an interest in paleontology. This particular presentation was about the discovery of a grave in the Bükk Mountains in Hungary, and there were drawings that accompanied it. I knew there was something familiar about the drawings, and several days later it came to me. They were more formal renderings of the sketches I'd seen in the diaries I'd purchased in Hungary. You can imagine my excitement. I went back through the diaries, and found the story of the expedition that had found a burial in the Bükk. How they became separated, I don't know, and why the diaries were back in Budapest, when the work had been presented in London, I'm not sure either. I'm making a rather long tale out of this, aren't I?"

"I'm enjoying this," I said.

"You're in the business. You have some idea how I felt, particularly when I got to the part about finding a skeleton in a cave with a lot of beads and a carving of the head and torso of a woman. There and then began my search for the Venus."

"And you found her where?"

"I got her from a dealer in Europe. He'd been shopping her around. You get to hear these things. I tried to be pretty cool about it, but the dealer either knew what he had, or could sense my excitement, as much as I tried to hide it. He'd been trying to flog it to various museums, without success. There's a lot of skepticism out there these days about these kinds of antiquities. The authenticity of several of our most treasured "goddesses' has been called into question, and a few of them are now quietly acknowledged as fakes. So, several of the people this dealer approached didn't think she was real, and frankly, the only reason I knew she was, was because I had Piper's diaries that detailed the discovery. Add to that the fact that most museums don't have budgets of any size for acquisitions, and it was possible for me to get it."

"So the learned paper by Piper was in London, the diaries in Budapest, and the Venus in Europe somewhere. Hungary, as well?"

"The dealer refused to tell me whom he was selling it for," he said. It had not escaped my notice that he hadn't answered that last question. "That bothered me, of course, although it does happen. I wouldn't have touched the Venus with a barge pole if I didn't have the other documentation. And yes, I thought about that fact, that the pieces of the puzzle were in entirely different places. Why would the diaries still be in Hungary, when Piper came back to England for good? I have no idea. He simply may have lost them, or left them behind thinking he would be back, but not returning for some reason. Or perhaps he needed money and sold both the Venus and the diaries to support the find. But I've had the ink and the paper tested on both documents, and they check out."

"Handwriting?"

"You are a suspicious woman, aren't you? Quite right, too. One is handwritten—the diaries obviously—and the other is typed. But I've been able to corroborate the presentation because there was a newspaper report of it at the time. Nothing very flashy. I'm surprised the paper didn't elicit more interest, but that may be because this was not a formal meeting of the Royal Geographic Society, or anything like that. This just seems to have been a group of men who got together once a month to hear someone talk on a subject that had to do with their interest in bones. It may simply have been an excuse to get out of the house and drink and smoke cigars for all I know."

"So where did Piper find the Venus? Did you not say we didn't know exactly where?"

"The diaries detail Piper's excavations in a cave in the Bükk Mountains of northern Hungary, not far from a place called Lillafüred. But there are hundreds and hundreds of caves there, and we don't know exactly which one Piper found the skeleton and the Venus in. But there was enough evidence in the diaries, and a very detailed description of the Venus and I knew I'd found her. The dealer told me the asking price. I laughed. There was no way the Bramley would have purchased it. But then I ended up in Toronto for various reasons, and I managed to find a donor for it in Lily Larrington. I went back with Lily's lovely money and made the dealer an offer he couldn't refuse.

"I still had a few bad moments, you'll understand, while the tests were being done, but the Venus panned out. She's real, and she is, despite what you think of my male chauvinism, so beautiful she takes my breath away. If a man can be in love with an inanimate object, I am that man."

"I can't disagree with you," I said. "She is beautiful. There is something almost magical about her. Especially when you think how old she is. And now what are your plans? This will surely make your reputation. You could go and work anywhere you want, couldn't you?"

"I don't know whether that is true or not, but at this point, I am very happy to be here. I like the Cottingham very much, and I think it has all kinds of potential. Major didn't have a clue about running a museum. He just wanted the tax receipt and the ego massage. There is much that can be done, and Courtney, bless her, is very amenable to the kinds of things I am proposing. You probably noticed that Major is more than a little out of it, so she is the person I deal with.

"I don't want you to think I'm enjoying a paid retirement, or anything. I work hard there, but I often think of Piper, who apparently felt his work in the Bükk was enough. When I was working on the book, I went and found his favorite haunts. I even know where he is buried. I found the graveyard in Devon. He was considered quite the expert, and was consulted widely on ancient man during his later years. I can't find any record of his having done much after the work in the Bükk. Perhaps it was enough that he could dine out on it indefinitely, lucky sod. I'm hoping to do the same now, of course, that the magic of the Venus will rub off on me." He smiled rather sheepishly.

"I'm sure it will," I said. *One way or the other,* I thought. We were both quiet for a minute or two.

"Do you remember your favorite antique purchase?" he said. "Or the first?"

"The first, for sure," I said. "And because it was first, it may even be my favorite. I have it in my den still. It was a carved daybed and side table, and I found it in a barn and restored it myself. I used it as a bed all through college. It was in my studio apartment on Dovercourt."

"God, it was uncomfortable," he said. "Not that I cared."

"It was just fine for one person," I said.

"Exactly my point," he laughed. "That was a slum, really, when you think about it. But those were wonderful days. What was it you called yourselves? The Dovercourt . . ."

"Divas," I said. "And I believe you dated all of us, more than one at the same time, if the revelations in the bar the other night are anything to go by."

"Mmmm," he said. "Did I?"

"I think so," I said. "Although, obviously I refused to admit it to myself at the time."

"I may have been dating more than one of you at first, but you are the one I was with exclusively for quite awhile. I was enamored, you know."

"Me, too," I said. "But that was a long time ago."

"I suppose it was," he said. "You called yourselves divas, in other words, goddesses. Now that I think about it, you all had goddess names. Diana, Roman goddess of wisdom and the chase. Anna, a very ancient goddess, Ana or Anu, Cybil is Cybele, an Asiatic fertility goddess, and in Rome, the consort of Attis, Vesta was the Roman goddess of the hearth. Vesta still has a goddess name, incidentally. Morgan is Celtic. As for Grace, not a real goddess, perhaps, but the three Graces, companions of the goddess of Love."

"All goddesses except me," I said.

"No, no, you too," he said. "You don't know about the Dea Muta?"

"I guess not," I said.

"Lara was a Nymph, one that was asked by Zeus to help him in his planned seduction, or should I say rape, of another Nymph. Lara not only refused, but she told Hera, Zeus's wife, about his plans. In revenge, Zeus ripped out her tongue and banished her to the Underworld. She became known as the Dea Muta, the Silent Goddess, because she could no longer speak. She is supposed to be the averter of malicious gossip. Some consider her a Muse. In Roman times, she became Tacita, from which we get words like *taciturn*. Appropriate name for you, I think. I have spilled my

guts on my marriage and my parents, and my guilty conscience, and you have told me very little. That is perhaps
because, like the male chauvinist I undoubtedly am, I have
done all the talking."

"I've told you all kinds of things!" I protested. "My shop,
my marriage, my just-ended relationship."

"You have given me a chronology of events. I did this, I
married him, I did that. You have not revealed your heart to
me. I think there is something you are holding back, but
that's an impression only. Perhaps I'm imagining it, or perhaps you are just reserved because it has been so many years,
and you're not sure whether to trust me."

Sometimes inadvertently people say things that come
just a little too close to the bone. Here I was flirting with
this man, all the while trying to get information out of him
so that I could help my former college mates destroy him,
professionally speaking. At least I thought that was what I
was doing. Or maybe not.

"I suppose this evening must come to an end," he said,
when I didn't reply. "I'll get the bill."

"I'll split it with you," I said.

"No, you won't," he said. "In the first place, I invited
you, and in the second, I have not done nearly enough
groveling yet to make up for the other night. Excuse me for
a minute, will you?"

So he was off to the men's room, leaving his glasses sitting on the table. How tempting it was to reach over and
put them on, to see if his vision was anywhere near as bad as
he implied it was. My hand reached out, but then I drew it
back. Some things it's best not to know.

I looked about the restaurant and was surprised to see
Morgan and Woodward Watson at a table on the far side,
although I don't know why I should have been. It was a very

popular neighborhood bistro. So engrossed had I been in my conversation with Károly that I hadn't seen them come in. She quite obviously knew I was there. I gave her the slightest nod of the head, but she didn't acknowledge me, and her expression was unreadable. I turned my attention back to the glasses.

I was still looking at them when he returned. "Did you try them?" he said. If he'd seen Morgan he didn't mention it.

"Try what?" I said, as if I didn't know.

"My glasses. To see if my vision was sufficiently bad that I wouldn't recognize you."

"No," I replied. "I'll take your word for it."

"Maybe you shouldn't," he said.

"Okay, let me rephrase that, since you have accused me of holding back. I wasn't sure my fragile ego could cope with the truth. Is it time to go?" I said, in as casual a voice as I could muster.

"The truth?" he said sitting down and reaching across the table to take my hand. "Let me tell you about that evening. It should have been a triumph. I accepted the job at the Cottingham with no great expectations. My marriage to the British aristocracy was over. I hadn't got along well with many of the curators of the Bramley. I thought they were resistant to any kind of change, and certainly, museums do have to get more in touch with what the public wants or they will just molder away. They thought I was ignoring their advice, and running roughshod over good museum practice. Dumbing down, I think they called what I was trying to do, which was to get people in the door. I had the support of the board of governors, but I got tired of all the battles—both personal and professional. I just wanted to come home, and Toronto is the place I consider home, even after all these years. At that point in time I was prepared to stay, to lick my wounds, to languish forever in a small museum like the Cottingham.

"But through what some would call serendipity, others, less generous, dumb luck, I had happened upon an almost twenty-five-thousand-year-old Venus. It should have been one of the best nights of my life. But minutes before I walked to the podium I was told by our accountants that someone I'd hired, someone I'd known a long time, and had placed in a position of trust, had violated that trust. I fired the person that evening. It was unpleasant, no, way beyond unpleasant. It was ugly.

"If that wasn't enough, I'd been in a relationship—one's judgment immediately following a marriage breakup is, I'm sure, impaired. Bad idea, I know, taking up with someone on the rebound. Just how bad an idea it was became very clear to me that evening. I broke it off. So when I was sitting there signing books, Sophia Loren, Queen Elizabeth, Jennifer Lopez, you name it, could have shown up and I wouldn't have recognized her. All I can say is I'm sorry, please forgive me."

"Okay," I said.

"Okay?" he said. "Okay what?"

"Okay, I forgive you."

"Just like that?"

"Just like that," I said. He could not know that I'd been lurking outside his office and knew exactly what he was talking about. But I felt better somehow. It did explain rather a lot about what I'd seen that evening, enough that I was prepared to give him the benefit of the doubt. Besides, it was very good to see him again.

"Did you drive?" he said.

"I took a taxi," I said. "My car is in for repairs for a couple of days."

"I'll take you home," he said.

He walked with me along the lane way that led to my house from the street, then past the white picket fence, right up to my door. There he kissed me lightly on the lips, before walking to the gate. He turned then, and looked back at me. For a moment or two I thought he was going to ask to come in, and I think I wanted him to.

"The Dea Muta," he said instead. "I wonder what it is you aren't telling me." Then he blew me a kiss and was gone.

CHAPTER FIVE

September 11

"YOU SLEPT WITH HIM. I KNOW YOU DID," MORGAN SAID.

"Whaaa?" I said, or something like that. I was sure I had just dropped off to sleep, having wandered around most of the night, and there was that persistent ringing sound again. Being awakened by an unpleasant phone call was becoming an annoying part of my daily routine.

"I saw the way you looked at each other last night," she said. "You were practically gobbling each other up with your eyes."

"Oh, please, Morgan. I did nothing of the sort." Not that I wouldn't have, if he'd asked. At least that is what I'd concluded at three A.M. And it was rather funny she'd said gobbling, after that story of his about the goose.

"Honestly?" she said. "You didn't go to bed with him?"

Why is this happening to me, I wondered, as the door bell rang. "Honestly," I said as, holding the phone in one hand, I accepted a large box that promised flowers.

"So why were you there?" she said.

"I believe we discussed how I would need to talk with him about the Venus's provenance, did we not?"

"And?" she demanded.

"He told me how he found the diaries, and from them the Venus," I replied. "I could see nothing very wrong with his story." That wasn't entirely true, but having opened the box with the phone cradled between shoulder and chin, I'd found twenty-three gorgeous long-stemmed roses. Presumably I was supposed to be the twenty-fourth rose. It was a bit of a cliché perhaps, but it had been a long time since anyone had sent me roses.

"Whose side are you on?" she said.

"Will you please stop asking me that question? Either you want my help or you don't." I hit the End Call button. There was much to be said for these fancy phones, but there was no question it would have been a lot more satisfying to slam the phone down very loudly instead.

May I see you again? the card said. There was no name, but that would hardly have been necessary.

The phone rang again. Fancy technology told me it was the Watson residence. I debated about answering, but finally did.

"I'm sorry," Morgan said. "Look, I am going to trust you with something. I know you won't let me down and rat on me." She was almost whispering. "I had an affair with him. Károly I mean, and I don't mean in college. Very recently. He threatened to tell my husband. I made a significant donation to the museum at his request to prevent him from doing that. He's far too subtle to ask for the money for himself, and large donations make him look good. I'm telling you this because even if you didn't sleep with him last night, you need to know what kind of person you're dealing with. He is slime of the worst kind." She sobbed just once, then blew her nose.

I sighed. It did not take a genius to realize that either Károly or Morgan was lying. She had been holding a check in her hand when I saw her, and he'd thanked her for the donation. But he'd said he'd broken off with her. Maybe she'd thought a donation would get him back?

"Thanks for the warning," I said.

"What next?" she said.

"I'll have to think about that. I got a lot of information last night that I need to digest before deciding."

"Okay," she said. "But remember what I told you. Be careful around Károly Molnár!"

What to do? Part of me had wanted to tell Károly that his former classmates were out to destroy his reputation by proving that his most cherished achievement was a fake. The other part of me didn't trust them either. Having spent a little time getting reacquainted had reminded me why I hadn't bothered to stay in touch after I graduated. Cybil was always running herself down in a way that very quickly became tiresome, and when she'd left a year before she was to graduate because, as she'd put it, she got knocked up, she'd got into the married couple thing with a vengeance, and her single friends found themselves left out. Diana was just plain crabby much of the time, and absolutely certain her opinions, which she stated with firm conviction, were correct.

Grace had been nice enough but always a little distant, and she sure hadn't been kind to me while I was seeing Károly for reasons I had finally understood only a few nights ago. It would have been a lot more sensible if she'd just told me what the problem was, rather than sulking for a year, although to be fair, I was so besotted with Charles I might have overlooked the obvious. Now, in my opinion, she was just downright sanctimonious, particularly where her opinions about my drinking habits were concerned. Morgan I'd always liked, but she'd gone off to Africa or somewhere upon graduation, then taken up modeling in Europe and we'd completely lost touch. One of the things I'd always liked about her, though, was that she had a vivid imagination. In other words, one was never entirely sure when she was telling the real truth, or the truth as she saw it.

Károly I had been wildly in love with, no doubt about it. I still found him very attractive, but it did strain credibility to think that he was always telling the truth, while the Divas never were. While I had told the Divas that I could find nothing questionable in what he had to say, that was simply not the case. He had reeked of sincerity the previous evening, and there was no question he hadn't forgotten our college experiences, but that, to my mind, meant very little if I left my emotions out of it, difficult though that might be.

So again the question. What should I do? If there were not still a lacuna, a hole, in my recollection of events, a rather worrisome one, about what had happened that evening, the part when I was a semiconscious drunk, I would simply have walked away. I didn't need a new romance, or even an old one revisited. And I'd managed quite nicely without the Divas for many years. The people I held most dear I had met after I graduated, when I'd found an occupation I loved. What I did need was to know what happened the night the Venus was unveiled. I couldn't live with even the slightest doubt about my possible culpability in either the break-in at the Cottingham, or much worse,

Anna's death. As tempting as it might be, I couldn't just forget it. Not with the vision of that little piece of blue cloth caught in the railing of the Glen Road Bridge. Not with the memory of a dent in my car that no body shop could ever erase, and the slash of silver paint on the rock near the bridge. Not with Alfred Nabb's words echoing through my mind.

Desperate for something to take my mind off these anxieties, real or otherwise, I picked up *The Traveler and the Cave*, noted briefly the dedication, to Lillian Larrington, then turned to the foreword by one Károly Molnár, and started to read.

In 1995 I was working in the Bramley Museum in London, England, on a collection of papers belonging to a man by the name of C. J. Piper who at one time held the same position I did at the museum, that of Chief Curator.

One of the files caught my attention, although I would not appreciate why for some time. It was an account of a meeting of a group of scientists, including some from the Bramley Museum, at which a paper had been presented on a discovery in the Bükk Mountains of northern Hungary. The paper itself was in the collection, although it took me several days to find it. It was dated February 15, 1901. The paper was presented by Piper, and given the rather excited tone of the minutes of that meeting, he had made quite an impression. In it, he claimed to have found evidence of prehistoric man in a cave in the Bükk Hills. The site, located at a depth of two meters, contained evidence of fire, and of cooking. There were remains of animal bones, the skull of what Piper maintained was a cave bear, as well as primitive implements. In another part of the cave, Piper found what he believed to be a sacred site, a grave containing the skeleton of a man touched with red ochre, and garlanded with shell necklaces and bracelets. Judging from the skull, Piper determined that this was not a Neanderthal, but indeed early Homo sapiens. He also found what he believed were votive offerings.

Piper's paper included some drawings of the site, a very convincing description of the actual excavation, and some sketches of the grave goods. A drawing by Piper, an obviously talented artist, of the skeleton in situ was a very prominent part of the presentation, and the minutes of the meeting made much of it.

I am not an anthropologist. I am an art historian and curator. So it is doubtful that I would have paid much attention to this file, nor have reason to remember it later, but for one aspect of the drawing of Piper's discovery. That was that amongst the profusion of beads and some primitive tools that lay with the skeleton, there rested an exquisite small carving of a woman's head and torso, which had apparently been found in the grave. It was impossible to tell the material, but Piper's paper did make reference to ivory objects.

I was enchanted by it. What, I wondered, would motivate early man, if indeed that was the case, to carve such an object and place it in a grave? Was the body that of a person of some importance, or was the object itself imbued, in the minds of the inhabitants of that cave, with magical power? Did this tiny carving tell us that the people of that time could comprehend the idea of an afterlife?

There was one other question that was to haunt me for many months. Why did some of the drawings of that cave site look familiar to me?

Months later I was back in Budapest, working for the Bramley Museum on a joint exhibit with the Hungarian National Museum. Somewhat nostalgic for the two happy years I had spent in Budapest as the proprietor of an antique shop on Falk Miksa, I revisited that site.

I skimmed the following paragraph or two, the account of the old woman coming into his store and his purchase of the diaries. It was exactly as he told me, except for the conclusion, which was somewhat self-serving, no matter what he said.

I bought the papers, paying, I thought, rather too much for them. I did not expect a reward for what I had done, but rewarded I have been many times over. Because standing there on Falk Miksa, I remembered seeing something very similar to the drawings I'd more recently uncovered, the paper written and presented by C. J. Piper. Hardly able to contain myself until I was back in England, I took out the box I had purchased at least three years earlier, and which I had kept simply because in my profession it is difficult, if not impossible, to throw anything out, and quickly rifled through it. The box contained some diaries dating from about March 1900 to the winter of 1901. And included with the text were rough sketches that matched, I was certain, the drawings in Piper's presentation.

I read through the diaries with great haste, stopping neither to eat nor to sleep. I had found by dint of what seemed to me a miracle, the diaries of C. J. Piper, the same man who had presented his paper in London, of that I was certain, although the author had not put his name to the page. Imagine my excitement when I realized that the drawings were the same, although the ones in the diaries are only sketches, those in the presentation fully realized. On reading both, side by side, I found the description of the work and the cave and its astounding contents the same. Here was the real life story behind the learned paper. And what a story it is.

"I am quite decided that I will travel," the account begins. "Indeed I feel quite giddy at the prospect." We learn early on that the writer, whom we now know to be Piper, lived in London, was a rather solitary sort, quite resolved not to marry—although I can tell you that Piper did marry some years after his return to London and his triumphant presentation to his peers in 1901. He was a handsome man, as sketches of his talk that appeared in local papers attest, and I would expect he was in demand as an escort. For whatever reasons, here only hinted at, and influenced no doubt by the Victorian gentleman's love of travel, an enthusiasm that bordered on mania, the author embarked on a voyage of

discovery, both personal and collective. Armed only with two books,
The Art of Travel *by Francis Galton, and* On the Origin of
Species *by Charles Darwin—Darwin and Galton were cousins,
incidentally— Piper left Britain for the continent.*

*Despite his eagerness for new experiences, his first few days were
not a success. He reports to us that he was seasick crossing the channel after eating a rather poor meal just before boarding the ship,
and most unexpectedly, from his perspective, he finds he misses his
home. But as the journey proceeds, he is clearly more and more
enchanted by all he sees, most particularly Budapest, which seems to
have come to him as a wonderful surprise.*

*But this is not merely an account of a voyage. Giddy though he
might profess himself to be as he set off, this is not a slapdash effort
in any way. Rather, it is a meticulously recorded scientific expedition. Piper left Britain determined to find examples of early man,
or what was then called the Missing Link. He reasoned that if
Darwin was right, it should be possible to find examples of early,
less evolved man.*

*To put this journey in some kind of historical context: the Victo-
rian era was one of great discovery, new lands of course, but also
science. Indeed together, exploration and science almost defined the
age. By the time Piper embarked on his personal odyssey, David
Livingston had completed his historic journey in Africa, Heinrich
Schliemann had laid claim to finding Troy and had excavated at
Mycenae, the cave paintings at Altamira had been discovered,
although the question of their age and authenticity was not resolved
until the early 1900s. Prehistoric art had been found in the caves
of France as early as 1830, and in 1857, two years before the publication of* Origin of Species, *an ancient skull had been discovered
in a limestone cave high above the Neander Valley, Neanderthal
in other words, thus giving its name to Homo neanderthalensis. In
1864, a Venus figure had been discovered at Laugerie-Basse in*

France, the first such find in modern times. So Piper knew what to look for.

Science was also very much the rage during that time. Charles Darwin had been dead for eighteen years when Piper set out, and it was generally recognized that the principles Darwin had outlined need be applied to man, although there were still many who refused to accept Darwin's evolutionary theories.

It is in this context that Piper set off for the continent, stopping eventually in what is now northern Hungary after a sojourn in Budapest, and beginning his study of the limestone caves in the Bükk Mountains. Piper seems to have scoured the caves alone for a period of time, but once he settled on one, he assembled a team of workers. We know their names because of the detailed account of the work: in addition to Piper himself there was a fellow Brit, one supposes, by the name of S. B. Morison, two Hungarian brothers, Péter and Pál Fekete, and another Hungarian by the name of Zoltán Nádasdi.

Piper, overcoming hardship and initial disappointment, found what he sought, an ancient burial in one of the caves. We still don't know which cave, but his account of his efforts, the careful detailing of the excavation, the recording of every inch of the site, continues to impress today. Dr. Frederick Madison, a preeminent anthropologist who very generously assisted me in assessing these diaries and indeed the Venus itself, assured me that the work was done in a way that would be acceptable practice today. Professor Madison was also most helpful in arranging for me to test the inks and the paper on which both documents were written, and I am most grateful to him for that. The tests showed that both paper and ink dated to the time period in question and neither he nor I have any difficulty considering both documents authentic.

Piper returned to England to some acclaim. His findings were considered "convincing" by several of those present, according to the *minutes of that historic meeting. His achievements were heard beyond the meeting itself. "Mr. Piper has given us an admirable account of his studies on the history of man in the far reaches of Hungary. The illustrations he has shown us are superb, and one cannot find fault with his conclusions," one of the newspapers at the time reported.*

The diaries unfortunately end rather abruptly, and make no reference to Piper's return to England. Perhaps later accounts are lost. In the early pages of the diary, Piper confesses that he hopes that he may profit from travel, and it appears that indeed he did. From sources other than his diaries, we learn that he settled again in London where his reputation seems to have ensured that he was much in demand as a dinner guest. What we would now call society columns seem to indicate that he dined out on his adventures for some years. He was also able to purchase a country property in addition to his London residence. He married rather well, which cannot have hurt his fortunes. We can find, however, no hint that he ever made another journey to rival his first. He died at his country property in Devon on July 30, 1945, having borne witness to two terrible world wars.

As readers will doubtless learn, or know already, these diaries led to a most extraordinary discovery, a Paleolithic Venus figure now named the Magyar Venus. It is for this, I am convinced, that Piper will be remembered best.

Here, then, are the diaries of an extraordinary adventurer and a keen man of science: Cyril James Piper.

WELL, WEREN'T THERE holes big enough to drive a truck through in that one? While I couldn't dispute that the forward to the book and the explanation that Károly had given me over dinner were absolutely consistent, indeed absolutely the same—and that is what one did, after all, in tracing the history of an object, that is, look for the inconsistencies—

there was the odd little matter that bothered me, in both the official preface to the book, and our dinner conversation. Why were the diaries in Budapest when Piper obviously went back to England, not just to present his findings, but, if Károly's research was valid, to stay? Was it really possible he would just leave them behind? Surely that is not what one does with diaries. If he took them with him, how did they get back, particularly given the catastrophic events that engulfed Hungary in the past century?

And why was the discovery of the Venus relegated to a paragraph or two, and not even named in the foreword? Had Károly found her after the book had gone to print? Possibly. Did he plan a second book all about her? Probably. Still, there were questions.

And finally, were there just too many coincidences? Károly had accidentally found Piper's paper, and he had then just as accidentally found the diaries, and then, my goodness!, up pops the Venus. Maybe, horrible thought though it was, the story was just too pat, the two explanations way too consistent, as if they'd been rehearsed over and over. Maybe Diana was right. There could be something wrong here. Some additional research of my own was required. I picked up the phone.

"Hi, Frank," I said, once I was connected by a receptionist that sounded to be five years old. "It's Lara."

"Lara!" he said. "Hello." He sounded a little diffident, shall we say, hardly surprising given I'd propositioned him rather loudly and inappropriately that night in the bar. I could hardly believe I'd done it, and couldn't even think about it without turning pink with embarrassment.

"I called to apologize for the other night. I didn't get a chance to do so at the funeral. I don't know what got into me. I don't normally drink like that, nor act like that. It's just that I've recently ended a relationship of several years, and I suppose I wasn't really myself. It's been tough," I added. Now I'd see if this blatant and only marginally truthful appeal for pity would work.

"Oh, dear!" he said. "That's really too bad."

"I was hoping you'd let me take you to lunch somewhere hideously expensive to make up for it," I said.

He laughed. "Of course you can."

"How about today?" I said.

"I think that would be fine. Give me a sec to check my calendar." There was a brief pause, then, "Sure, where and when?"

"Bistro 990 at one?"

"That ought to do it," he said. "Make up for the other night, I mean. As long as you don't proposition me again."

There was no question I'd be paying for my evening of indiscretion for a long time. "I promise," I said. "See you at one."

I insisted we have a very fine bottle of wine, and carefully sipped mine as he quaffed his with enthusiasm.

"I'm reading Károly's book," I said. "I'm enjoying it. I expect given all the hoopla over the Venus it will do very well. It's gorgeous, by the way. The illustrations, the photographs, the cover, everything. It's really well done."

"Thanks. I'm happy," he said. "Initial sales are fine. The chains are starting to pick it up which is good. We'll see how it goes on the reorders. It's got everything, though. A twenty-five thousand-year-old Venus, an author the TV cameras love and women reporters swoon over, and a real-life mystery solved. The diaries themselves almost don't matter. Please don't tell anyone I said that, especially Károly. You won't, will you?" he said, taking another gulp of wine.

"Given what you have on me, it would be rather silly of me to tell your secrets, wouldn't it?" I said.

He smiled. "Thanks for reminding me. A case of this wine and you will be forgiven forever. Just kidding! Actually, you weren't that bad, and I was an eligible bachelor when you last saw me. It was long after college that I was prepared to accept where my true, um, inclinations lay. I was rather flattered. I even gave your offer due consideration."

"You're being very kind. The book must have been astronomically expensive to produce. Very fancy paper, lots of design work."

"It was. I was afraid we wouldn't even be considered for it, that the Cottingham and Károly would go to one of the big art or university presses, but Courtney Cottingham put in some money, which helped. Károly talked her into it, silver-tongued bastard that he is. He could talk the birds out of the trees, that guy."

"I heard from him yesterday," I said. "Did you give him my phone number?" Okay, so that question wasn't part of the research, but I had to know.

"How could I do that?" he said. "I don't know what it is."

"I was surprised he called, because he obviously didn't know me that evening at the Cottingham."

"You mentioned that in the bar. More than once. I reminded him about you, that you'd been an item and so on, when I talked to him the next day. I'm glad he called you."

Ouch, I thought. Sometimes it's better not to know, as I'd had reason to say on this subject more than once. I hadn't really believed that glasses story, but still. . . . "So Károly just walked into your office with the manuscript in his briefcase?"

"Pretty much," he replied. "He didn't have an agent or anything. He was just shopping it around. At the time, he hadn't acquired the Venus, so I guess there wasn't much interest in it. There are lots of Victorian travel books, and unless there's a special hook, like King Tut's tomb or something, they don't elicit much interest. If it hadn't been Károly, I wouldn't have paid much attention to it. I mean, we at Kalman and Horst try to publish books by Canadians, on subjects of interest to Canadians. Naturally, we were quietly going broke doing so. Károly might qualify, but the book in and of itself might not have. But you know how persuasive Károly can be. He said he'd do something that would make the book sell, and by George, he has. He may have single-handedly saved our bacon."

"Did you actually get to see the diaries themselves? That would have been exciting, at least for someone like me who likes old stuff."

"I didn't see the originals. Károly now has them in a vault somewhere, and he will probably donate them to the Cottingham. I expect he's just waiting until he's made enough money that the charitable tax receipt will be worth something to him. I saw copies, though. All handwritten, of course, and the sketches Károly talks about are there, no question about it. I've seen the Piper presentation at the London club, too. Also a copy. The original is still in the Bramley Museum. Károly is trying to see if the Bramley might consider sending the diaries to the Cottingham, either as a temporary exhibit, or better still, on permanent loan—unless he can convince the Bramley to sell them, and sweet-talk some old dear into paying for them. Speaking of Károly," he went on. "I got the distinct impression in the bar that night that the Dovercourt Divas were not entirely enamored of our Károly. That wouldn't be the case, would it?"

"I don't know," I said, shrugging my shoulders. Who was

pumping whom here? "I think he loved and left a lot of us, so there might be some residual resentment. It would be odd if we weren't pretty much over it by now." If Frank Kalman thought he was going to get information out of me, he was mistaken. I was the one asking the questions. Obviously he didn't know he was dealing with the Dea Muta.

"What was that business with Anna, though?" I said. "All that 'how could you?' stuff. What was that about?"

"That was unpleasant, wasn't it?" he said. "I have no idea."

"But she seemed to be looking right at the group you were in: Károly, you, Courtney Cottingham, Woodward Watson."

"I suppose it looked that way. From where I was standing it was difficult to tell. I can only speak for myself, but I can't think what it would be that would make her direct that comment to me. One hates to speak ill of the dead," he said, "but one cannot help but feel Anna was a little, shall we say, unhinged. Didn't someone tell me she had that condition where you can't leave home? What's it called?"

"Agoraphobia," I said.

"Right. They'd declared her an unfit mother, too, hadn't they? Taken her kids away from her? I can't take too seriously anything she might say."

"I guess," I said. "Too bad about what happened to her."

"Terrible," he agreed. "Very sad. Are the Dovercourt Divas planning another get-together?"

"I haven't heard of any plans," I said.

"I wouldn't mind coming along if they are, and if you'll permit it, of course. It was great to see everybody the other night, even if it ended badly. I'm referring to Anna, of course, not your um . . . you know."

Frank and I seemed to have run out of things to say,

which I suppose is what often happens when former class-mates get together after twenty years or so. I paid the bill. Forgiveness, coupled with very little additional informa-tion, had not come cheaply.

There was a voice mail message from Diana waiting for me. "The Divas, what's left of them, are getting together again for a planning session," she said. "Please come. Bloor Street Diner at five."

I left a message for Diana to tell her I'd be there, and that Frank had indicated he'd like to join the group any time we got together. I said I'd leave it up to her, but she could call him if she chose to. I didn't think she would.

On the way to the so-called planning session, I went to the Cottingham and had another look at the Venus. I hadn't noticed the other night, besotted, like everyone else, by the Venus herself, but the exhibit was an interesting one. Sec-tions from both the diaries and Piper's presentation had been greatly enlarged and mounted on panels. Particularly interesting was the formal drawing of the grave site show-ing the skeleton, the beads, and the Venus. It was unques-tionably the Venus on display in the case. The detail was exquisite. I knew that archaeological expeditions often had an illustrator as part of the team, given the nature of pho-tography at that time. Even though there were cameras then, it would not have been easy to take photographs in the cave.

I liked the handwriting on the diaries. It was neat, pre-cise like the drawings, and despite the fact that the passages chosen were about the project, there was someone very real and personable behind the science.

I left a note for Károly, thanking him for the roses, and telling him I'd like to see him again, then I headed for the diner.

"Okay, now that we're all here, let's get started," Diana said. "What have we got so far, Lara?" She sounded rather officious.

"Not much," I said. "I'm sure Morgan has told you that the Venus was never in Lillian Larrington's possession, that she put up the money to purchase her, that's all. I talked to Károly—"

"You didn't!" Grace exclaimed. "You talked to him about this? Does he know our plans?"

"Of course not," I said. "We had dinner together, that's all." Morgan raised her eyebrows. "I just asked him about the Venus. Why wouldn't I?"

"Are you sure that was a good idea?" Grace said.

"Give her a little credit," Morgan said. "She's an antique dealer. Why wouldn't she ask him about it?"

"Can we get on with this?" Diana interjected. "What are we going to do next?"

"We," I said, emphasizing the word, "aren't entirely sure, yet." How did I manage to get myself into these situations? "I have to try to find the name of the dealer from whom Károly purchased the Venus, talk to that person, and see if they'll tell me where they got it, which is very doubtful, even if I can find this person in the first place."

"That's not a problem," Diana said.

"What do you mean it's not a problem?" I said. "If Károly won't tell me, how am I going to get it?"

"I can find out where he got it," she said.

"How would you know that?" Grace said.

Diana looked at us all as if we were clearly of subnormal intelligence. "I expect I wrote the check," she said. "I was the bookkeeper until very recently, if you recall."

"So who is it then?" I said. This conversation was starting to set my teeth on edge.

"I don't know offhand, but I'll get it for you."

"How would you do that?" Morgan said. "Given that you no longer work there. Are you planning to drive through the plate glass window and get it?"

"Are you implying that I'm the one who tried to break into the Cottingham?" Diana demanded.

"Ladies," Grace said irritably. "To the subject at hand, if you please? We are too old to be bickering like children."

"I kept copies of all the documents I handled in the last six months," Diana said. "I have them at home. If you can give me more information, I'll get you a name."

"It should be a check for about a million," I said.

"I don't recall any that big, and I'm sure I would. Not in the entire time I was there. I'll have a look through the stuff, though. Can you give me any more information that might help me narrow it down?"

"Europe. It was a dealer in Europe."

"Okay, I'll go through everything when I get home and call you with what I have," she said. "Assuming I find it, which I will, what then?"

"I'll get in touch with this person or company, and see what I can find out. I have to tell you though, that Károly told me that the dealer wouldn't tell him who had owned it. If he wouldn't tell the man with the check, he probably won't tell me."

"Maybe you should take Morgan along with you, and have her vamp him," Cybil said.

"Oh, puh-leeze," Morgan said.

"Just kidding," Cybil said. "Sorry."

"Is it a good idea to purchase something as expensive as the Venus without knowing who owned it?" Grace asked.

"Normally no," I replied. "If I remember correctly, Károly said he wouldn't have touched it with a barge pole if he didn't have the other documents that would appear to authenticate it."

"Could this not be part of an elaborate hoax?" Morgan asked. "The paper, the diaries, everything?"

"It could be, sure," I said. "But according to Károly, the ink and paper on the diaries and the presentation check out."

"So they are authentic," Grace said. "Both the diaries and the Venus?"

"It's still possible to fake these things, even the Venus. But it wouldn't be easy. You'd have to find a piece of mammoth ivory twenty-five thousand or so years old, for starters, and most of us don't have that kind of thing lying around. You couldn't use modern metal tools to carve it, because the metal would show up, tiny fragments of it, and the Venus, if you will recall, dates to the Stone Age. As for the diaries and the presentation to the science club, you'd also have to find old paper, not too difficult given it's only a hundred years ago, and you'd have to know the composition of ink at that time, also not so difficult, given the relatively recent date on the documents."

"So it's still possible this is all a fraud, and Károly is part of it."

"It's possible, yes. It's also possible it's a fraud and Károly was duped along with everybody else."

"This is fraud, and he's part of it," Diana said. "I just know it." I thought for a minute she was going to break down and cry, but she got up and went to the washroom.

"Seriously," Cybil said. "What if, like you said, this dealer won't tell you where he got it. If he wouldn't tell Károly, why would he tell you?"

"That too is a good question," I said. "We'd be at something of a stalemate."

"What would you do then?"

"I'd start at the other end," I said. "With the Venus, and then trace it forward, rather than back."

"From 1900, you mean?"

"Yes."

"That wouldn't be so difficult, would it? It's only a hundred years."

"That would be a hundred years that contain two world wars, a Nazi occupation, about forty-five years under Soviet domination, to say nothing of the 1956 Hungarian Revolution when two hundred thousand people left the country. So, no problem," I said rather caustically.

"Would we have to go to Hungary?" Morgan said.

"Another drink, ladies?" the waiter said, before I could answer.

"Not for me," I said.

"Good idea," Grace said.

"Why don't you just let that one go, Grace," Morgan said. "If we want Lara's help, maybe you should just let that one go."

"I'll second that," Cybil said.

Grace looked nonplussed. "It's time we got going," Diana said, returning to the table. "The trail is not getting any warmer. I'll get you that name, and you can take it from there."

I stopped to do some shopping on the way home, and when I got there one of the people I least wanted to talk to at this moment was sitting on my front doorstep. "I think I spoke too soon," Diana said. "I've brought the whole file for you to look at. I didn't copy everything, only the big ones, or ones I thought were suspicious. As I think I told you, there isn't one here for a million dollars."

I didn't want to invite her in, so I told her I was busy that evening, so she'd have to leave the files with me, and I'd have a look through them later that night.

She didn't want to do it, but I didn't give her a choice. It was an interesting selection of documents to be sure, and while there was a lot of material, it was pretty obvious that what had captured Diana's interest were Károly's expense claims. She had marked several for special attention, many of them meals in rather fancy restaurants. When he traveled, Károly showed a definite preference for both hotels and restaurants with lots of stars. Where he had listed guests for lunch or dinner, she had put a little yellow sticky on the invoice with the note "check guests". On the hotel bills, there was a question about the minibar usage.

I suppose this kind of thing is what a good bookkeeper is supposed to do. However, she seemed to me to be overly diligent, if not downright enthusiastic. She had kept a clipping of a newspaper feature on Károly written while he'd been director of the Bramley, one that referred to his difficult relationships with the Bramley staff, but also his high-rolling tastes. In my opinion, it was none of her business as a freelance bookkeeper, what he chose to spend the Cottingham's money on, as long as the board of directors agreed, and assuming there was no fraud. I doubted there'd be a peep out of the board of the Cottingham now that Károly had snagged the Venus, no matter how much he'd spent doing it. The lines at the ticket booth would put all thoughts of that right out of their minds.

Still, for my purposes and whatever her reasons, the fact she'd kept these invoices proved useful. Stuck in the invoices for a trip to Budapest, there was one receipt that I found much more interesting than where he ate. This receipt made reference to a head of a woman, believed to be old. Wasn't that an understatement of some proportion!

There were two disturbing things about the invoice. One
was that the company was in Budapest. Károly had dodged
my question about where he'd found the Venus, but in saying Europe he had implied it was somewhere other than
Hungary. The second, even more glaring, was that the
invoice was for $600,000, not a million.

As if on cue the telephone rang. My fancy phone said it
was the Cottingham Museum. I decided I didn't want to
talk to him. The conversation with Frank earlier, in which
he'd told me that he'd had to remind Károly who I was, and
even that we'd been, shall we say close, still rankled. And
while I wasn't going to spend my life tracking his expenses
the way Diana did, I needed some time to think about the
discrepancy between Lillian Larrington's money and what
he had paid for the Venus, if indeed that was what the
receipt was for. Perhaps there was some logical explanation,
a final payment, perhaps, although that was not how I
would have done it. Any receipt from me would show the
total amount of the purchase. Perhaps it was one of those
receipts you get to try not to pay too much duty on something you've purchased, much less than the ticket price,
although why he would need to do that for an object so old
that was destined for a museum, I couldn't imagine.

Whatever the explanation, I didn't want to see him, so I
let the message go to voice mail, and stomped around my
house in a snit for about an hour. But then I had a thought.
Károly had never actually said he had paid $1,000,000 for
the Venus had he? He said he'd taken Lily's lovely money and
made an offer the dealer couldn't refuse. I had thought a million because that's what Lily had told Morgan and me she'd
donated to the Cottingham. It was not necessarily all for the
purchase of the Venus. Part of it could have gone for the
exhibit, which was impressive, and perhaps also something

toward the publication of the book, which was essentially the exhibit catalog, or indeed for something else entirely. I picked up my message.

"Hi," he said, once again not introducing himself. "I was wondering if you would let me come over later this evening. Or, if you'd prefer, you could come to my place." He gave me an address in a fancy downtown condo. "Or failing either of these, and this last is my least-favored option I want you to know, would you meet me for a drink in the bar at Canoe around nine? I'm at the office. I'll be here until about eight-thirty or so. I think I gave you the number, but if I didn't here it is." He dictated both his home and office numbers. "Call me back when you get this. If I don't hear from you by the time I leave the office, I'll assume you're out."

"Oh, why not?" I said aloud, and dialed his office. I got his voicemail. "Hi," I said. "It's just after eight. Sorry I missed you. If you're still free, I think I'll go with your least-favored option. The bar at Canoe at nine. See you there." There then followed another wardrobe frenzy—I really needed to get out and shop, or at least get to the dry cleaners—and I was off to the bar. I didn't yet have my car back, something about sanding still needing to be done before paint could be applied, so I grabbed a taxi on Parliament Street.

We spent a pleasant hour or so. He was late, but then so was I. We talked about books, films, wines we liked, just about anything but business, and it was fine with me. When it was time to go, he said, "I have a feeling we're both going home alone, is that right?"

"I think so," I said.

"I was afraid of that. Where is rohypnol when you need it?" he said.

"What?"

"I'm sorry. I should not have said that. It was in poor taste. Forgive me."

"What is whatever that thing you just said?"

He looked at me in some embarrassment. "It's a date rape drug," he said. "You know, you slip it to the woman in question, and she gets all amorous. The trouble is she's barely conscious and can't remember a thing afterwards. Hardly ideal. As I said, my comment was in poor taste."

"How do you spell that?" I said. He looked at me as if I was mad, but he told me.

"Is this stuff easy to get?" I said.

"Apparently. Honestly, I have no idea. Please tell me I am forgiven."

"This is all very edifying," I said. "And yes, you are forgiven."

"Thank you. Is your car out of the shop, yet?"

"No."

"Good. I'll take you home then."

"I think I'll take a cab," I said.

"I would never do anything like that," he said.

"Like what?"

"Slip you a drug," he said.

"I know that," I said.

"So I'll take you home," he said. "I'll behave myself, if that's what you want."

"I'll see you soon," I said, kissing him on the cheek.

"It's not as if we're exactly—how to put this—strangers?"

"It was a long time ago. I'll see you soon," I repeated.

"I hope so," he said. He sounded a little grumpy.

WHEN I GOT home, the message light on my phone was flashing. The kitchen clock said it was 12:15. "Tomorrow,"

I said to it. Because I had things to do. I went on the Internet and did a search of rohypnol. My symptoms all were there, right down to the retrograde amnesia: blurred vision, dizziness, disinhibition—I cringed to think about propositioning Frank, and chatting up all those young men at the bar—difficulty speaking, the works. Apparently the stuff took only twenty or thirty minutes to kick in, and peaked in a couple of hours.

I looked at the phone. It was still flashing, and I finally gave in and put in my password.

The first message was from Cybil. "I'm feeling a little blue, and could use a chat," she said. "It's about 9:30. Please call me when you get in. It doesn't matter how late it is."

The second message was from Károly. "Hi. Just checking to see you got home all right. Sorry I was such a jerk."

I ignored them both. No doubt Cybil was going to tell me what horrible thing Károly had done to her that would make her a member of the new Vengeful Divas. Károly was going to apologize one more time, and maybe make another pitch to come over. I made myself a cup of herbal tea that claimed relaxing powers, sat down in my favorite armchair at the back of the house overlooking my garden, and decided it could wait. I had rather a lot to think about.

Was it possible someone had slipped a drug into my drink? Did I want to believe so because it would make me feel better, absolve me of responsibility, or did it really happen? And if someone had slipped me a drug of some kind, one that made me appear drunk, and leave me with no memories of what happened, who would it have been, and more importantly, why would they? I went over and over the events of that night in the bar, insofar as I recalled them. What had happened just before I started feeling peculiar?

Anna had come into the bar and made a little scene. So what could that possibly have to do with it?

As I sat there, at 3:30 by my watch, the motion detectors I'd installed at the back of the house suddenly kicked in, and the yard was awash in light. I got up and peered into the yard, but could see nothing. The lights switched off after a few seconds, but then switched on again.

My property backs on a cemetery, one that starts at my back wall and ends down in the valley where Anna met her death. Other than having to endure repeated jokes on the part of everyone who notices this for the first time—ones about how people are dying to get into the neighborhood and so on—the location has much to recommend it. The cemetery is a very old one, rife with history, acres of old, gnarled trees, and yes, the neighbors are really quiet. The gates are locked at sunset, presumably to keep out the un-desirable elements in society, but quite frankly, most people, no matter how malign, don't like to spend the night in a graveyard. I've often considered it one of the safest places in the world.

But perhaps not at this very moment. The moon was full, casting shadows across the yard. My porch lights kept flick-ing off and on. I turned out the light in the back room, and when the lights came on, peered toward the back of the yard. I still couldn't see anything, but I knew with absolute assurance that something was out there, something in the graveyard, just a little beyond where the beam of my lights could reach.

I thought of waking my neighbor Alex Stewart, a lovely man who is both friend and occasional staff in the shop, but I remembered that he'd gone to his cottage in Ireland for a couple of weeks. I couldn't call Rob, and certainly not Károly. I grabbed a flashlight and headed out into the yard.

The moon went behind a cloud for a moment just as my flashlight failed, and a spectral vision rose above the gravestones and floated toward me. It was Anna, one arm up and pointing, the same way she had in the bar. It appeared she was pointing at me. In the other hand she held the Magyar Venus, which she held out toward me. Her mouth opened and closed as if she was trying to tell me something. She was crying. I tried to speak, to ask her what had happened and to tell her I was sorry if I'd been involved in any way, but the words stuck in my throat. She turned and gestured across the graveyard, and I knew she was pointing in the direction of the bridge where she'd met her death. Then she turned back to me, her eyes grew very large, her mouth gaped wide in a scream, and she started straight for me.

I awoke, heart pounding, gasping for air. I was sitting in my favorite armchair and the garden outside was dark. As the stark terror of the nightmare subsided, I realized that I would never find any semblance of peace of mind, nor sleep through the night, until I knew why and how Anna died. I also knew that I'd spent enough time wallowing in my own anxieties and insecurities, and not enough actually doing something that would let Anna's soul, and my conscience, rest. My subconscious was telling me that Anna's death and the Magyar Venus were related. My conscious brain was telling me that one of the people I'd thought were friends had drugged me. That's all I had to work with.

And then it came to me. I would check out the Venus's provenance, just as I'd been asked to do. I'd prove it was a fake, or I'd prove it was genuine. It didn't much matter which, in terms of what I really needed to know. If it was genuine, it would go a long way toward making me trust my old love again. If it was a fake, and he'd covered it up, then I'd vindicated the others. Either way, I was sure to find out what happened that night. Either way, the road ahead was the same. I sat down at my computer and booked a flight to Budapest for the very next night. I left a voice mail for Clive at the shop to say where I'd gone, and how he could reach me. Then I sent e-mails to the Divas, Károly, and Frank telling them only that I was off to Hungary. At least one of them would have to wonder why.

CHAPTER SIX

April 30

My Journey to Budapest was a difficult one, not because my accommodations were unacceptable, nor even because of the mal de mer that afflicted me as soon as the ship left England, but because of anxiety as to what I would find on my arrival. As to the city itself, Budapest is a wonder. Although I had heard much from T, who extols the beauties of his native city with great enthusiasm, I believe I still laboured under the Englishman's staunch belief that of London there is no equal. I have seen with my own eyes that this is not so.

I felt great apprehension, almost oblivious of the splendid vistas on the river, as the steamer from Vienna made its way through the gorge and turned almost due south toward the city. Or to be precise, I should say cities. To my right, I saw Buda, its castle, not yet completed, but still impressive, having a fine vantage point high *atop cliffs over the Danube. To my left lay the city of Pest, not so grand perhaps, but rather to my liking with its industrious nature. I am pleased that I chose to reach my destination by steamer rather than by train, and happy indeed that the disagreeable condition that plagued the first part of my journey did not reappear on the river, because it seems to me that arriving by boat is to capture the essence of the city, the Danube being so great a feature of it.*

I am most fortunate in my choice of lodging, having found an apartment that is clean and well situated in what is called the Lipótváros not far from the Danube for a price that I am able to manage with some care. The building is owned by a family called Nádasdi who live on the piano nobile, *the first floor, in what I am told are quite splendid accommodations, although they summer at their country estate in the mountains. The smaller apartments are above them, mine on the fourth, the top, floor. The janitor lives on the main floor near the front door, but behind the rather wide main stairway to the first floor. His name is Fekete Sándor, his wife Marika, whom I am to refer to as Fekete Néni, which means, I believe, Mrs. Fekete. The Hungarians put their family name first. My little apartment looks over the central courtyard, and yet, as I am on the corner of the building, if I stand just so, I can see the Parliament, and beyond it, just a glimmer, the Danube. The Parliament is not yet complete, but nonetheless rather grand. I walked the short distance to view them the day after I moved into my lodgings.*

I am happy to find that many here speak some German, and my pitiful efforts in that same language are by and large understood. While we do not understand each other well, Fekete Néni is very kind and much concerned for my comfort.

I am most taken with the city. My walks about my neighbourhood are quite agreeable. The building in which I now stay is rather pleasing in aspect, neoclassical, with four columns in front. The main portal, up a few steps, is protected by a wrought-iron gate and there is some interesting tile work which I am told is porcelain from a famous Hungarian factory called Zsolnay. Across the street is an apartment one storey higher than mine, modern and lavish in aspect. If I walk south and a little bit east, I come to the Basilica of Pest, and a little beyond that is a magnificent street which is referred to as a Sugárút, a radial avenue. If I am correct, út in Hungarian is a word for street or avenue. This avenue is shaded by chestnut trees, is wide and most impressive, and flanked by very beautiful buildings in many styles. One of the most beautiful of all is the Opera House, quite the equal of any in London, and if I husband my allowance, it may be that I will be able to see a performance there.

The admirable avenue, where I most like to walk, ends, or is it begins in a grand square, which like so many structures in this amazing city is under construction. It is to be a monument to the Magyar conquest of the Carpathian basin, built to honour its millenary year, already past, although the monument is not completed. It seems to me that the Magyars are a proud people much interested in their history and their heroes. They will tell you that Budapest is one of the oldest settlements in Europe. The Magyars themselves were a fierce nomadic race who came into this area from the east under the leadership of one Arpád, conquering the area in 896, hence their millennium celebrations four years ago. While the monument to Arpád is not finished, there are buildings to either side, one of which, a palace for the arts, is constructed to resemble a Greek temple with six Corinthian columns.

Beyond that, there is a city park which is endowed with a castle, quite an extraordinary one. On Sundays, many families gather in the park at an outdoor restaurant called Wampetics, and I am quite determined to take a meal there at some time during my visit. Should one become weary on the walk along the avenue, which must extend, by my reckoning, for two miles, there is an electric subway, the Franz Josef Underground line, which is a marvel. I find the trip in the yellow cars beneath the street exhilarating, but mindful of mounting expenses, I walk almost everywhere.

My lodgings are also most conveniently situated near the Danube. There is a splendid walk along its banks. The bridges across the Danube—bridges are híd in the local language which I am making every effort to learn—are a marvel of both engineering and aesthetics. I find the Lanchíd, the chain bridge, which is very near my apartment, particularly attractive, but the Erzsébet Bridge, now under construction, will be equally impressive, I'm sure. It may well be that it is named for their Emperor Franz Josef's late wife, the Empress Erzsébet, Elizabeth we would call her, whom Fekete Néni tells me was adored here. They called her Sisi, but she died about two years ago, assassinated by a madman. They mourn her still.

The coffee houses seem to me to be a very important part of the life of the city, where like-minded men gather to discuss issues of importance, like politics, or great literature and the arts. Perhaps when T arrives we will visit one of these together so that he may translate for me the discussions. As it is, I rather enjoy the smell of coffee, slightly burnt, that permeates the air almost everywhere I walk, competing with the scent of violets this spring. The weather has been very fine since my arrival. It is such a relief from the rains that so depressed me in February when it seemed to me to be the worst such winter as I could recall.

I have left a letter and packet for T as we arranged before he left England for the continent. I have not received a letter back, but am not concerned. Nor am I idle. I am continuing my studies on ancient man, and indeed find myself quite taken with the idea that it should be possible to find evidence of his existence nearby. It now seems quite laughable to me that our immediate forebears believed as they did, that the world was created in 4004 B.C. I am much taken with the reports of the skeletons found in the Neander Tal, and also of reports of caves north of the city.

I have already made enquiries and find that a journey of reasonable duration will take me to the region in which limestone caves are to be found. When T arrives, I will question him closely on this subject, and it may be that he will accompany me there.

I am quite convinced that my decision to journey here was the right one.

September 13

Many questions had surfaced in my reading through the excerpts from Piper's diaries, the identity of T and the need for his anonymity being only one of them. The decision to choose Budapest was another. In 1900, most of the discoveries of evidence of early man had been in France or in Germany. If I were looking for an old skeleton in 1900 or so, the Dordogne in France was the place I'd go. Altamira in Spain was another possibility. The famous cave drawings there had already been found, and while many disputed their authenticity, someone like Piper would not. That was with the benefit of a century of hindsight, of course. Still, it was a question. Did T have something to do with it? Did Piper strike up a friendship, or perhaps even a business relationship, with a Hungarian so persuasive that Piper chose Hungary for his scientific explorations, other evidence to the contrary? The fact that the choice was such a happy one would surely be merely serendipitous.

On one point Piper and I were in total agreement. Budapest, to my surprise, is lovely, with broad tree-lined avenues reminiscent of Paris, the gleaming Danube its Seine. On one bank, Buda Castle reigns over its surroundings; on the other, the Pest side, cafés along the river's edge were filled with people enjoying the last of the sun before the cold weather took over, laughing and talking and sipping their drinks. I expected a city of Soviet-style gray concrete bunkers and prominent statues of heroes of the Revolution. I was wrong.

Only thirty hours after I'd been visited by Anna's specter in my dreams, I was sitting in the Café Gerbeaud, a very old coffee house not far from the Danube on Vörösmarty tér, a place that my guidebook told me everybody visited.

I was not, however, there because the guidebook said I should be. I was there because my hotel room on a back street off Andrássy út near the Opera House was not yet ready for me, and because Károly Molnár had, according to his expense claims, been there four times on the trip that netted him the Venus, in the company of someone by the name of Mihály Kovács.

It's amazing what you can find out about a person from their expense claims. I knew that Károly usually stayed at the Hilton in Buda, came to the Gerbeaud almost every day, and, if I'd been able to read Hungarian, which I couldn't, I would have known what he ate. What I didn't know was anything about the city in which I found myself. It had been a very long time since I'd been somewhere I'd never been before, and where I spoke not so much as a word of the language. While I do get to travel all over the world, I have a regular route for my buying trips, agents and pickers at every stop, and at a very minimum, I know how to say hello, thank you, and goodbye. Not here.

Right at that moment I couldn't think what had possessed me to come. I was jet-lagged, fatigued beyond endurance, to say nothing of rumpled and scruffy. All I'd brought with me, other than clothes and toiletries hastily assembled, were Károly's file and the book on the discovery of the Magyar Venus. The guidebook, I'd acquired at Heathrow.

I could see it was a business kind of place, as well as a tourist haunt. The tourists were there, certainly, in their jean suits and trainers, money belts strapped around their middles, but there were locals too, people with papers spread out on the marble-topped tables, talking very seriously to a companion or their cellphone.

I'd managed to order an egg sandwich and a coffee, and thus encouraged, decided to try to ask the waitress whether she knew a Mihály Kovács.

"Please?" she said. "More coffee for you?"

This is not going to be easy, I thought. I tried pointing at the name on the invoice.

"American Express?" she said. "Yes, here."

'Perhaps I could help," a very attractive woman a table or two away said.

"I'm supposed to be meeting someone here," I lied. "I don't know what this person looks like. I was just hoping the waitress would know him."

"Let me try," she said, and I pointed out the name. "It is pronounced Kovash," she said. "Despite what it looks like. That explains your problem."

She spoke to the waitress who shook her head. "She doesn't know him," the woman said.

"Thank you for your help," I said. "My name is Lara McClintoch, by the way. I'm an antique dealer from Toronto. As you have already guessed, I'm new to Budapest."

"Laurie Barrett," she said. "A lawyer, also from Toronto. I'm here keeping my husband company. He's in insurance."

"But you speak Hungarian," I said.

"Not particularly well anymore," she said. "But yes, a little. My mother is from Hungary, and I spoke it a bit when I was young. Her father's name is Lorand, and she found me an English name that was close. My father was

British. It was only with my grandmother that I spoke Hungarian. My husband comes here regularly. He's opening an office here for his firm, and I often tag along. I take Hungarian lessons when I'm here, and it helps a little. I wouldn't bother trying to learn it unless you'll be here a great deal, by the way. More and more people speak English, now that the Soviets are gone. It's a difficult language, not related to any of the romance languages you might stand a chance of comprehending."

"My guidebook says it's related to Finnish in some obscure way."

"Apparently so."

"Do you still have relatives here?" I asked.

"No. I did try to find the family home. It wasn't there, bombed, I expect during one of the wars. Hungary has a bad habit of being on the wrong side of just about every war going. I was disappointed not to find the house, as was my mother to hear about it. We're so accustomed to moving all the time, in North America. You know, bigger and bigger houses as the family grows, then back to an apartment at retirement. But here people don't move as much. My mother's family had lived in the same house for several generations. That's the way it is, I guess. So are you here to buy antiques?"

"Yes," I lied again. "Well, sort of. This is really just a reconnaissance trip, I guess you'd call it. I've seen some really attractive antiques that have come from here, and given I had to be in Europe anyway, I thought I'd take a side trip to see what I could find."

"I love antiques," Laurie said. "Where are you going to look?"

"Umm, Falk Miksa," I said, naming the street on which Károly claimed to have had a shop and where, as it turned out, the firm that had sold the Venus also did business.

"Where's that?" she said.

"The Pest side of the Margit Bridge," I said, trying to sound authoritative. This lying business takes a lot of energy. "Not that I know exactly where that might be from here."

She pointed over her shoulder. "That way," she said. "I could show you."

"That's very kind of you to offer, but you don't need to do that. I'll manage."

"Are you saying that because you don't want company? If so, that's fine. But to tell you the truth, I'm rather bored. My husband is at meetings much of the day, and it isn't as if I haven't been here many times before. I would be happy to show you around. If you are here alone, perhaps you would have dinner with my husband and me one evening, or perhaps we could go to the opera. We do that regularly while we're here. You really must see the Opera House."

"That is extremely kind of you," I said. "And I would appreciate being shown around. Right now, all I want to do is get to my hotel room, get cleaned up, and get some sleep. It's supposed to be ready at four."

"You've just arrived then?"

"I did."

"The overnight transatlantic nightmare. I'll give you one of our cards with our address and phone number on it. My husband and I stay in an apartment his company owns. I'll give you one of his business cards as well, in case you have a problem reaching me at the apartment. His name is Jim McLean, and you could always leave a message with his office. Just call when you would like a tour guide."

"Thank you," I said. "I will."

Despite what I'd told Laurie, sleep wasn't on the agenda.

As hard as I tried, I couldn't sleep more than a couple of hours that night, and spent most of it reading guidebooks, studying maps, and trying to figure out what approach I could possibly take to Mihály Kovács. Making an appointment was pretty much out of the question. If I told him what I wanted, he'd be sure to be on his guard. A surprise attack seemed the only answer, but I felt so out of my element, I couldn't figure out what to say.

What if he doesn't speak any English, I fretted. It was possible I could ask Laurie Barrett to accompany me to act as translator, if she'd be willing to do so, and with that thought in mind, I dug out her number and her husband's card. Then, just looking at it, I knew what I could do. J. R. McLean the card said, and he was a vice president at a very well-known international insurance company. It was a good card for my purposes, suitably vague as to the sex of its owner. I carefully copied out all the information on it, and early the next morning, headed for Falk Miksa.

Falk Miksa utca was right where Károly said it was, at the Pest end of the Margit Bridge over the Danube. The little street, or *utca,* runs off the much larger Szent István körút, and on that corner was a large BAV store, which I had learned from my guidebook was the government-run antique chain. The street itself was lined with private antique shops on both sides. The antiques on display were impressive to be sure, virtually acres of beautiful mahogany furniture, jade and ivory, huge crystal chandeliers, miles of Herend and Zsolnay porcelain, art deco everything, including some quite stunning jewelry. I was practically salivating by the time I'd walked a block or two.

The shops weren't open yet, so I had a cappuccino in a little coffee house called Da Capo, where the walls were lined with glass cases containing an extraordinary array of espresso cups, and where patrons sat on brown pseudo-leather banquets, and drank their coffee from mahogany tables.

At ten, I presented myself at Galléria Kovács Mihály and asked to speak to the proprietor. "Janet McLean," I said, holding up my card. "As you can see, I'm an insurance adjuster."

I believe he gave me his name, but I couldn't understand him. Fortunately he went back to his office to get his card. It was Hungarian on one side, and, praise be, English on the other. Kovács Mihály, proprietor, it said. Now wasn't that a break! I tried to hold on to McLean's card, but Kovács insisted upon taking it and looking at it closely.

"How may I help you?" he said at last, in impeccable English.

"I'm here in regard to the insurance on an antiquity that I believe was purchased from you." I got out the copy Diana had made of the receipt from Károly's expense claim, and waved it under his nose. "I'm sure you know it. It's called the Magyar Venus, and it's at the Cottingham Museum in Toronto."

"It hasn't been stolen?" Kovács exclaimed.

"No, no, nothing like that," I said. "Now, first of all I will need to confirm the purchase price, which according to the receipt was six hundred thousand dollars. Correct?"

"Yes," he said.

"That's a very good price. I expect we'll be insuring it for considerably more than that, perhaps in the millions. Does that sound about right to you?"

"I would think so," he said. "If you would like a professional evaluation I would be happy to be of service."

"Thank you. I'll pass that information along to our valuation department. The seller was rather keen to unload it, was he?"

Kovács looked annoyed. "It was a reasonable price. Dr. Molnár took a chance when he bought it, of course, but the arrangement allowed time for the tests, and the seller was very happy with the transaction."

"Well, assuming the Venus checks out, Dr. Molnár certainly got a bargain. You know Dr. Molnár personally, I take it? Didn't he tell me he once had a shop around here?"

"Yes, yes, of course I know him. And he had a shop just down the street a few years ago. But you said 'assuming the Venus checks out'. There can't be a question as to its authenticity!" he said. "Dr. Molnár told me he had submitted it to the most stringent of scientific testing—"

"Yes, indeed. And the tests, which we were intimately involved in arranging, were very reassuring. But you do see what I am getting at, do you not? There is that pesky matter of provenance. As you will know far better than I, in places like Hungary—as one of the Axis countries during the last war, and then afterwards under Soviet occupation— the question of ownership is something an insurer must consider. If someone claimed that it had been stolen, that would be a problem, now wouldn't it? As you are no doubt aware, most countries do not have a statute of limitations on genocide, and if a work of art were to be identified as Jewish cultural property confiscated by the Nazis, for example, and the true owner found, then the object is either returned, or the owner is compensated. I'm not saying that is the case with the Venus. I'm not saying that at all. But as you have already pointed out, the value of the authenticated Venus could well reach into the millions, and due diligence must be exercised. So, if you could just show me your records, that would be extremely helpful. A copy of any documents proving ownership that you have will be fine. I will take copies of them with me, and not take up too much of your time."

Kovács looked at me very, very carefully. I tried to look crisp and authoritative. "I am afraid that I am not able to help you," he said after a few seconds pause. He was trying to look as if he were consumed with regret. "I understand your reason for asking, but if you have been insuring art for some time, you will know that there are times when the seller asks the dealer not to reveal his name, and I'm afraid this is one of those times. You might speak to Dr. Molnár at the Cottingham, however. I was able to get permission for him to speak to the seller, and he was quite satisfied that all was in order. Now, if I may help you with anything else?"

"I will have to go back to my superiors on this, you understand," I said, pulling Jim McLean's card out of his hand. "I will be back in touch when I've done that. Thank you for your time."

"It has been a pleasure," he said. "I am so sorry I was unable to help." I reached out to shake his hand. He looked at mine as if he thought there might be a gun in it, and then reluctantly shook it. I could understand why he had hesitated. His hand was shaking rather badly.

I had held out faint hope for that conversation, and was not surprised by the outcome. I wouldn't have given someone that kind of information if they'd just wandered into my store, but I had been hoping that decades of Soviet rule had instilled such a fear of authority in people that Kovács would simply do what he was told if I was sufficiently officious. It had been, I supposed, worth a try. The visit was not without some benefit, in a negative sort of way, in that I had spotted a discrepancy. Károly had claimed that he hadn't talked to the previous owner, Kovács said he had. It wasn't a huge lapse, and in and of itself probably meant little, simply a miscommunication between Károly and Kovács, perhaps. But still, it was there.

I realized I was hungry and went out to Szent István körút to find myself something to eat. Eventually I discovered a pleasant restaurant in the basement of an old building just off the *körút,* the name of which, Keresztapa, I couldn't even guess until I was inside and discovered, from the photos of Manhattan in what was probably the thirties, and the English menu, was called The Godfather. I had a delicious soup of smoked sausage, mushrooms, sour cream, and the ever-present paprika that the waiter, who spoke some English, explained was called *bakonyi betyárleves,* something to do with young rogues. He recommended *palacsinta* for dessert, essentially crepes with cottage cheese and lots of whipped cream, dusted with sugar and flavored with vanilla. I was a new person when I was done.

But I was no further ahead. Unless I could think of some other way to persuade Kovács to tell me at the very least who had owned the Venus most recently, I was in a bind. It certainly made it way harder. The only tack I could take now was to start at the other end, as it were, that is, start with Piper's discovery and try to work forward to the present. In some ways a hundred years is not long where an antiquity is concerned, in others it's an eternity. Right now it could have been a thousand years, not just a hundred as far as I was concerned, sitting here in a restaurant where I couldn't even read the menu without help. Should I start in Budapest with the discovery in the Bükks, or should I head for London and Piper's presentation to his colleagues in the pub? I just didn't know. And so, not defeated exactly, but certainly discouraged, I made my way back to the hotel. I thought I might try for an afternoon nap, given I hadn't slept much at night, and might awake to a more positive attitude. When I got to my hotel, however, I was handed a note.

We're here! the note said. *We thought you might need some help. We're having a rest now to get over our jet lag, but meet us in the lobby around seven and we'll all go for dinner. Diana picked a place in her guidebook on the flight over, and the nice people at the desk say it's good. See you at seven. Morgan, Diana, Grace and Cybil.*

My plan for shaking one person loose from the pack of suspects in the drugging of my drink had been stunningly unsuccessful, although at least two, Frank and Károly, hadn't shown up. Not that Károly was a suspect in this particular matter. He hadn't known who I was at that time, as I'd had occasion to mention since. It now behooved me to try to find out whose idea it had been to come here, and then figure out a way to distance myself from them all.

I thought of changing hotels while they slept, but when it came right down to it, it was probably just as well they were there. They were just as much a part of this puzzle as the Venus was, and perhaps having them where I could see them was for the best. I called Clive, though, to find out who he'd blabbed to.

"Rob called asking where you were, but I didn't tell him," Clive said the minute I reached him. "Wild horses wouldn't have dragged your location out of me."

"But you did tell somebody," I said. It was entirely predictable, and indeed, I'd been counting on it.

"No, I didn't," he said.

"Yes, you did," I said. "I'm betting Morgan. Tall woman, rather attractive, high heels."

"Morgan, of course," he said. "You didn't mean her, did you? Nice-looking woman. She said you were classmates, one of those Divas you occasionally talk about. I didn't think you'd mean her," he said. "When are you coming back?"

"When I'm done," I said.

"Done what? What are you doing over there?" he said.

"I'm not sure. Having a mini-nervous breakdown, maybe?"

He snorted. "Over what?"

"I don't know. Middle age, breakup with Rob, suicide of an old friend." I couldn't believe I was actually saying these words to Clive, of all people. I really needed to get some sleep.

"I see," he said. "I have two words for you, Lara. Shit happens. Get over it."

"That's five words, Clive," I said.

"And here's three more. Get back here."

"I thought you told me I should get away," I said.

"That was before I knew you'd be acting so silly," he replied. "Stay out of trouble, please." Lovely man. But maybe he was right.

The five remaining Divas had dinner at a restaurant off Váci utca, the main shopping drag, very near the Erzsébet Bridge over the Danube. The place claimed to be one of the oldest restaurants in Budapest or something, and maybe it was. It was also my introduction to that Budapest institution, the surly waiter. Within two minutes of dealing with him, he had me longing, for the first time in my life, for someone who knelt beside my table to tell me his name was Jason and it was his pleasure to be my server that night. The man forgot just about everything we asked him for, argued with us when he brought the wrong entrée, managed to go for very long stretches without ever making eye contact with any of his patrons, and took forty minutes to bring the bill. But that was the least of my worries.

"We're a little bit surprised that you just took off for Budapest without telling any of us that you were going," Grace began rather belligerently the minute we were seated.

"I don't recall anything about having to tell you where I was going," I said. "You asked me to trace the Venus's provenance and that is what I am here to do."

"You didn't return my file," Diana said.

"I'm glad you brought up the subject of your file," I replied. "Because I've been asking myself, is it normal to keep copies of all the documents you deal with when you're a bookkeeper? To keep copies at your home?"

"I was freelance. I worked from home," she said.

"I'm sure Diana has her reasons," Grace said.

"These were not all current files," I said, ignoring her. "Some of them went back to the day Károly started at the Cottingham, I believe."

"So?" she said. "I brought the whole file home with me, that's all."

"Actually, they were not all expense claims either," I said. "Technically they shouldn't have been in the same file." I could see the others watching this exchange with some interest.

"When he fired me, I went back and got some of the files I thought would be useful," she said. "I had been wrongfully dismissed, and I wanted to prove my innocence, so I went back and got some of the files."

"No, you didn't," I said. "They changed the locks on your office before they fired you."

"You don't know that," she said.

"Yes, I do," I said.

"How do you know that?" she demanded. "The only person who could have told you that is Károly Molnár!"

"I saw you, Diana. You couldn't get into your office."

That was not true, but I wasn't about to say I had been hiding behind a curtain when I heard the news.

"What are you getting at?" Diana demanded.

"I'd say she is wondering, as I now am, why you would have been collecting files on Károly for all that time," Morgan said. "If I have interpreted this conversation correctly, there seems to be more to this than your being fired, perhaps?"

"Absolutely not," she said.

"So why did you, then?" Cybil demanded. "Keep the files for so long."

"Okay, if you want to know, I'll tell you," Diana said. "I have nothing to hide. I have my PhD, and I'm working part-time as a frigging bookkeeper, that's why. I live in a crummy apartment, I don't own a car, I can never take a decent vacation, and it is all because of Károly Molnár. Do you know the magic word when you're teaching at a university? It's tenure. I'd got my doctorate, slaved as a student, a teaching assistant, and finally a professor. And then it came time for me to apply for tenure. However, I'd written my thesis on a subject that Károly considered his own. Furthermore, my conclusions contradicted, no, not just contradicted, destroyed, one of his prize theories, and when it came time for my application for tenure at the university to be considered, he vetoed me. I'm told he spoke very eloquently, as only he can, against me. I expect I don't need to tell you that that ended my academic career on the spot. No other university was going to touch me, and I'd already invested years of effort where I was for nothing. I had to scramble just to earn a living, and have been working at pathetic jobs ever since."

"So when he came back to Canada you saw your chance for revenge," Cybil said.

"Yes, I did," Diana said. "I got a job at the museum.

Károly even hired me. He's probably forgotten what he did to me, it was so inconsequential from his perspective. I had heard about his big spending habits from a former colleague of mine who works in England now, and I figured I'd bide my time and I'd find a discrepancy somewhere in his expense accounts, and the board would fire him, for a change. But then the Magyar Venus came along, and I was sure it was a fake. I still think so. And I don't care what you think of me keeping his files."

"I don't know why you wouldn't have told us this before," Cybil said.

"I agree," Grace said. "You shouldn't keep this bottled up. We are your friends, you know. Talking about it will enable you to move on."

"Whatever," Morgan said.

"It does rather beg the question of why we're all here, sitting in this restaurant tonight," Cybil said. "I guess I just want to believe that it was not my insensitivity, my negligence as a friend, that allowed Anna to die. I suppose I'd rather believe that Károly had something to do with it, although I can't think what it would have been. I have no reason other than my personal demons to come to such a conclusion."

We all sat and thought about that for a minute. Grace reached over and patted Cybil's hand. "You mustn't blame yourself for what happened," she said.

Morgan made a face. "Lara knows why I'm in this, but right this minute I think I'd rather not say," she said. "Lara, tell them I've confessed already, please."

"She has," I said. "What about you, Grace? Do you have some reason you haven't shared with us. Can it really be because he dumped you in university? Surely not."

"I have my reasons," Grace said. "I prefer to leave it at that."

"And you, Lara?" Diana said. "Why are you here, exactly? Surely, to use your expression, it is not because he didn't recognize you that night. I will not believe that."

"Maybe I'm here to prove you all wrong, Diana," I said. "Had you thought of that?"

CHAPTER SEVEN

June 1

I have received word from T that he has *been delayed in his arrival
due to business matters in Vienna, and may indeed not reach
Budapest for some weeks.* As a result, I am determined to visit the
hills north and east of the city to ascertain whether the account of
them I have heard is true, and if so, whether or not they might lend
themselves to the sort of scientific study I am of a mind to do. If the
hills are, as I am told, formed of sedimentary limestone, clay, slate,
and dolomite, and marked throughout by caves, what better place
for the earliest man to live? I am intrigued too by some small pieces
of stone and flint that Fekete Néni has shown me. Her two sons,
Péter and Pál, work on the Nádasdi estate near a place that was
named, fairly recently if I understand correctly, Lillafüred. The
two young men like to explore the caves, and have given these objects
to their mother. I have studied these very carefully, and have reason

to believe that their form is due not to natural forces but rather to the workings of man. I am therefore most interested to visit these caves.

I am not blessed with the gift of making friends easily, and am therefore most grateful for the kindness of Fekete Néni, but also the Nádasdi family whom I admire very much, their every word and action of such grace and refinement. The children are schooled at home by private tutors, and speak several languages, French quite beautifully. I was fortunate indeed to take dinner with them one evening, invited, I believe, in order that I might speak French with the children. The furnishings in their sitting room would rival anything I have seen in London or indeed anywhere. I was particularly enchanted by a lovely painting, a landscape with mountains. The family tells me that it is the site of their country home.

I have booked transport with Fekete Néni's help, and have packed my trunk with clothing and supplies that I hope will be useful. Mr. Galton's advice, I now see, is rather more suited to darkest Africa or the deserts of the Maghreb than to the lands under the dominion of Franz Josef. However, I have purchased clothes which I hope will suffice, most especially a pair of rather splendid leather boots. No doubt I will make quite a good impression in my cotton shirts, black trousers and those boots. My pistol cannot help but add to the impression of my seriousness.

I am told the towns that I shall pass on my journey are rather more provincial than Budapest, and I am certain that will prove true. But I am told that I will be able to find a meal and lodging, and perhaps some workmen to help with the tasks ahead. First, though I plan to explore the area on horseback, and where the terrain requires, on foot.

HADN'T THAT JUST put the cat among the pigeons, hinting that I might be on Károly's side of this little drama. Diana went off in a huff immediately, without even leaving her share of the bill. The others tried to carry on as if nothing had happened, until at last dinner was over. Grace and Cybil took a taxi back to the hotel. Morgan and I walked out to the Danube. The bridges were all lit up, as was Buda Castle across the river. It was a really beautiful sight. I travel to a lot of places, and like a lot of them, too. But every now and then I happen on somewhere new and lose my heart, and this, I knew, perhaps because it was such an unexpected pleasure, I was in danger of doing in Budapest.

Morgan felt it too. "You want to walk for awhile?" she said. We ambled up Váci utca to Vörösmarty tér, and headed into the Gerbeaud for a nightcap.

"Are you really on Károly's side?" she asked.

"I'm on no one's side right now," I said. "The point I was trying to make, which is the one I've been trying to get across all along is that—"

"I know," she said. "You will trace the provenance of the Venus, but it won't necessarily come out the way we want it to. I think all of us except Diana know that. She is just so convinced she's right, that she can't imagine another outcome, and therefore you will be her enemy if you don't prove her right. It's something of a bind for you, but I want you to know that I do understand. I did have to smirk quietly to myself when she said she had nothing to hide, and then proceeded to tell us that she'd essentially been stealing documents from her employer. What did you think of that business about tenure, by the way?"

"I don't know what to think. It's true, of course, that if you want a long career in academia with a nice pension at the end, you have to be tenured. But could one person prevent her getting it? I don't know. Does it have to be unanimous? I don't know that either, but I wouldn't think so. And would she be denied it if everyone but Károly thought she was fabulous? I doubt it."

"Just what I was thinking," she said. "I'm not sure where the truth lies there."

"Speaking of truth, I have a question for you," I said.

"Shoot," she said.

"What happened that night in the bar, after I, you know, passed out."

"You didn't pass out, exactly," she said. "You were acting a little peculiar, though. I wondered if you were ill. Your eyes looked funny. The thought crossed my mind that you might be on drugs, actually. Sorry. I'm sure you weren't. Were you? Anyway, we all left shortly after that. Diana said she'd get you home. I had to drag Woodward away from Courtney. He's boinking her, of course."

"Are you sure?"

"Yes," she said. "Have I caught them in the sack together? No. Have I even seen them smooching in a restaurant? No. But yes, I'm sure. Was your husband unfaithful to you?"

"Yes," I said. "But not until, as he'll tell you, it was essentially over. And did I know at the time? Yes, I did. I gather you've met Clive."

"Yes," she said. "Cybil told us she'd called you the other night, but that you hadn't responded. And you didn't answer calls the next day either. Then we got your e-mail. So I was delegated to see if I could find out what hotel you were in. Clive is rather cute, by the way. Are you still in love with him?"

"No. I like him a lot better now than I did when I was married to him. He probably feels the same way about me. We were a disaster as marriage partners, but we are a good business combination. And he never lets me wallow in self-pity, which is a good thing, because I am inclined to do so from time to time."

"I've been wallowing in it a bit myself, lately," she said. "I could use a Clive. Are you wallowing in self-pity now?"

"A bit, I suppose. There is no question I have not been my usual optimistic self. I broke up recently with a man I'd been with for a few years. A lovely man really, by the name of Rob Luczka. I don't know why I left him, other than that we'd hit a rough patch. His daughter had some bad things happen to her, and we tried to help, but neither of us really talked about it, how we felt, what we thought we needed to do. Perhaps it was all just too painful. I've always thought we discussed everything, but it turns out we didn't. I didn't feel that I could. I think maybe it was like a worm eating its way into my feelings for him."

"Too bad," she said. "I wish I could confront Woodward on the subject of his philandering, but I just carry on as if I don't notice. That night at the Cottingham he wanted me to chat up some bank president because his company has run into some financial difficulty, and needed extended credit, so of course I did it, even though I felt like a whore. It was 'darling this' and 'darling that' all evening while he's making goo-goo eyes at Courtney. Pathetic, isn't it?"

"I suppose I could say to both of us what Clive says to me on a fairly regular basis these days: Shit happens. Get over it."

She laughed until the tears ran down her cheeks. "I'll try," she said. "I'll try."

"Me, too. Why did all of you rush to follow me here?"

"I don't know. Perhaps it was because Diana insisted. I just wanted a break from Woodward. I think maybe Cybil just wanted to get away, too. None of us had been to

Budapest before, so it seemed like a bit of a lark. Diana couldn't pay her airfare by the way, even though she was the one insisting on coming, and we got these fabulous last-minute tickets. I paid for her ticket. She says she'll pay me back, but I'm not sure how she's going to do that, given her circumstances. Was she that sour in college, do you recall?"

"Not quite so bad," I said. "But there always was an edge there. And Cybil always ran herself down, and Grace never really shared her thoughts with any of us."

"I don't remember her being quite so sanctimonious, though, do you? You know, we're too old to be bickering like children, that sort of thing," she said. "She is rather tiresome, isn't she?"

"I guess!" I replied.

"And you and me?" Morgan said.

"I always admired you because you had so much courage," I said. "You did things the rest of us wanted to, but didn't, and you didn't give a hoot what people thought."

"I'm not very courageous now, am I?" she said. "I should leave Woodward, get my own place, and find a real job. But somewhere along the line I lost my nerve. As for you, speaking of courage, I always thought that beneath that very refined exterior of yours, the daughter of a diplomat schtick, the person who tried to do the right thing and say the right thing at all times, there was someone else. I only looked like the rebel, you know. I was the one that cut classes, smoked and drank, and slept around, but I was a fraud, and the real rebel of the group was you. I thought in many ways you were absolutely fearless, and I still think so."

"I don't know," I said.

"Oh!" she said. "I almost forgot. Have you seen this? Where is it?" she said, pulling at least three cosmetic bags out of her bag before she found what she wanted. "Here. What do you think? It ran the day after you left. I ripped it out of the newspaper on the plane."

"It" was an article from a a local Toronto paper. "Forging the Past" was the headline. The subhead said something to the effect that on the unveiling of the Magyar Venus at Toronto's Cottingham Museum, it was interesting to note how many of the museum world's most treasured objects had been found to be fakes. The author argued that the advent of better and better testing methods had set the museum world on its ear as more and more of the world's most treasured antiquities were found to be fakes and forgeries, or at least suspected as such. Amongst the Mayan incense burners, the gold mask of Agamemnon, the Minoan Snake Goddess, and other antiquities that someone at some time had questioned, there was an ivory head of a woman called the Venus of Brassempouy, that was supposed to be about the same age and material as the Magyar Venus, but which some expert somewhere had decided was suspect. There were photos of several of these objects, and one of the Magyar Venus. Are they real? the cutline asked. By the time most people had read through to the end, they'd be forgiven for concluding that the Magyar Venus should be added to this ignominious list. It was a rather cleverly done hatchet job on the Magyar Venus. Without ever saying so, its authenticity was called into question.

"My, my," I said.

"Yes, indeed. I wonder who the author, this Dr. Thalia Lajeunesse, is. It doesn't give any credentials."

"No idea," I said. "Never heard of her. I assume it's a her, with a name like Thalia."

"I confess I was rather wondering if it was Diana under a pseudonym," Morgan said. "I asked her if she'd written it, but she denied it. She did not deny enjoying reading it, though."

"I'll bet," I said.

"I know everybody keeps asking this, but where do we go from here?" she said. "I'll help you any way I can."

"There'll be assignments," I said. "Don't you worry."

And there were. The next morning at breakfast, I handed all of them copies of a list I'd spent a good part of the night drawing up—I'd slept for about four hours, making it a very good night. Early the next morning, I'd arranged to have the list copied at the front desk, one for each of them.

"Okay, here's the drill," I said in my chirpiest voice. "These are all places that the diaries mention," I said. "Some of them you should be able to find easily. Others will be a little harder. Sugárut, for example, does not exist today, at least not on my map. But the diaries say the Opera House is on it. That might mean it's an early name for Andrássy út, which is just a couple of blocks away. You'll need to go over to the Opera and see when it was built, if it was in that same place in 1900. Your assignment is to make sure these places exist, that they are where the diaries say they are, and where there is a discrepancy, make a careful note of it."

"Why are we doing this?" Diana demanded. "I think you're just sending us off on a fool's errand while you do something else."

"She's checking to make sure there are no mistakes, no anachronisms, in the diaries," Cybil said. "Isn't that right? If there's a mistake, then it calls the whole thing, the Venus and everything, into question."

"Exactly," I said.

"What are you doing then?" Diana asked, in a somewhat mollified tone.

"I'm tracking down the lab that tested the Venus to see what they have to say, and——"

"What about the invoice?" Diana said. "You said you found the invoice in the stuff I gave you."

"I've already been there," I said. "I talked to the proprietor."

"And?" she demanded.

"And he refused to tell me who owned the Venus previously. I will, of course, be asking him to reconsider, but we can't count on it."

"That's very suspicious, isn't it?" Cybil said.

"Not really," I said. "If Mihály Kovács walked into McClintoch & Swain and asked who had previously owned an object I'd had in the store, I wouldn't have told him. It was worth a try, but it didn't work. Now, be back here at four, and we'll go over what we've learned."

By ten, I was in an Internet cafe, *googling,* to use the new term, Dr. Frederick Madison, the person Károly had thanked in his preface to the book for testing the Venus. Madison headed up a lab in Arizona, and I managed to find his phone number reasonably easily. With several time zones between us, however, I was going to have to wait until the afternoon to call. I sent him an e-mail telling him what I wanted and that I would call him in the morning his time.

Next I tried to see what I could find out about weather in the British Isles over a hundred years ago. Piper had obliquely referred to an extraordinarily hot season the previous summer and an equally unpleasant February. It took me about half an hour, but the Internet is a wonderful research tool, and I was able to confirm that indeed the summer of 1899 was an unusually hot one over much of Britain, and February 1900 was one of the rainiest months on record. I'd see what the others had found in their expedition, but so far the diaries were tracking just fine.

Then I went to a pay phone, managed to figure out how to use it, and called Mihály Kovács.

"Janet McLean," I said. "I was in yesterday?"

I heard a rather pronounced intake of breath on the part of Mr. Kovács. "I've run into some, shall we say, anomalies in the accounts of the Magyar Venus," I said. "I haven't been able to reach Dr. Molnár to question him about them, given the time difference, but I am asking you once again, to provide information about the previous owner."

"No, I cannot," he said. "That is not possible." He almost croaked out the words.

"Okay, then," I said. "I suppose I may have to call in the authorities. Thanks for your time." I paused for just a moment to see if there would be any reaction. Instead of a goodbye, or whatever, there was this annoying clatter and banging, and I realized that Kovács had dropped the phone. I waited until the line went dead. Mr. Kovács was rather, shall we say, high-strung, and I seemed to be making him very nervous. If you've lived under the Communist regime, you would have some anxiety around officialdom, and perhaps my call, and my use of the term *authorities,* had touched a nerve. On the other hand, maybe there was something he didn't want me to know.

I decided to make it even worse for him. I went back to Falk Miksa utca, the street of antique shops, and just hung around. I looked into Kovács's shop, and caught a glimpse of him scurrying quickly into the back room. I went in and asked for him, whereupon the assistant pretended not to speak English, but managed to convey that Kovács had gone out. I hung around outside then, peering into store windows until I was rather bored, and then hungry. Giving up on Kovács, I set off to find the restaurant I'd happened across the previous day, the one with the delicious soup and dessert, but I couldn't retrace my steps. I tried to ask a policeman on one corner if he knew of the place, but either he didn't understand me, or he didn't know. As I stood beside the officer at a traffic light, I saw Kovács at the window table of a cafe on Szent István körút not far from his store, and he saw me. He literally paled before my eyes. I couldn't understand why until I realized that he was looking not just at me, but at the policeman beside me, the one to whom I had just spoken. As I'd already concluded, something was really bothering Mihály Kovács, and I'd undoubtedly spoiled his lunch. Maybe I'd call him again later in the day.

I went back to the hotel, stopping at a coffee shop for a bite to eat, and thence to my room to place the call to Frederick Madison. I had told him via e-mail that I was writing an article for an antique dealer's newsletter on the Venus—in my defense, I did write articles from time to time, although this wasn't one of them. I said that I had interviewed Dr. Molnár, which was true, although some might call it a date, and that Károly had told me that Madison's lab had authenticated the Venus, and suggested I call. I got through to him right away.

"I got your e-mail," he said. "I'm happy to talk to you."

"I'd just like to know a little bit about the testing that was done on the Magyar Venus," I said. "Dr. Molnár told me your lab did the work."

"Lovely piece," Madison said. "And yes, we did the testing. The mammoth ivory was found to be in the range that Dr. Molnár claims."

"So the Venus is twenty-five thousand years old, or there about."

"The mammoth ivory is about twenty-five thousand years old."

"You're saying that someone could have carved it much later."

"We couldn't find any indication of that. There were no metal knife marks or anything," he said, chuckling.

"So are you completely comfortable that the Venus is authentic?"

"For me to be completely comfortable," he said. "I would want stratigraphic documentation. Do you understand what I'm saying?"

"Sort of," I said.

"We use provenance a little differently from you antique dealers," he said. "You look at the hands the object in question has passed through. In archaeology, we consider the provenance, or provenience, of an artifact to be the find spot. There are cases in the authenticating of antiquities where it is possible to know who owned an object at any given point of time over decades if not centuries but where no one can say with any assurance where the object was originally found. This is apparently one of those times.

"Despite all the science of dating, stratigraphy is still the principal way to evaluate objects at an archaeological site. We call it archaeostratigraphy when it's used in archaeology, for obvious reasons. It all has to do with where exactly an object was found, on a horizontal matrix or grid and a vertical dimension as well, that is to say, in what layer, or stratum, the object was located, its relativity to other objects above or below it, or even in the same layer. If I'm being too academic here, please tell me."

"No, this is very helpful," I said. "Please continue."

"Ah, there's nothing like an interested audience for a lab man. You may have to stop me sooner or later. I'll try to be brief. The principles, the rules if you will, that govern stratigraphy are actually pretty obvious. Older strata are covered by younger strata, right? Material from an older stratum might make its way into a newer one, but not the other way around. If an object cuts across several strata, it can't be older than the uppermost strata in which it's been found. There are others, but this should give you the idea. Are you still with me?"

"I think so. If I were to excavate a site in, I don't know, Mesopotamia, or something, I would, as I go down, pass through several different civilizations and perhaps cities. If I found an object at one level, it could be older, and still in use. I'm an antique dealer, after all. I want people to use objects from an earlier era today. So for someone to have a pre-Columbian statue in their living room in twenty-first century New York, is not only possible, but it happens reasonably frequently."

"Exactly," he said. "But you wouldn't find a plastic baggy in the fourth-century level, or if you did, you would have a problem. You would definitely have had disturbance at the site."

"Right," I said.

"So stratigraphy is invaluable in assessing the sequences at a site, and the relative age of artifacts in context. Now these so-called Venuses of the Paleolithic," he said. "They've been found everywhere, and several of them are not documented properly. They just seem to turn up from time to time. They're found in a cave somewhere or other, nobody can remember which. They're found in the foundations of a house. One was found by the side of the road, if we are to believe that account, which I, for one, don't. We would be compelled to say that an exact stratigraphic determination would be pretty much impossible under these kinds of circumstances. Some, of course, were found by archaeologists in the course of excavation. Now with those, we can test the object, but we also have the stratigraphic evidence. We can date other objects in that stratum, using different dating methods, depending on the object. All dating methods have their limitations, you see. We used radiocarbon dating on the Magyar Venus, because it is made of mammoth ivory, and carbon dating works well on organic objects, that is objects that were once living things, up to about fifty thousand years old, no matter where they are found. Carbon dating is not much good beyond fifty thousand years, but the Venus is well within the range. For inorganics, ceramics for example, or flint which has been burned before it was buried, we could use thermoluminescence dating, or TL, which in principle lets us date way further back than fifty thousand years. So if we found the Venus in the same stratum as flint tools or ceramics, then we might be able to date both, and if they matched, then we'd be much more confident about the results."

"So for this particular Venus, we have a radiocarbon date of about twenty-five thousand years, and only anecdotal evidence as to where it was found," I said.

"Exactly. It is said to have been found in a cave. Which cave? Where in that cave? In what context? Dr. Molnár showed me the diaries of that fellow . . . what was his name?"

"Piper."

"Piper," he agreed. "We tested the diaries too, and the ink and paper checked out. Now Piper seemed to know what he was doing, and everything he did was well documented, so the anecdotal evidence is better than most. But we don't have the site, do we?"

"So what are you saying, exactly?"

"I'm saying that the mammoth ivory is about twenty-five

thousand years old, that we could find no evidence, no smoking guns as it were, pointing to forgery, that the ink and paper on the diaries dates to about 1900. That is all I can say. I suppose I could add that most of the Venuses tend to date to that approximate time period, so at least it's consistent. And it fits the pattern. They're all essentially rather large around the middle with large drooping breasts, but small heads and tapering heads and limbs. This Venus is consistent with that, too."

"What about the ochre?"

"Right. There were traces of ochre. Dr. Molnár tells me that ochre was mined not far from there between about thirty and forty thousand years ago. Older than the Venus by quite a bit, but it does show that ochre was valued in that part of the world."

"Thank you for all of this," I said.

"My pleasure. I hope I didn't bore you."

"Not at all," I said. "In fact, it is all fascinating. Thank you."

"A pleasure," he said.

"Can I ask you one last question?"

"Shoot."

"My personal theory about testing is that you do it when you have a bad feeling, for want of a better term, about an object. I mean if I look at an antique, and there is something about it that bothers me, even though I can't point to anything specific about it, then I'll have it tested. So, leaving all that stuff about archaeostratigraphy aside, and trying to forget for a moment all the provisos you have to give when you're asked about the testing, do you have some sense about the Magyar Venus. Do you think it's genuine?"

"I can't really do that," he said. "But I suppose . . . my answer would be yes, I think it's genuine."

"Thank you," I said.

"Send me a copy of your article, will you?"

"Sure," I said. I would, too, if I ever wrote it.

It was hardly absolutely definitive, and there was certainly wiggle room no matter which side of this puzzle you were on. If you wanted to believe the Venus was genuine, there was evidence it was. If you didn't want to believe it, if you were Diana, just to pick a name out of a hat, then there was enough there to give you some small measure of satisfaction. To my mind, though, this was starting to look like a convincing if not airtight case for the Venus. I looked at my watch. It was time for the report from the Divas.

They were down in the lobby bar having tea, and looking rather well pleased with themselves. "We're done," Cybil said. "All of it."

"I'm impressed," I said. "What have you got?"

"You first," Grace said. I told them about my lengthy conversation with Frederick Madison. I did not tell them about Kovács.

"Now it's your turn," I said.

"You go, Cybil," Morgan said. "You're the one that made the big discovery."

"What big discovery?"

"Wait for it," Morgan said. "Cybil?"

"We went along Andrássy út," Cybil said. "We checked some guidebooks, and, as you suspected, Andrássy was called Súgarut early on. And the buildings, now shops and other businesses, do look like mansions. We walked right up to the top of Andrássy, or is it the bottom, to Hősök tér, Heroes Square. There is a building that matches the description you gave us. It's called the Palace of the Arts, or something, and it has what Grace assures us are Corinthian columns, just like the diaries say. Then we went into the city park. It's neat, by the way. There is a castle and it is peculiar-looking. We bought a guidebook, and according to that, the castle was built in 1896 for the Hungarian Millennium celebrations—theirs, not the century to come. There is also a restaurant in the park. It's called Gundel's, and we wished we could afford to eat there. We had a look at a menu, though, and it would have been there in 1900, but called Wampetics, just like Piper said.

"We also took a tour of the Parliament Buildings, but it seemed to us that they were open in 1900, while the diaries say they were under construction. So we went for lunch nearby, and that's when I found this great book. It's a book of photographs of Budapest in guess which year?"

"Nineteen hundred!" they said in unison.

Cybil waved the book in triumph. "See, the Parliament Buildings and the Elizabeth Bridge really were under construction that year, as was part of Buda Castle. Look, here's the bridge with the scaffolding on it. There's a photograph of the Emperor Franz Josef and his wife, Elizabeth, although I don't know about the reference to her death."

"I do," I said. "I checked some of the historical stuff on the Internet this morning. Elizabeth, or Erszébet, was in fact called Sisi by the adoring Hungarians, and she was stabbed to death by an Italian anarchist in 1898. I also looked up the weather in Britain, by the way, in 1899 and 1900, because there are references to that, and it also checks out."

No wonder Diana was quieter, and more sullen-looking than ever.

"That doesn't necessarily mean that the diary, and by extension the Venus, are authentic. Someone wanting to fake the diaries could pick up the same book you did." I said. Diana brightened considerably. "But the details do bring an air of authenticity to the pages of the diary, there is no question about it," I said. Diana's face fell again.

"So what next?" Morgan said. "Are there assignments for tomorrow?"

"I'll have to think about that. I'm going to my room to do some more research. I'll see you in the morning." What I really wanted to do was have a nap. Despite all the walking, however, I just lay there, rigid and wide awake, until the ringing of the telephone jarred me to my feet.

Once again the caller felt no need for a salutation of any sort. "Will you have dinner with me tonight?" the voice said.

"I'm in Budapest, Károly," I said.

"That is just as well," he said, "Because, as it turns out, so am I. Let me pick you up at your hotel around 7:30."

"The Divas are here," I said. "All of them. They arrived yesterday." I found myself wondering if the airlines had noticed this sudden spike in air travel to Budapest. Certainly it wasn't panning out exactly the way I'd planned it. "I don't think you want to show your face in this lobby."

He laughed. "Does this mean you don't want to be seen with me? Okay. You're near the Opera, correct? Off Andrássy út? There's a very nice bistro nearby. If you walk out to Andrássy and turn right, you'll come to it within a block or so. It's called Vörös és Fehér." He spelled it for me. "That means red and white, as in wine. It's a wine bar. I'll meet you for a drink there at, say, seven, and then we'll go somewhere far away from your hotel for dinner. If you need to call me in the mean time, I'm at—"

"The Hilton," I said. Didn't he always stay there? At least when he was on an expense account. "What are you doing here?"

"The Hilton, yes. How . . . ? Never mind. I could ask

you the same question, what you're doing here, but in answer to yours, Frank dragged me here. Some book deal he wants to put together about the Venus. I have an appointment with some people at the Magyar Nemzeti Múzeum, the Hungarian National Museum, as well, to see about an exhibit on prehistoric art in Hungary I want to mount at the Cottingham in conjunction with the Venus. They are interested in doing a joint exhibition that would include the Venus. Frank will want to do the catalog. He's discovered art in his old age. And you?"

"I'll tell you when I see you," I said. I set down the phone and called Clive.

"Clive," I said. "We've already had this conversation. You are not supposed to tell anyone else where I am!"

"I haven't told anyone," he protested.

"You did so. You told Károly Molnár."

"Who's he? Not that guy at the Cottingham? Why would he be asking where you are? Speaking of Molnár, though, have you heard the Venus may be a fake?"

"No. Frank Kalman, then?"

"I don't believe I know Frank Kalman, either. Look, it is true that, as is my wont, when I saw the particularly comely Morgan, I lost all sense of space and time, as well as all discretion. Yes, I blabbed your whereabouts. But I haven't told anyone else."

"Okay, sorry," I said. "I'll talk to you soon."

"Is that all you called for? You haven't called to tell me what flight you're on, when you'll be back pulling your weight in this store we share?"

"Bye, Clive," I said, hanging up before he could protest some more. It was a puzzle though. If he hadn't told Károly, who had, and what did it mean? That one of the Divas was not entirely frank about her reasons for being here? That was hardly a surprise. One of them had spiked my drink, too. I hoped it wasn't Morgan, but I really couldn't be sure. She was the one, by her own admission, who'd gone and seen Clive to find out how to find me. It would hardly have been Diana who had told Károly, would it?

Vörös és Fehér was indeed a rather lovely wine bar. Károly ordered me a glass of red from the wine country around Eger, and it was a pleasant surprise. I associated Hungarian wines with the plonk I'd drunk in my poverty-stricken student days, but this was rather good. I would have been happy staying there for dinner, too. The food looked and smelled just fine, but Károly had other ideas. We took a long taxi ride across the Danube, and then some miles to a restaurant called Rémiz. It, too, was a splendid place, a series of little rooms framed by French windows and doors, and a lovely garden outside. I let Károly order for me without protest this time, given I hadn't a clue what was on the menu. He ordered goose liver on toast to start, and fish for the main course, something he called *fogas*, a fish he claimed could only be found in Hungary's Lake Balaton, a kind of pike/perch. Whatever it was, it was delicious. The wines were very tasty, the dessert divine, and the conversation quite companionable, once we got a contentious subject or two out of the way.

"Is there any chance the Dea Muta would tell me what she's doing in Budapest?" Károly asked. "I believe I've told you why I'm here."

"You didn't mention you were coming here when we had drinks at Canoe," I said.

"No, because the plans were not firmed up. I did call you to tell you where I would be once I heard from the museum here that the person I needed to see would be available for only about three or four days. I was going to suggest that you come with me. You weren't there. I don't recall receiving a message from you. I thought perhaps, despite what you'd said, that I'd offended you. The comment about the drugs."

"You can let that one go," I said. "I found it educational. As to why I'm here, it's kind of hard to explain, even to myself," I said. "I decided a few weeks ago that I needed a break from the store, and I wanted to go somewhere different, somewhere I don't usually go on my business trips. I didn't want a beach, and when I was looking to see where I could get a cheap last-minute flight, Budapest came up. We'd talked about it, and you'd told me how lovely it is, so I booked the flight and here I am. The rest of the gang, the Divas, just kind of tagged along. I'm sorry I didn't tell you. I suppose I'm still a little confused about our relationship."

"I'm not," he said. "I want us to have another go."

"I don't know," I said, for possibly the hundredth time. "Perhaps it's too soon after the end of my last relationship. How did you find me? Did Clive tell you?" I would believe Clive over Károly any day, I was sorry to say, so this was definitely a test.

"Frank told me," he said.

"How would he know?" I said.

"I have no idea. I can only assume one of the Divas must have told him. He knew where you were staying as well. Why don't you want to be seen with me?"

"I don't mind being seen with you. It's just that some of the Divas are not your biggest fans at the moment. I believe you fired Diana. That's whom you meant when you told me that you had had to fire a person in a position of trust that night at the Cottingham, is it not?"

"Will I get sued if I confess?" he said. "Yes, I fired her, but please don't ask me why. It would be inappropriate of me to tell you."

"She says you blocked her getting tenure at University," I said.

"What!" he exclaimed.

"She said she got her doctorate, and everything, but you spoke eloquently against her, or something like that."

"I did nothing of the kind. In fact you might inquire where—" He stopped, midsentence. "No, I am not going to get into a slagging match here. I will say nothing more."

"And the woman you broke up with that night? Morgan, by any chance?"

"Did she say that?" he said, hesitating. "I don't like to kiss and tell."

"I'm putting two and two together here."

"I see. And do the rest of the Divas have a bone to pick with me as well?"

"Nothing specific that I've heard, but they are all friends, so if one of them is mad at you, there is a reasonable chance the rest of them will be."

"No doubt," he said. "You Divas always were a rather closed circle. Look, I know I was a love 'em and leave 'em kind of guy. I suppose I'm paying for that now. But I left you because I felt like a fraud. I've already told you why. I am not going to answer to any more of these accusations. You are going to have to decide for yourself if you believe them, or you believe me. So which is it? Where are you on the subject of Károly Molnár?"

"I'm here having dinner with you, aren't I?" I said. He didn't say anything for a moment or two, but he looked a little sad, really, and with good reason. I hadn't answered the question, nor was I capable of doing so at that moment.

"I feel as if I've spent the last several years searching for something, love, success, my roots, peace of mind, you name it," he said finally. "I've hopped from museum to museum, every job a little better than the last, certainly, but I haven't stayed long. I went through a string of women until I married Peggy, and still I wasn't happy. I had a good job at the Bramley, we went to all the best parties, and I felt like a complete fraud. I came back to Toronto tail between my legs, broke, publicly humiliated by the wife, fired from the Bramley because I couldn't get along with the curators, or something equally ridiculous. Did I mention that my wife's father was chair of the Bramley board?

"Then, out of the blue, I discover that everything I wanted was here all along. The Cottingham may be a fraction of the size of the Bramley, but I'm happy there. You know I was always trying to make the institutions I worked in more responsive to what the public wanted. At the Bramley, I tried some innovative exhibit design, I tried to popularize the subject matter. And I was blocked at every turn by the staff, most of whom had been there for decades. The truth was they didn't want to change. The museum could gather dust, and become increasingly irrelevant, and they would be working away at what they'd done for years and years and calling it scholarship, even though there was no one interested in it any more. The Cottingham is different. I told Courtney and Major that I wanted to build a cave exhibit for the kids to play in, maybe have a make-believe archaeological dig site right in the cave where kids could pretend to be archaeologists looking for the Venus. They loved the idea. And what Major and Courtney say, goes. I think I can do some truly innovative things there.

"And, best of all, I found you again, after all this time. I want us to be together. I want to be able to hold hands in public, go to the same parties, neck in the back row at the movies, just like we used to, no matter who is there. I don't care what the Divas think, or anybody else for that matter.

I'm not divorced yet, but I soon will be, so the only impediment from my perspective are your feelings for me. I know I'm pushing too hard on this, but I feel I've wasted a lot of time."

"Károly, I am very glad to see you again after all these years. Really, I am. And I like being with you. I'm thrilled the Cottingham is working out well for you. But for now we are going to have to leave it at that. There are a few, what will I call them, outstanding items in my life that need to be resolved before I can make that kind of decision."

"I'm not sure what you're saying. Can we continue to see each other?" he said.

"I would like that," I said.

"I suppose that will have to do," he said. "I'm not going to give up, though."

That last statement made me think of Rob, something I didn't really want to do at that moment: Rob when he'd said he was going to put his effort into getting me back rather than getting over me. "Could we talk about something else?" I said.

"Of course. I'm sorry. Whatever you like."

"Budapest, then. I went to Falk Miksa utca. I suppose I can't get too far away from antiques. I remembered you'd mentioned it. Where exactly was your store?"

"I take some comfort from this, that I was obviously on your mind." He made a bit of a face, but he got out a pen and a piece of paper and drew me a map. I asked him what other places I should see, and after a minute or two, the conversation naturally moved on to safer topics.

At the end of the evening, when it came time to go, Károly helped me with my coat. He was standing behind me, and rather than stepping away, he put his hands on my upper arms, very gently, and just stood there. I could feel his breath on the back of my neck, and the pressure of his hands through my coat. *Don't lean back,* I told myself. *If you do, you know how this will end.* But then I felt a wave of emotion wash over me, part loneliness perhaps, part nostalgia, and also, to be honest, a large measure of desire, feelings so intense, I felt as if there wasn't enough air for me to breathe. I very slowly leaned back until we touched, his arms came around me, and my resolve vanished.

CHAPTER EIGHT

July 19

The countryside is extraordinarily beautiful. The people here call *them*
mountains, but really they are hills. The wooded hillsides are covered in beech trees with lovely silvery leaves interspersed here and
there with dark green evergreens. There are meadows, and lakes the
colour of emeralds. The feature of the landscape of most interest to
me are the limestone outcroppings. Even from below I can see they
hold much promise. The going is fairly steep, but not impossible to
someone young and in good health.

Once again I am the most fortunate of individuals. The
Nádasdi family has insisted that I should stay in a cottage at their
estate. It is right in the mountains, on the eastern edge of a great
plateau, a beautiful place with cascading waterfalls and streams,
surrounded by magnificent slopes. The town is small and rather

quiet, its main industry, a foundry, having relocated almost thirty years ago. There are hopes it will become a resort, a place for people from Budapest to spend their summers away from the heat of the city, and has been named Lillafüred. I am grateful to be here, as I am told that Budapest is very hot and dusty in summer. I remember only too well the extremely hot summer we endured at home last year, and am glad to be in the cool of the mountains.

Still no word from T, but I must be patient. His business affairs are of the utmost importance, I am convinced, or he would be here by now. Sometimes at night I fear that something untoward has happened to him, but then comes the dawn, and my work in the caves, and these morbid thoughts vanish.

There are so many caves. I despair when I think how many lifetimes it would take for me to explore them all. I have eliminated several as not fit for habitation even by most primitive man, and others because they are devoid of any soil, and therefore all is revealed with the most cursory search. If ever man lived there, his signs have long disappeared.

I have decided to restrict my search now to two caves. Both are very high above a valley, and quite difficult to reach, and commended themselves to me because of their good aspect. One has two chambers off the entrance, the other a single one. They seem to me suitable places to live if one must live under these conditions, as ancient man did. The entrances to both are high so that a cooking fire would not cause serious problems, the single chambered cave in particular having a very high cathedral ceiling. Both are approximately 100 feet or more in depth, and, being situated at the narrower end of the gorge, would provide a good opportunity to watch for game from relative safety. I have found small pieces of stone which may well prove to be altered by man rather than the elements in the two-chambered cave, and a skull which I believe to be a bear in the other. Tomorrow I will choose one, perhaps with the *toss of a coin, given no more scientific solution, and contrive to make a start.*

September 16/17

You'd think spending the night with the first great love of your life would cure any case of insomnia. Any case but mine, that is. At least I had something more interesting than maps of Hungary to look at that night. Károly slept soundly, and, with the cares of daily life temporarily at bay, the lines of a couple of decades smoothed by sleep, he looked much as he had in college, the charming, funny, affectionate man I'd loved. It was difficult for me, with him so close beside me, to think he was capable of anything the Divas accused him of: blackmailing Morgan, cheating on his expense account, forging a diary and a twenty-five thousand-year-old artifact, and, if Cybil's rather emotional ramblings were to be given any credence, saying something so terrible to Anna that she threw herself off a bridge. Somehow, lying there in the semidarkness, none of it seemed even remotely possible.

But then, of course, came the dawn, and with it harsh reality. Surely all of the Divas couldn't be wrong. Surely they couldn't be caught up in some collective hysteria that made them invent all of these things. And what did I really know about Károly? What did I know about any of them? Time, life in fact, had intervened, and all of them were, to some extent, strangers to me. I went over the previous evening's conversation, at the restaurant, and the things he'd said in the night. But I had not been truthful, not at least in response to his questions over dinner. How could I be sure he was being honest with me?

The thing was, ever since I'd started reading the diaries, I'd had this sense that something was amiss. Diana had felt it, too. In my rather lengthy conversation with Dr. Frederick Madison, I'd told him that I thought that scientific testing was a second line of defense, really, that came into play after someone who had a bad feeling for the object in question had doubts as to its authenticity. And the more I read the diaries, the more I felt that way. Something was wrong with them. So far, however, I couldn't point to anything specific. I'd sent the Divas off to verify the landmarks that were mentioned, and they all checked out. Even the weather was right! Not only the paper on the original, but the ink had come through with flying colors! But here I was lying in the dark beside the man who'd published them, who'd used them to find the Venus, which, of course, also checked out, and I was having my doubts.

Had I felt the same twitch when I'd looked at the Venus, sitting in her spotlight at the Cottingham that first night, that signal that told me something was not right? I had not. This could be explained by the fact that I knew nothing at all about twenty-five thousand-year-old artifacts. Or it could be because the Venus, quite simply, was real.

But what, exactly, I had to ask myself, did this have to do with Anna Belmont's death? Nothing except that she'd been to the gala unveiling at the Cottingham, and she'd left, come back to the bar, and yelled at a group of people standing there before jumping off a bridge. That, and my dream of course, or should I say nightmare, of Anna floating over my back fence with the Venus in her hand. People said she was crazy. Maybe the crazy person here was a certain antique dealer.

Except—except that she had had her little spell, if that is what we could call it, when Károly had mounted the stage and started talking about the diaries. I was certain that was when it was. Had she seen the Venus? I didn't think so. I knew she hadn't left the building, because she'd been in the women's washroom still in some distress, but I hadn't seen her filing past the Venus with the rest of us. After that she'd come to the bar, and she'd pointed to a group of four people, two of whom, Károly and Frank, were intimately associated with the diaries. A coincidence, surely. But was there any evidence that it could have been Courtney Cottingham or Woodward Watson? I'd ask Morgan about the latter, but I was certain the answer would be no. Morgan had been unaware of the tragic events of Anna's life when we'd first met in the bar before the gala. That had been clear from her reaction, which paralleled mine. And I remembered that Woodward had asked Anna if he knew her. Courtney had not looked guilty, it seemed to me, but rather just plain baffled by it all.

These were not the kind of thoughts I wanted to have, given my present location, but they somehow seemed unstoppable. By about six in the morning, I decided that breakfast with Károly wasn't something I wanted. I had a quick shower, gathered up the clothes that seemed to have scattered themselves about the room, and after a quick glance at Károly, let myself out. I had a feeling he was awake, but he didn't say a word.

It was barely dawn, but when I crossed the lobby, I heard my name. "Good morning, Lara," the voice said. "Changed hotels, have we?"

"Hello, Frank," I said. "Not a bad hotel for a penniless publisher." He sounded a little peevish, and for a moment I wondered if he was jealous, although why he would care what his heterosexual acquaintances were up to, I couldn't imagine.

"I'm traveling on Károly's tab," he said. "Cottingham official business."

"So I've heard."

"I was just going to pick up a coffee and take it out to the Fisherman's Bastion," he said. "Care to join me?"

"I don't know what that is," I said.

"Then you must come. We'll have the place to ourselves before the tourist buses get there. It's a bit chilly, but worth it."

It was. The Hilton is located in Buda, on top of the hill, a short walk from Buda Castle. The Bastion, a rather frivolous white colonnade, interrupted by turrets and towers, neo-Romanesque I guess you'd call it, runs right along the edge of Buda hill. Frank found us a couple of chairs from the cafe there, not yet open, and we sat high over the Danube. The dawn light was gray with just a hint of pink, and mist swirled around and under the bridges: the Lánchíd, the Chain Bridge, almost directly below, farther away, to the right, the Elizabeth Bridge. To our left, Margit, or Margaret Island, in the middle of the Danube, looked like a magical ship, floating in the mist. Across the river, Pest was waking up, a yellow tram making its way along the Danube Corso, cars, headlights still on, edging along the streets. It was really lovely. I'd thought the previous day that I was in danger of losing my heart to this city. That morning I believe I did.

Hearts, lost and otherwise, seemed to be on Frank's mind as well. "Are you going to break his heart?" Frank said, bestirring himself at last.

"I don't think his is in any more danger of being broken than mine," I said.

"I'm very fond of Károly," Frank said. "I think of him as this little lost soul, somehow, almost naive in his acceptance of people at face value. He sees in people what they want him to see. I think people like that are almost certain to be disappointed, if not betrayed."

"Is that right?" I said.

"Things are starting to go better for him now," he said. "He's had a difficult time, you know, with his divorce, and the rather abrupt departure from his job at the Bramley. I don't think he expects this winning streak to last, of course. He may have been raised in North America, but he is cursed with an acute case of Hungarian pessimism. It's a national characteristic, you know. It's in the DNA, I suppose. I suffer from it a bit myself."

"Frank, this conversation is a little byzantine for me. I'm born and raised in North America, don't have a drop of Hungarian blood as far as I know, and I need something a little more straightforward. So, forgive my direct approach, but what are you trying to tell me?" I said. "Is it stay with him forever, or is it buzz off?"

"I don't know," he said. "Now that you mention it, the indirect approach may be very Hungarian too."

"You're the one who told him where I was," I said.

"True."

"How did you find out?"

He laughed. "I've infiltrated the Divas. There is a mole in your midst."

"Who?"

"If I told you, she wouldn't be a mole anymore. You have a one in four chance of being right the first time."

"My guess would be Cybil. She knows you better than the rest of us. She thinks that maybe Károly said something to Anna that would drive her to suicide."

"She what?" Frank exclaimed. "That's ridiculous! I knew Anna, you know. I went to see her a few times when she was holed up in that ghastly apartment with her equally ghastly mother. Cybil suggested I visit, and I did. Let me tell you: Anna was stark, raving bonkers. I told the police that, too. Some fellow who lived by the bridge told police he thought she might have been chased out on to the bridge and over the side. That is absolute bullshit. Losing her child was a terrible thing, but other people survive it. She locked herself up in that little apartment, with her dotty mother, and went quietly mad. She was always a little nuts. Think back to college. She did some really crazy things. Admit it!"

"I suppose," I said. "They seemed more like pranks, though. I remember she talked us into climbing over the wall to one of the men's colleges. We had to pile up garbage cans to do it. We got caught, of course. But the headmaster invited us for sherry."

"Did you happen to notice that she stole some of the silver?"

"No!" I exclaimed. "Well, yes, I do recall that, now that you mention it. You are exaggerating. She took a spoon or something, to prove we'd been there, but she returned it."

"No, she didn't," he said. "It was a silver soup ladle. Sterling, no less. I found it in her stuff when I went to help Cybil clear out the place after she died. The emblem of the college is quite clear. I sent it back to them with a note."

"It was still a prank," I said. "Although I suppose she should have returned it."

"I'm trying to tell you that Anna was nuts, and not just nuts, dishonest. I helped Cybil clear out her room. There were clothes in that closet with the tags still on them. I think she shoplifted, too."

"Without leaving home, you mean?" I said. "Rather hard to do. Wouldn't it be more logical to assume that her mother, or Cybil, bought her new clothes to try to entice her to go out?"

"I'm just saying she may have been dishonest. For sure she was crazy."

I thought about that for a minute. Anna, it had to be said, had been a little manic in college. Her pranks could be, at times, annoying. But dishonest? I didn't think so. Stark raving bonkers? I simply couldn't agree. I decided, however, that there was no point in saying so to Frank.

"So why did you go to visit her?" I said. "If you thought she was so crazy."

"I guess I felt sorry for her," he said. "More to the point, Cybil asked me to."

"I suppose it doesn't much matter now," I said.

"It does, if Cybil is saying those kinds of things about Károly," Frank said.

"I'm sure she'll get over it," I said. "She's upset, and casting about for a reason for what Anna did, when there isn't one, not a logical one, that is."

"What could he possibly have said to Anna to make her jump off a bridge?" Frank said.

"I have no idea. But why let it bother you? As you have pointed out, life is improving for Károly. You, too, I expect. Both of you have rather benefited from the Venus, haven't you?"

"No question about it," he said. "While Károly was breaking up with his wife and getting offed from the Bramley, I was going broke. The large chains had completely revolutionized bookselling, and I couldn't make a living on their terms. I couldn't even find a buyer for the tattered remains of my company. And then Károly walks into my office and I get the book deal, plus I'm going to do a catalog for the

Cottingham, and I'm here to do a deal for the catalog for a special touring exhibit. Not bad for the kid of immigrants. I'm not rich by any means, but I'm not broke anymore, either. I don't live as high off the hog as Károly, but then I don't have his huge debts."

Huge debts? I wanted to say, but I didn't. Perhaps this was Frank being byzantine again, trying to talk me into leaving Károly. "You weren't entirely truthful when you told me at lunch a week or so ago that you had to remind Károly that he and I had been an item in college, were you?" I said instead.

"No," he said. "I should not have said that. He was very distracted that evening, but he remembered you all by himself. I have to admit you're good for Károly, even if he doesn't think it will last. He thinks there are things you aren't telling him."

"The two of you seem to discuss me a fair amount," I said.

"Not really," he said. "I'm surmising really. You're thinking it's none of my business, and you're right."

"No, I'm thinking I'd better be on my way," I said. "The Divas will be wondering where I am. I'm hoping you won't tell them, by the way. Not even your mole."

"Wouldn't dream of it," Frank said.

In the taxi on the way back to my own hotel, I decided that I wanted to spend the day with the Divas even less than I'd wanted to talk to Károly that morning. I'd been thinking about heading out of the city and into the Bükk Mountains, just to get a sense of the place, and see, once again, if the diaries reflected reality. I'd even bought myself some lovely old binoculars in one of the antique shops on Falk Miksa to help me find the caves. This, I decided, just might be the day to do it.

This course of action was confirmed when I got back to the hotel, because sitting in a café across from the hotel entrance I spotted Mihály Kovács. He must have followed me back to the hotel that day, after I'd seen him in the restaurant. I made a dash for the door from the taxi in hopes that he hadn't seen me. It was definitely a good time to get out of town.

The people at the desk told me that they could have a rental car for me by eleven, so it was back to my room to pack, and to work on the day's assignment for the Divas. I took a small bag, in case I needed to stay overnight, with some reasonably sturdy walking shoes and a waterproof shell, a change of clothes, and then I pulled on jeans and a warm sweater.

By the time the Divas were down for breakfast, I was ready to go. "So what's our assignment for today, Chief?" Cybil said. She was obviously raring to go, with her fanny pack at her side, jeans and a sweatshirt, and her white and red walking shoes on. "I think we served with distinction yesterday."

"Yesterday was the easy part," I said. "Today will almost certainly be more difficult. Today, you are going to try to find Piper's apartment."

"How on earth would we do that?" Diana said. "Unless there's an address or at least a street name."

"Sorry," I said. "There are clues, however, and I've written them out for you. According to the diaries, it's in an area called Lipótváros, named for Leopold, who would have been one of the Hapsburgs. It's near Leopold körút."

"What's a *körút?*" Cybil said.

"I think *körút* is another name for a type of street. We have streets, avenues, lanes, roads. They have *körúts, úts, utcas,* which would probably be little *úts*. A *körút* would be a major street, I think. Now Lipótváros is an area that still exists. It's part of the fifth district, I think, right here," I said, spreading the map out on the the table and pointing. "It is, as the diaries point out, near the Danube. In fact it goes right down to the Danube. It's one of the oldest parts of the city. The rest of the clues are as follows: close to Parliament, a little bit north and west of the Basilica. There may be an old coffee house nearby. It's a four-story building, neo-classical in style—think four columns, straight lines. It has some interesting porcelain tiles around the entranceway, a large staircase inside. It has a courtyard in the middle, which you may or may not be able to see. It's across from an art nouveau-style building of five stories. And if you got the corner apartment on the fourth floor, and if you stood just so, you can see the both the Parliament and the Danube, at least you could in 1900."

"I don't see a Leopold körút," Morgan said.

"Get out the book about Budapest in 1900," I said. "If I knew exactly where it was, I wouldn't be asking you to find it."

"How do you know it will still be there?" Diana demanded.

"I don't," I said.

"Even if it is, it might not have the porcelain tiles in the entranceway," Cybil said.

"That's right," I said.

"There isn't even a street name," Grace said.

"Exactly," I said.

"Let's get going, girls," Morgan said. "We have our assignment. We can talk all day about what we don't know about it, or we can go look for it. I, for one, intend to find this place, if it exists, and pin it down very closely if it doesn't."

"The difficult we do immediately. The impossible takes a little longer," Cybil said. "I expect to have buns of steel after all this walking."

"What are you going to do?" Diana said.

"I'm going to move a little farther afield," I said. She looked at me suspiciously. I wondered how suspicious she would be if she knew about my previous evening's activities. I didn't think I wanted to be nearby if she ever found out.

THE CAR WAS at the front door as promised. I'd seen the Divas off on their assignment, had left a note for them at the desk to say I might not be back that evening, had done the same at the Hilton for Károly, and was ready to roll. I looked around after the man from the rental agency and I had concluded the formalities, amazingly uncomplicated, much to my surprise, but there was no sign of Kovács.

I pulled the car, a little teal-colored Opel hatchback with animal hairs all over the seats, out on to Andrássy út and headed east, past the city park, before hitting the M3. Driving in Budapest, no matter for how short a time, seemed a foolish and life-threatening thing to do, but I managed it. I'd been warned by the rental company that I would have to get a permit for the tolls, which somehow I also managed to do at a station on the side of the highway just out of Budapest. Once on the highway, the driving wasn't bad, flat at first, but then, as I got farther out, some rolling hills, and farmland, vines, and little towns with orange-tiled roofs. It was very pretty. There wasn't too much traffic on the well-maintained four-lane road, so I made good time, stopping once for the permit, and a second time just for a stretch, and a check of the map. Piper had referred to the town of Lillafüred in the Bükks, had stayed there, in fact, and I could find it on the map. But it seemed just a little bit too far to drive at that time of day, so I opted to go instead to Eger, on the western edge of the Bükks, rather than Lillafüred, farther east. Either place, I reasoned, would give me a feel for the diaries' contents.

When I took the turnoff for Eger, a dark green Toyota Camry pulled off at the same time, and pretty much stayed with me right into the city. It made me nervous, thinking as I was of Mihály Kovács standing at the hotel, but the car stayed far enough back that I had no chance to see the driver. I decided I was imagining things, and kept going.

I was in Eger by midafternoon. It was autumn, and already the sun was fairly low in the sky. I wasn't too keen on wandering around caves in the dark, and it was pretty clear to me that I wasn't going to get all my exploring done and get back to Budapest in one day, so I found myself a room at the Flora, a hotel that boasted a spa and hot springs, and spent what was left of the day exploring Eger. It's an attractive town, baroque in style, all pinks, peaches, and yellows, topped by red tile roofs, particularly pretty in the late afternoon sun. There's a handsome brilliant yellow cathedral, Italian in style, a castle, or what's left of one, and even a Turkish minaret. And there was wine to be drunk in the many cafés, grown in the vineyards in the rather charmingly named Szépasszony-völgy, the Valley of Beautiful Women.

While being there alone without the Divas, and doing all the tourist kinds of activities, gave my afternoon the air of a holiday, it wasn't. All the while I kept checking over my shoulder, but neither Kovács nor the green Camry were to be seen.

I THOUGHT THAT after all that driving, a couple hours of sightseeing on foot, and some really lovely wine, I'd sleep that night. For days, if not weeks, I'd been telling myself I'd sleep if I got tired enough, but I had long since passed that point, and still I was wandering around most nights like some restless wraith. On this particular occasion, every time I dozed off I dreamed of Anna, holding the Magyar Venus, crying and pointing. This time she was pointing toward a rather dark and menacing cave.

IT WAS EARLY morning when I packed up and left the hotel. Steam was rising from the warm pools outside, where already people of various shapes and sizes were taking the waters. Two men were playing chess at a table in the pool. I supposed I might benefit from a spa treatment or two, but I didn't have time.

With the help of directions from the concierge, who spoke excellent English, I headed into the Bükks to find a *barlang,* a cave. I knew I wasn't going to find Piper's cave. As guidebooks to the area made clear, there were hundreds of these *barlangs* in Northern Hungary stretching right into Slovakia, and it was ridiculous to think that I'd just strap on my walking shoes, head into the Bükks, and happen upon the right cave.

What I wanted to do was essentially what I'd been doing all along, which was to test Piper's narrative to see if the descriptions of the surroundings remained credible once outside Budapest. I was still looking for something, the whatever it was that was bothering me, but so far, no go. On the other hand, if the diaries were consistent that would lend some weight, if not assurance, to the story of the discovery of the Venus.

And indeed, the description of the countryside rang true. I took a road that wound first through many vineyards, this being the part of the country from which the famous Egri

bikavér wines come, but which then started to climb higher
through steep turns right into the hills. The beech forests
interspersed with dark evergreens matched the diaries' description perfectly, as did the alpine meadows, grass gleaming with the previous night's rain, and the tiny, brilliant
green lakes. The leaves of the trees were a gorgeous yellow
in the autumn sun. As the road climbed higher, I began to
see the limestone outcroppings, and then the cliffs that
Piper had written about, where the caves of the region were
to be found.

I'd put about thirty kilometers on the odometer, when I
saw what I was looking for, a cave entrance, high up over the
road, but quite visible from it. I trained the binoculars on it,
and on the ground leading up to it, and decided I'd give it a
go. The Hungarians might call these mountains. Where I
come from they'd be called hills, and climbing them didn't
seem insurmountable by any means, a hike up a reasonably
gentle slope.

I found a place to pull off and park as close to where I
knew the cave to be as I could, although from directly below
it couldn't be seen. There were trail markers, however, and a
rather overgrown but still distinguishable path heading
upwards. I decided to follow the trail as long as it kept
going up, on the assumption it would probably lead to the
bottom of the rocky ridge in which the cave was situated. I
hauled out my walking shoes, and sitting sideways in the
driver's seat, with the door open, put them on. As I did so, a
dark green Camry passed me. I didn't look up in time to see
who was in it, but it sent an unpleasant shiver up my spine.
I watched as it took the turn ahead, lost sight of it in the
trees, but caught a glimpse of it again farther along the road
at the next turn. There too it kept going. In fact, it didn't
even slow down. I told myself that there was more than one

green Camry on the road, and even at that I couldn't say the driver of any one of them was looking out for me.

As I'd predicted, the climbing was not particularly difficult, none of it of the fingernail-gripping-stone variety, simply a walk up a reasonably steep hillside through a forest of beech. I stopped to catch my breath after climbing over a large fallen tree that blocked the path, enjoying the exercise and fresh air—until I heard what I thought was the crack of a branch behind me. I turned and looked back down the trail, saw nothing, but realized just how silent the woods suddenly were. There wasn't a chirp from any bird, nor the sound of any cars on the road.

Stuffing down incipient panic, I kept climbing until I reached what I thought was the bottom of the rocky ridge high over the road, only to find it wasn't. I stopped and again heard what I thought could be an animal in the woods below me and to the right. The other sound had been below and to the left, which either meant that I was imagining things or there were small animals about, or, and this was my least-favorite option, there were three of us in the woods. The cave, which from the road had been quite visible, was from my current position, nowhere to be seen. I kept climbing steadily upward—it was higher than I'd thought—until at last I saw the rock face, at which point I left the path, now almost extinct anyway, and took the last few steep steps to the rock. It was relatively smooth, and there was no way I was going to go straight up from there. Again I heard a sound in the woods behind me and lower down. Perhaps I should have made a dash for the road, but I would have run into whoever it was down there, and it just didn't seem like the best idea in the world. I couldn't go up, and I didn't want to go down, so there was only one other option, which was to edge along the rock face—there was only one direction where this was possible—and hope to find a hiding place. The rock was damp and clammy, the smell of mold in my nose as I edged my way along. The footing was slippery, precariously so, but I hung on.

The sounds below were louder and closer when I saw it at last: the entrance to the cave I'd seen from the road. I hauled myself up over another ledge of limestone, slipping a bit as I did so, and then, with a quick few steps, I was in the cave. It was a spectacularly large space, the forefront of which was reasonably well lit due to the sunlight outside, but rapidly disappearing into darkness toward the back. I scrambled my way in to a large stone and crouched behind it. If someone was following me, I reasoned, they would be caught in silhouette in the entrance to the cave. I knew I was trapped, but by now I'd assembled a little pile of rocks beside me which I was prepared to use if pressed, and I had the advantage of having become accustomed to the dim light at the back of the cave, something a new intruder would not.

I sat there for what seemed an eternity, but was maybe ten minutes, waiting for something to happen. Nothing did. No one came. No bats swooped over my head. No cave bears roared. Nothing. So gradually I let my eyes slip away from the entrance and had a look around. I was in a huge chamber, maybe 150 feet deep with a roof that tapered up to a point, like a vaulted ceiling. I could see that this would be a place where people could live. Several families could survive and make their home, however temporary, here. The roof was high enough that fires could be lit against the cold, and up on the ridge it would be possible to watch for game. This, then, was the place where Piper had toiled in what he referred to as considerable inconvenience. Not this specific cave, maybe, but one just like it. And it could not have been easy, climbing up here every day. Light must have been a problem. For a few hours a day, perhaps, if the opening were situated just so, there would be enough light shining into the cavern, but otherwise there would be only this gloom. And this was 1900: no flashlights, no floodlights, only torches against the dark.

This cave, or one just like it, must have been the find spot for the Magyar Venus. I found this thought extraordinary, that people who had lived under these conditions had managed to create something as beautiful as the Venus. Like everyone else, I suppose, I thought of cave dwellers as primitive creatures of subnormal intelligence. But they couldn't have been. They must have been able to see beyond the walls of the cave, in their minds at least. The people who had lived in this cave at the time the Venus was carved had brains the same size as ours. They must surely have loved and cared for their children, and found some way of working together, or we would not have survived as a species. And if that was true, then maybe I would have to rethink my idea of progress, that Darwinian idea, or at least everyone's interpretation of it, that we were becoming increasingly advanced and civilized. What, after all, made us more advanced? Was it technology? Perhaps we should be judged not just by the fact we had it, but by the purposes to which it was put. Were we increasingly more generous toward our fellow man? I hardly thought so. Were we any less superstitious, for example, than the people who had lived here? Not if daily horoscopes and such were anything to go by. There was a lot to think about hiding in this huge cathedral in stone, ideas that became, as I sat there, an absolute conviction that the Venus was real.

This little riff on the Venus, however diverting for me, was not going to solve my immediate problem, which was how to get out of here. My eyes flicked back to the cave

entrance. There was nothing to be seen but rocks and trees.
The cave had no back entrance in sight, and while I could sit
there for days, I supposed, thinking philosophically about
cave dwellers before I shriveled up and died, it wasn't a particularly entertaining idea. There was nothing for it but to
head out, and hope my fevered imagination had been at
work, nothing more.

I carefully edged my way back to the entrance and peered
out. Nothing. I looked up, but no face hanging over the top
of the cave entrance looked back at me. I went out to the
ledge in front of the cave and scanned the terrain in all
directions. Still nothing.

I picked my way back along the ridge, face to the rock, a
rather unpleasantly exposed position, until I was back at the
edge of the woods. I waited there for a minute, heart in
mouth, listening as carefully as I could.

Then, my face still to the rock wall, I stepped back and
down, one foot suspended for a moment feeling for the
ground below. The surface found, I shifted my weight down
and on to—something squishy. That something was an arm,
and it was attached to the body of the former Mihály
Kovács, antique dealer. I hurtled down the path, stumbling
and falling most of the way, got into my car, and drove away.

CHAPTER NINE

August 19

This cave is proving much more fruitful than the last. The work,
while slow, has gone rather well this month, with much progress
being made. We have continued to dig down and have reached a
depth of approximately six feet now. We have found some pot-
sherds near the surface, and some crude implements of stone lower
down. We have also found some indications of fire, and a skull
that I believe to be that of a cave bear, but no sign of human bones.
We have not yet reached bedrock, and so I remain optimistic that
we will find the evidence of early man I so devoutly hope for. I
hope so. Summer is wearing on, and my time here is limited to fair
weather.

I have some help with the digging at last, the excavation team
now being constituted as follows: Zoltán Nádasdi, second son of my
landlord who is interested, as I am, in science, Péter and Pál

*Fekete, sons of the redoubtable Fekete Néni, and of the same good
character, and S. B. Morison. Péter's wife, a lovely girl from the
village by the name of Piroska, brings us our midday meal so that
we may continue working.*

*While the others rest after the meal, I walk. I find it calms me,
although today I came to a place where it is said that lovers, fated
to be apart, leap to their deaths. If one can forget that, the vista is
spectacular. I wonder how desperate these lovers must be to cast
themselves off the cliff.*

September 17/18

Mihály Kovács's green Camry was found two twists and
turns away from where I'd parked my car, after I'd led police
to the spot where I'd found him. His head had been bashed
in. I suppose if I hadn't spent a half hour or so huddled in
the cave, it might have been possible to save him, but I
doubt it, given the good thirty minutes or so it took me to
drive back down to a village and make myself sufficiently
understood that police were called. After I found the spot
again, with some difficulty, the police had a good look
around, while one of them, who spoke a little English, sat
me down on a log and asked me a lot of questions. I couldn't
understand a word the others were saying, but I could tell
they'd reached the same conclusion I had. Kovács had tried
to edge along the rock face, just as I had, but in his case, he
hadn't quite managed it.

I was in a turmoil of conflicting emotions, and thoughts
that ranged all over the map as well. My first thought was
that I'd been very lucky. Those unnerving feelings I'd had
weren't just paranoia after all. Kovács had been following
me. I just wished I knew why. Given he'd been prepared to
track me all the way into the Bükks and up the side of a hill

on to a narrow rock face meant he must have been pretty serious about it. Had he come to do me in because he believed I really had found some anomaly in the records on the Venus and was going to get him sent to jail? That could only mean that there was something wrong, and so far I hadn't found it. Given the developments in my love life, I wasn't sure I wanted to.

The other thought I had, and one that there was no point in trying to discuss with anybody in my immediate vicinity, was that there seemed to be rather too many people taking headers off high places. Yes, the ledge was very narrow, and yes, it was slippery. He hadn't had the shoes for the expedition, that I knew. His city shoes were the second thing I'd seen, right after I'd stepped on his arm. He hadn't known where I was going. Even I hadn't known only a few hours before I left. I hadn't told anyone where I was going, either. He couldn't have come prepared.

I asked the young policeman what he thought had happened, and he seemed to think it was all pretty clear. The man had fallen, pure and simple. He did, however, have to ask me to go with him to the police station to discuss one or two things.

I spent several hours in Miskolc, a city that stretches on endlessly and not in a particularly attractive way. But maybe it was my mood. While I waited for them to check that my passport was valid, I was asked a number of questions about what I was doing in the Bükks. I told then I had Hungarian friends in Toronto who had raved about how beautiful they were, that I loved hiking and climbing, and that I'd just decided to go and have a look. They asked me if I'd come alone. I said yes. They asked if that wasn't a bit unusual for a woman. I just shrugged.

They asked me several times if I'd come with Kovács. I

said no. I told them I'd stayed at the Flora Hotel the night before, and that I'd been alone, something I thought the hotel would verify. I then waited while they checked. They did not ask me if I knew the victim, which was a jolly good thing, because I had no idea what I would say. If they found out later, I'd just have to pretend I hadn't understood them, which was not so far-fetched, because by and large I couldn't. All the while they were asking, they kept looking at the car rental papers, my passport, my driver's license, my birth certificate. This was clearly a country in which papers matter a very great deal.

Then I waited some more. I picked up the diaries and reread the sections on the Bükks.

September 14

Today is the most exceptional of days, so much so that my hand shakes as I write this. Our work, undertaken at considerable inconvenience has reached a happy conclusion. I will put it simply. We have found a skeleton in the second cave! It is, I am certain, very old, and a most distinguished individual, judging from the decoration of the cadaver. On the bones there are traces of a red substance, and it is much garlanded with necklaces and bracelets, made, I believe, of shells. What is particularly interesting is that we have some idea of how this person died. There is a smallish stone which has been worked into a point and surprisingly sharp, that, for all the body has been disturbed, it is still possible to hypothesize once rested between the ribs. It can only be that this person was stabbed and died of the wound.

With the skeleton we have found a carving, the like of which I have never seen, but very fine in character. It is of a woman, but unfortunately much damaged, except for the head and part of the torso. It is, I believe, of some sort of bone or perhaps ivory. I am

much taken with it, not just because it is beautiful, but because it is
an indication that this man and those of his time, capable of such
artistry, are worthy ancestors indeed. That this object could have
been carved with the crude tools we have found in the same stratum
as the skeleton is a wonder.

My companions are quite as excited as I. We will carry the
skeleton down to Lillafüred to study it more carefully.

"IS LILLAFÜRED FAR from here?" I asked my English-
speaking policeman.

"Not far, no," he said. "It is very beautiful."

"I'd like to see it," I said.

"You can go now," he said. "No climbing on rocks,
please, alone." I went. The restriction was just fine with me.

Lillafüred is indeed beautiful, situated as it is where two
rivers meet, in a long and narrow gorge with waterfalls cascading out of dense woods. It has a rather grandiosely large
and semi-elegant hotel in a turn-of-the-century hunting
lodge kind of way, the Palota, in which I had no trouble getting a room. Indeed, it looked as if the season in Lillafüred
was almost at an end. It had a kind of "last days at Marienbad"
feeling what with the spa downstairs and the dining room
empty except for a few desultory visitors like me, and except
for the decor, which was what Clive would call ye olde En-
glishe, a medieval theme with the waiters in silly costumes. I
suppose it might, under different circumstances, be rather
romantic there, but right now, romance was far from my
mind. I called the hotel in Budapest and asked for Morgan.

"Where are you?" she said.

"Lillafüred," I said.

"Lilla what?"

"It's a town in the Bükks where Piper stayed," I said.
"When he was digging in the caves."

"Have you found the cave yet?"

"I'm afraid not. I did find a body, though."

"What?"

"Some guy fell," I said. "I had to spend most of the day in a police station, and I am still a little shaken, so I decided not to drive back to Budapest tonight."

"I guess not," she said. "You poor thing."

"How did you all do on Piper's house?" I said, trying not to burst into tears at this expression of sympathy.

"This is really difficult. Grace keeps saying that we mustn't complain in her usual schoolmarmish way, and Diana keeps grumbling that this is just not possible, because there have been two wars since Piper lived here, and the city was rather badly bombed. Both points of view have some validity, I suppose. Cybil on the other hand is right into this. She's convinced she's lost five pounds already. I can't tell you how far we walked. My feet will never recover."

"Does the term *sensible shoes* mean anything to you?" I said.

"No, it doesn't," she replied. "Despite all of the above, we have three possibles. We figured out from our 1900 book that Leopold körút is now Szent István, St. Stephen, körút. Then Grace and I walked north and west from the Basilica—also called Szent István, by the way—while Cybil and Diana walked in from the Danube near the Parliament buildings. We think the house has to be a little bit north of the Parliament, actually. There's one place on a street called Honvéd utca, and another one on a street called Falk Miksa utca. The third is on a street that crosses both, Markó I think it's called."

"Did you say Falk Miksa?" I said.

"Yes," she said. "Neoclassical building just up from the Parliament. Do you know it?"

"I think so," I said. Of course I did.

"Are you all right?" she said.

"Yes," I said. "I wish I was in Budapest right now, though. The hotel is practically empty and it's starting to rain. But Piper was here, so I'll have a look around and come back in time for dinner tomorrow."

"That reminds me," she said. "I picked up your messages. You're invited to dinner with Laurie Barrett and Jim McLean. Do you know these people?"

"I met Laurie in the Gerbeaud," I said. "That's nice of her. Give me the number and I'll call her."

"There's another message, too," she said. "From Károly Molnár. Perhaps you know him too."

"See you tomorrow," I said.

"Hold it!" she said. "Since when was Károly in Budapest?"

"A couple of days, I think. Gotta go, though. This call may be expensive."

"No, you don't," she said. "I'll reimburse you. How would he know where we were?"

"Frank told him," I said. "And don't bother asking me who told Frank, because I don't know. I'd like to, though."

"So would I," she said. "I'd vote for Cybil."

"Talk to you later," I said. She sounded genuinely surprised about Károly and Frank, but right now I was too tired to think straight, and I wasn't convinced my antenna for deceit was working as well as it should.

I ate my dinner in the medieval-themed dining room which was in the basement, when it came right down to it, a round, tower-shaped room with stained glass windows that were supposed to represent territories stolen from Hungary over the years. The waiters' costumes had not improved any since I'd peeked in on my arrival. I sat there feeling as if the walls were moving in on me. I suppose spending time hiding out in caves will do that to you, especially if you find dead people when you venture forth. I was more shaken by what had happened than I would ever be prepared to admit out loud. It was bad enough that he was dead. What was worse was that I had no idea why he'd followed me. I'd made him very nervous, asking all those questions about the Venus's provenance. He knew where my hotel was. If he wanted to say something, why didn't he just talk to me there? If I'd really rattled some skeletons on the subject of the Venus, maybe he intended to kill me, and a nicely isolated spot in the country was the place to do it. Maybe it was a really lucky break for me that he'd fallen.

Besides me, there was a family of six obviously enjoying their meal, and another solitary diner nearby, a rather robust woman of about sixty with rosy cheeks and awfully sensible shoes. "Enjoying your stay?" she said, in German-accented English.

"I just got here," I said. "Late this afternoon."

"Here for the hiking, are you?" she said. "Or is it the caves?"

"I've seen enough caves," I said, in something of an understatement.

"Hiking, then," she barked. "Lots of fresh air. It's supposed to be a sunny day tomorrow. You should get out. You look a little pale."

I felt pale. Having said that, I did not feel much like hiking. I did, however, want someone to talk to, seeing as how I was going slightly barmy all by myself. "Perhaps you could tell me a relatively easy route to get me started," I said.

"All the hiking around here is easy compared to what I'm used to," she said. "Although for you—"

"I'm just a beginner," I said.

"I'll tell you my favorite, then, shall I? Nice vistas, that sort of thing. At your age you should still be up to it. Bring some color to your cheeks."

"Okay," I said. That I was participating at all in this conversation showed just how desperate I was for someone to talk to.

She then proceeded to give me directions, something about walking out the northeast side of the hotel property, along the highway, which wasn't much of one at this point, crossing the Hámor Lake dam, then up to some peak. "Lovely view over the valley of Also-Hámor," she said. "There's a legend about the place. There was a mill at the base of the cliff. The miller took a very young wife, who loved another, a young man from the area. In some versions, the young lovers threw themselves off so they could be together in heaven or some hogwash like that. In the other, the miller climbed up on the cliff because he suspected his wife of infidelity, and when he saw the young man creep into the house, threw himself off in despair. Apparently people have been doing the same thing rather frequently ever since. The cliff is named for the mill, the miller, actually. It's called Molnár-szikla. *Molnár* is the Hungarian word for miller," she added. "All very dramatic, of course. But it's a good walk. You should try it."

"Perhaps I will," I said. I wasn't in the mood for stories about people being thrown or choosing to heave themselves off a cliff. What was interesting, I suppose, was *molnár* being the Hungarian word for miller. Károly had called himself Charles Miller, hadn't he? He hadn't just made up a name. He just translated the one he had. I didn't know whether that made me feel better about him or not.

"I'm off to bed," the woman said. "Must get my beauty sleep. Perhaps I'll see you out on the trail tomorrow."

"I hope so," I said. *Not a chance,* I thought.

My beauty sleep consisted of listening to rain pelt against the window, wondering why I was there. When I did doze off, horrible things, for example Mihály Kovács with his head bashed in, were creeping up on me as I sat trapped at the back of a cave. To keep myself from drifting off to this unpleasant vision, I tried my version of relaxation: I shopped. In this case, I made my way down Falk Miksa, choosing treasures for the store. Usually I don't get further than a store or two when I do this, but this time, instead, I found myself shopping for Jennifer and Rob, a fine bottle or two of Hungarian wine for him, and a red leather jacket I'd seen in a store window near the hotel for her. I knew she'd look fabulous in it. Given the state of my personal life, this was not only depressing, it was downright stupid. It also made me homesick.

But, as predicted, the sun was shining the next morning, and I left the hotel in a more positive mood. I'd see Károly that evening. I'd phoned Laurie and asked her if I could bring a colleague from Toronto who'd arrived in Budapest unexpectedly.

"Not *the* Károly Molnár," she exclaimed. "That divine fellow from the Cottingham? I can't wait to meet him!"

I WAS ON the outskirts of Lillafüred when I saw the sign. Antik Bazár, it said. This is a sign that someone like me finds almost impossible to pass by. In this particular case I had two good reasons to go in. The Antik part, and a second sign that presumably gave the name of the proprietor, Nádasdi Gyula.

It was an unusual shop, it must be said. There were a

number of paintings that probably dated to the turn of the
century, some nice old furniture, but primarily there were
bugs, rocks, and stuffed animals. By stuffed, I am not referring to plush children's toys, but rather animals once alive,
and now staring at me from various vantage points through
glassy eyes. There was a huge collection, under glass, of bee-
tles of some sort, and butterflies pinned everywhere. Boar
heads protruded from the walls all around the room. Various
birds stared at me from glass cases.

There were also old binoculars, guns, and a shelf of old
shoes. There was a particularly attractive pair of hiking
boots, handmade of beautiful leather, and for a moment I
entertained the idea they had belonged to Piper. I don't
know why, except that they looked to date to the same
time period, and Piper was much on my mind. But they
were very small. They certainly wouldn't fit my average
feet, and most likely had belonged to a small woman. I
wished I knew someone to buy them for, they were that
appealing.

The proprietor, who by sign language managed to
convey that he was Nádasdi Gyula himself, was interesting
in a frightening kind of way. He was obviously rather odd,
maybe even completely insane. His hair stuck straight up
from his head, his eyes resembled those of the animals
around the room, and he spent most of the time I was there
just giggling and chattering away, particularly after I
had introduced myself as McClintoch Lara. McClintoch
was too much for him, but he liked Lara. I showed him
my business card, and I believed conveyed that I was also
in the antique business, but I'm not entirely sure. "Lara,"
he kept saying, holding up yet another stuffed creature for
me to see, and collapsing with laughter when he was able
to sneak up behind me and startle me with some fish or

something. Such is the tough lot of a dedicated antique hunter.

Despite the proprietor, I love places like this. You never know what will turn up, and I've often found really quite valuable pieces hidden amongst the junk. Nothing, however, prepared me for my discovery at that moment.

I declined the animals on offer, but purchased a pair of bronze art deco bookends I was reasonably sure would fetch a decent price at home, and was turning to go when I saw something rather unusual, even for this store. "What's that?" I said, pointing to a very worn leather case.

Nádasdi turned and picked up a stuffed woodchuck, or something, and brought it to me.

"No, *nem*," I said, trying out one of the three Hungarian words I had mastered, and pointing again. After several tries he brought me the case. In it was an extraordinary collection of stones. The stone shapes were not random; they had obviously been worked. I was way out of my depth here, but I was pretty sure these were really, really old stone tools. A couple of them could have been hand axes, for example, another, pointed, the end of a spear or something like that.

"Where did you get these?" I said. He looked at me blankly.

"*Barlang?*" I asked.

"*Igen,*" he said. "*Barlang.*" Yes, they had been found in a cave.

There was so much I wanted to ask him, and it was terribly frustrating not to be able to do so. We just looked at each other for a minute, and then he beckoned me behind the counter, and into a back room which was even weirder than the first, where he pointed at a glass case.

I was dumbfounded. "What is that?" I exclaimed.

"Sztalin," he said, laughing.

"Stalin?" I said. He just kept laughing.

"How much for Stalin?" I said. He didn't understand me. I got out my wallet, and pulled out a few *forint*. A few thousand, actually, *forint* being one of those currencies that requires hundreds if not thousands of them for relatively small purchases. He named a sum, which I couldn't understand, so he wrote it down. I couldn't afford Stalin.

"*Nem, nem,*" I said, pointing to my head.

"*Igen,*" he agreed, sadly. We bargained, me pointing to my head and saying *nem,* no, over and over, and eventually I parted with rather a lot of *forint,* plus some of my U.S. currency, and my new friend Gyula Nádasdi put the wooden box with its clear plastic top that slid in to protect the contents, in the trunk of my rental car. Whereupon, Stalin and I headed for Budapest.

I spent half of the drive trying to figure out how to get Stalin into my hotel room without anybody seeing him, and the other half wondering if I was truly out of my mind. I stopped at a little town just off the M3 before I got to Budapest, and spent my remaining few *forint* on a blanket, which I wrapped around my purchase. When I got to the hotel, I had a quick look around the lobby to make sure none of the Divas were about, and then, spurning several offers of assistance, I carried the box, which was rather heavy, up to the room myself.

I double-locked the door, and, setting Stalin on the bed, carefully unwrapped him. What Nádasdi rather humorously—a little communist in-joke, perhaps?—had named Stalin, was a skeleton, minus the head, a deficiency that had enabled me to get the price down to something I was prepared to pay. In place of the skull, some wag, probably Nádasdi himself, given his rather immature sense of humor, had placed a Soviet military cap. The skeleton also came adorned with a gun, an old pistol. I had bought it, hat, gun, and all, not because this was my idea of funny, but because the skeleton itself was obviously very, very old, crumbling away even under glass. He or she—I didn't know enough about bones to say—had been decorated in shells, bracelets, and necklaces, thousands of them. The rib cage had collapsed, but I could see a piece of stone there, one that had been worked to a point. Stalin, who minus the hat and gun matched the description of Piper's bones just about perfectly except that he was missing his skull, had been in the possession of a man by the name of Nádasdi, which just happened to be the name of Piper's landlord in both Budapest and Lillafüred, and indeed the name of one of Piper's excavation team members.

As I stood there staring at this thing, there was a tap at the door.

"Who is it?" I called out.

"Károly," the voice said.

"Just a minute," I said, looking desperately about the room. Stalin was way too big to put in a drawer or the cupboard. In an instant, I hefted the box, and stuffed it under the bed.

"Aren't you a bit early?" I said. "I haven't even showered yet."

"Perhaps I'll have one with you," he said.

"The Divas will see you," I said. "I thought we were going to meet at the restaurant."

"I don't care if the Divas see me," he said, wrapping his arms around me, and guiding me in the general direction of the bed. "Although I suppose it might be a problem if you are sharing a room with one of them. I'm going to assume from the double bed that you aren't, unless you tell me otherwise."

From there it all went about the way you would expect it to, except for the moment when he stubbed his toe on something protruding very slightly from under the bed. "Ouch," he exclaimed. "Do you have something hidden under the bed?"

"Just a body," I said.

"No problem, then," he said.

I suppose that was one for the record books, *la grande horizontale* over what might well prove to be a twenty-five-thousand-year-old man. It was not entirely lost on me that while I was more than a little besotted with Károly, I did not trust him sufficiently to tell him about the bodies, either of them, that I had encountered in the last day or two, including the fact that one of them was in the room with us. Károly knew Kovács; he'd purchased the Venus from him after all. And he would surely, given he'd edited Piper's diaries, understand why I'd spent a lot of money on Stalin.

We spent a very pleasant evening with Laurie and Jim. We went to the Múzeum Kávéház, a beautifully restored nineteenth-century coffee house and had a great meal, with terrific wines, piano music, and conversation. Károly was charming, as were Laurie and Jim. I felt almost happy sitting there, for the first time in many months.

It didn't even bother me when the conversation turned to the article in the Toronto paper that had hinted that the Venus might be a fake. Apparently Jim stayed in touch with home through the Internet.

"I am firmly convinced the Venus is authentic," Károly told them.

"Who wrote the article?" Jim asked. "Was it an expert of some kind? I don't think I remember the name."

"Dr. Thalia Lajeunesse," Károly said. "Nobody knows

who it is. Nobody, that is, except me, which is the way it is supposed to be."

"So who is it?" I said.

"Someone who knows nothing about paleolithic Venuses, I can assure you. Somebody with an ax to grind."

I guess I looked baffled. "You'll have to delve back into Greek mythology," he said. "Then you'll know."

"Very mysterious," Laurie said.

Károly looked a little bothered for a moment, but then suddenly he laughed, and put his arm around my shoulder for a quick hug. Laurie gave me a little knowing smile, and the conversation moved on to happier topics.

But later, back at the Hilton, I spent the dark hours of the night awash in anxiety as to whether or not the next morning might be the day the housekeeping staff at my hotel cleaned under the bed, and puzzling my way through a series of questions. Assuming Stalin was Piper's skeleton—and this was a very risky assumption, I knew—what was it doing in Lillafüred? It had been found there, yes, but I thought the diaries made it pretty clear that the bones were going to England for study, and certainly England was where Piper gave his presentation. Had it been sent back, then? And if so, why?

And more to the point, if the body was in Lillafüred, where was the skull?

CHAPTER TEN

October 1

I believe I must admit to myself that the analysis of this find is beyond my capabilities. All of us are amateurs really, and I feel keenly the need of some expert guidance. The Nádasdi family, as enthralled as I am by the discovery and its implications, has offered to ensure that the bones make it safely back to England in the care of one of their most trusted servants. I will send it to the Bramley Museum where the distinguished scholars there will assuredly be able to instruct me as to its age. I have completed drawings of the site from my sketches, as well as a detailed description of the excavation which I will send with the bones. Together I believe they will assist the experts who have promised to study our work carefully. I would take the precious cargo there myself, and indeed will follow it to England, perhaps later this year, but I have word from T that he will be in Budapest soon, and I am therefore hastening to my lodgings in the Lipótváros to await him.

September 18/19

Once I'd recovered from the excitement of finding the skeleton, it became clear to me that I had come to something of a dead end in Budapest. I went with the Divas to the apartment buildings they had identified as possible homes to Piper. They all answered to the description, but I wasn't sure where that got me. I checked the list of residents at the doors of each, and there was no Fekete, and no Nádasdi either.

So there I was in Budapest with a skeleton I had no idea what to do with. I didn't think I was going to be able to take Stalin home with me. I was pretty sure carrying bodies across international borders was a no-no, even if there wasn't a possibility that they were twenty-five thousand-years-old— to say nothing of the gun. One could only imagine what they'd say as the box passed through the x-ray machine at the airport. The best solution would be to show it to Károly, and let him deal with it. He had all the connections in the museum community here. Who knows? The National Museum might be thrilled to have Stalin.

But Mihály Kovács was dead, and Anna Belmont still haunted my dreams.

By late that next evening I was in London. I'd told the front desk I would be out of town for one night, but that I was keeping the room. Hoping to keep incursions under my bed from occurring, I stressed they wouldn't need to clean the room until I was back. I went out and bought lots of kraft paper and wrapped Stalin and his case up tightly, and shoved him back into his hiding place. I then left a message for the Divas and Károly to the effect that I was going to London to look at some merchandise Clive had asked me to check out while I was in Europe, but that I would be back the following evening.

I was at the entrance to the Bramley Museum as it opened the following day. It was a rather stuffy old place. Károly had said he wanted to update it, and I could certainly see why. It lacked the interpretive experience that the best museums now offered, and showed instead row after row of display cases, each item marked with a sorry little number that you had to search out if you were interested in knowing at all what you were looking at. In the foyer there was an oil portrait of Cyril Piper, along with a number of chief curators. Károly was not there. Perhaps Károly's soon-to-be-ex-father-in-law, as chair of the board, had seen to that.

I had phoned from Budapest to arrange an appointment to see the material they had there on Piper, and was ushered into a carrel toward the back of the reading room by a short, plump woman with spiky hair. "I'm Hilary," she said. "Hilary Edmonds. You'll remember my name if you think of Mount Everest. My father was something of a mountaineer, and named me after Sir Edmund Hillary. Rotten sense of humor if you ask me. I've put out some books and documents for you, and I'll just leave you here to work away. You'll find me out at the front if you need me. I'd start with those," she said, pointing to one pile. "There's lots more when you're done with that."

"Thanks," I said. I looked at the mountains of material with some dismay. All I had wanted to do was to see for myself the presentation Piper had made to his colleagues, to

look at the original drawings, and get a sense of the man.
This pile of paper looked more like a doctoral thesis than
some casual research to me.

She must have noticed the look on my face. "Is it the
Magyar Venus you're interested in?" she said.

"Yes," I said.

"There's a shortcut, you know, a new book. It's called—"

"*The Traveler and the Cave,*" I said, pulling out my by now
rather worn copy. "I've read it, more than once."

"Then you are serious," she said. "Good for you. I'll leave
you to it."

I suddenly felt very tired. The task seemed more than a
little daunting. But I was here, wasn't I? I started at the top
and began to wade through. Most of it was almost impossible to read unless you had a lot of time. There was a great
deal of correspondence, all of it handwritten, the sheets of
paper now in a protective wrap. I'd asked for copies of the
minutes of the meetings in the Piccadilly pub, and there
was a rather large pile of those. The group met almost, but
not every, month, and the presentations were by and large
about bones. There was one about the ravages of syphilis
that was particularly revolting, and others comparing the
skulls of negroid peoples with those of the British. I will
not get into the content; let me just say that today one
might assume one had happened upon the minutes of a Ku
Klux Klan meeting by mistake. It was a reflection of the
times, perhaps, but reading it made me squirm.

I found Piper's presentation on the skull from the
Bükks, and it was rather more interesting reading. Piper's
hypothesis was that this was the discovery of very early man.
He hazarded a guess as to the age, and it was considerably
more recent than the carbon dating on the Venus, only ten
thousand years. Piper, of course, hadn't had the benefit of

carbon dating. The first radiocarbon dates weren't published until 1949, the result of studies by an American chemist by the name of Willard Libby.

The final item in the minutes was a statement by one of the members, a man by the name of William Llewellyn, that Piper's find would be rather difficult to top. It made me think this was a competition of some sort between a group of scholars, each striving to outdo the other. Not that this was any different from academia today, but there was something about the tone of the minutes that kept niggling at me. I decided I'd have a chat with my new friend Hilary.

"This group of people that met every month at the pub off Piccadilly," I said. "Was it a real club? I mean did you have to pay to join? Was it a professional association of some sort? I'm having trouble figuring out what its purpose might have been."

"I've often wondered the same thing," she said. "Are you hungry?"

"Hungry?" I said. "I guess so. It's lunch time."

"I'm heading out for a sandwich. Would you care to join me? I'm going to the pub where Piper and his pals met. It's something I do from time to time. The food isn't bad. There's a roast turkey, ham, with mashed potatoes and mooshy peas."

"You mean the pub still exists?"

"Oh yes," she said. "You may find the answer to your question there."

I didn't know what mooshy peas were, but onsite research with Hilary didn't sound like a bad idea. The pub was called the Brook and Hare, and the sign on the outside looked very old and authentic, with the requisite picture of a hare jumping over a brook. Inside it was a fine place, dark and pubby. I passed on the green goo, which I took to be mooshy, or was it mushy peas that must have been whirred around in a blender, and had a really good roast turkey sandwich on grain bread, and a beer. Hilary had the full meal with lots of gravy, and a beer to keep me company, she said. We took our food to a back room where smoking was not allowed.

"This is the room where Piper and his colleagues met just about every month," she said. "It probably looked about the same then as it does today. At that time it would have been a private room. It even had a separate entrance. You can see the door. It's a fire exit now."

I looked around as we ate. The room was paneled in dark wood, and windowless. I could imagine the men sitting around smoking cigars, drinking ale, and listening to each other speak.

"What do you think?" she said.

"It's a great place," I said.

"Notice anything different about the motif?"

"Motif?"

"Skulls," she said.

"Where?" I asked, but then I saw it. Up where the wall met the ceiling a row of grinning skulls, painted with a deft hand, circled the room. You wouldn't really notice them. They were done in such a way that they looked like a repetitive pattern of some kind, somewhat art nouveau-ish with swirls and leafy things. You had to be paying attention to see what they were.

"There's a reference in the minutes to the publican decorating the room to their specifications," Hilary said. "You asked what kind of group it was. I think it was just an informal gathering, nothing official. They were mostly anthropologists, interested in bones, and I suppose they thought the skull decor was cute, or something. I've always thought that the pub's name was a bit of a joke," she added. "And that perhaps it was chosen as the meeting place for that reason. The pub predates Piper by about twenty years."

Brook and Hare? A joke? "I don't get it, I'm afraid," I said after a moment's pause.

"The Brook and Hare, Burke and Hare," she said.

"Burke and Hare," I said, slowly. "It rings a bell, but you're going to have to help me here. I'm from the colonies, you know."

She laughed. "In that case, it behooves me as a representative of an imperial power to enlighten you. William Burke and William Hare were a couple of rather notorious mid-nineteenth century grave robbers in Edinburgh, Scotland. They made their money digging up bodies and selling the cadavers to doctors and other scientists. This was a time when science was quite the rage, and apparently supplying skeletons for research was a lucrative venture. Grave robbing, however, was frowned upon, even then. When the Bobbies posted a guard on the cemetery Burke and Hare favored, the two of them began to create their own cadavers, to put it politely. They murdered people in other words, so they'd have something to sell. They were caught eventually and executed for their crimes."

"Perhaps the group that met here thought the pub name was cute, then, too," I said. "I found some of the content, and certainly the tone, of those meetings a bit offensive. These people were—"

"Racist pigs? I know what you mean. I think you have to be sympathetic to the times, you know, the standards of the day. I mean we shouldn't judge the past by current thinking. Having said that, I would agree with you. I can't help but feel that this was a group of men who were not only racists, but misogynists, too. There wasn't a single woman in the group, and there are letters in the file from at least one woman asking to be admitted to the group, and others from the members making pretty clear this was not something that would ever be allowed. Does the name Francis Galton mean anything to you?"

"Sure," I said. "He wrote the book about travel that Piper used as a reference point, *The Art of Travel,* I think it was. And he was the man who coined the term *eugenics,* wasn't he? The idea that races can be improved by only letting the fittest, in all senses of the word, people marry? Piper attended a lecture of Galton's, and was not terribly impressed."

"Did you know that Galton developed what he called a Beauty Map of the British Isles, rating cities by how attractive the women were. London won, of course."

"Ugh," I said.

"Exactly," she agreed. "I'll take your word for it that Piper didn't approve of this kind of thing, but the fact of the matter is that some of the members of the group that met here would not have disagreed with Galton's theories. A rum bunch when it comes right down to it."

"A rum bunch, but not, perhaps, atypical, as you put it," I said.

"Maybe," she said. "Most of these men were scientists, you understand. They had an academic interest in the subject at hand. Having said that, some pretty terrible things were done in the name of science. And I'm not talking about murderers like Burke and Hare."

"You're referring perhaps to the bad habit some explorers had of bringing—what's the word I'm looking for here, live specimens maybe?—back with them, bringing native people back home from their travels and showing them off to an amazed public?"

"Yes. I know that we can't be self-righteous about it. When you think of the experiments the Nazis carried out, we could hardly say that we are past all that. But at the end of the last century, at the time Piper was our chief curator, leading anthropologists in both the States and here regularly plundered graveyards in the name of research."

"I have been struck more than once in the course of my research," I said, not telling her what that research actually entailed. "That perhaps my definition of civilization, my previously firmly held conviction that things are almost inevitably getting better despite the odd setback, needs to be rethought. I have to tell you, though, that Piper makes it quite clear he does not agree with these kinds of theories. I have trouble reconciling this room and the group you have described with the author of the diaries."

"I hope you're right," she said. "Sometimes working on this stuff leaves a bad taste in my mouth. Maybe it's just boys will be boys."

"On that score, I thought there was a little bit of of one-upmanship in that group," I said. "As if each presentation had to top the last."

"Exactly. Let's face it, these guys collected skulls. Not for sport exactly, but each month one of them had to come in with a skull and it was, as you've said, rather competitive. Piper was a big success with his skull from Hungary. No one else had come in with one anywhere near as old. Unfortunately, they had no idea just how old it was. They almost certainly didn't. I don't want to imply, when I talk about Burke and Hare, that the men who met in this room killed people to get the skulls or anything, but I can't help feeling it was entertainment as well as science, you know? Rather grotesque, when you think about it."

"Very." There was something niggling away at the back of my own skull at that moment, but I was focused on what I saw as a more immediate problem. "Where did the skulls go, then?" I asked. "Does the Bramley still have the skeleton Piper found with the Venus?" *Please,* I pleaded silently, *let her say yes, so I can show Stalin to Károly and get the thing out from under my bed!*

"No, we don't. We've looked. It's gone."

"You often read about fantastic things being rediscovered in a drawer somewhere in storage in a museum," I said, mightily disappointed, but not prepared to give up. "It may still be possible to find it. Couldn't it be there, somewhere?"

"I don't think so. Most of the stories you hear about that sort of rediscovery occur when someone is looking for something else, and just happens upon the object, whatever it is. But we've done a thorough search for this one. Once the Venus was confirmed, we got right on it. The Cottingham Museum in Toronto asked us to have a look for the skeleton, of course, but we would have, regardless. This isn't new. We had an inquiry from someone even before the Cottingham made it official. This person was looking for both the skeleton and the Venus. The Venus wasn't here, and the skeleton isn't either."

"Someone asked about the Venus?"

"Yes," she said. "Amazing, isn't it? It could have been someone working for the Cottingham, I suppose. They went on to find it, though, didn't they? Serves this place right, if you ask me. The man who found it, perhaps you know, is a former chief curator of this museum, a chap by the name of Károly Molnár. I really liked him. He was trying to pull us kicking and screaming into the twenty-first century. People said he got the job because of his wife. She was the chair of the board's daughter, don't you know. But I thought he was great. And he's the one who figured it all out."

"I've met him," I said. "I interviewed him for this article I'm writing."

"Weren't you impressed?" she said.

"Very," I replied.

"I adored him," she said.

We sat in companionable silence finishing our beers, she probably thinking about Károly, I about Piper. As I looked at the little row of skulls at the ceiling, the thought that had been worrying its way to the forefront of my brain, surfaced.

"Calvaria Club," I said. It was almost a whisper.

"Sorry? I missed that. What did you say?" Hilary said.

"Calvaria Club," I said. "The skull club. I think they called themselves the Calvaria Club." My mind's eye was staring at a little piece of paper that had been stuck in Anna Belmont's desk. Calvaria Club. The implications of those two words hit me so hard I could barely breathe.

"Latin for skull, you mean?" Hilary said, not noticing my distress. "Interesting idea. I'll have a look and see if there's any such reference when I have the time. I have to get back to work," she said, looking at her watch. "Are you finished with your studies, or are you going to come back with me?"

"I'm coming back with you," I said. "This has been very helpful." She had no idea just how helpful she'd been. "Thanks for bringing me here."

"I enjoyed your company," she said. "You're a kindred spirit."

I went back to the Bramley and had another go at the

pile of papers. This time I knew what I was looking for.
This time I paid attention. It made a huge difference. I
went immediately to the minutes of the meeting of the
men who collected skulls, the Calvaria Club. For an unof-
ficial group they had a pretty formal way of doing business. The minutes listed everyone in attendance, meeting
start time, who was chairing, and so on. Piper was obviously a regular. His name appeared at almost every meeting over a number of years. And there it was, the
discrepancy I'd been looking for. I grabbed my copy of *The
Traveler and the Cave,* and, hands shaking, started flipping
through the pages. Within only a few minutes, I'd found
the proof.

I then went back to the correspondence, glancing at
each piece just long enough to ascertain it wasn't what
I was looking for, before flipping to the next. It took me
a couple of hours to find it all, although further proof
was not necessary. There was just something else I had to
know.

Having found it, I just sat in that cramped study carrel
feeling awful. As the implications of everything sank in, I
began to feel literally physically sick. I'd started on this little exercise because I wanted to find out what happened the
night Anna died. Somewhere along the line—it was not
too difficult to identify when—the goal became instead to
prove that the new man in my life was right, that the Venus
was authentic, the diaries were authentic, the man was
authentic. Sitting in that cave in the Bükks, I had believed
it all so completely. And now I found I was wrong. The discrepancy was so huge, I was surprised I was the only one
who'd noticed. Except that maybe I hadn't been. That
thought turned my heart to ice.

The truth of the matter was this: On at least three separate occasions in 1900, Piper was listed as being in attendance at the Brook and Hare, at the same time there was an entry in the diaries from either Budapest or Lillafüred. Piper was not only not the author of the diaries about the discovery of the Magyar Venus in Hungary, he hadn't even been there.

It was all a lie. It had been a lie back then. It was a lie now. I hadn't been able to reconcile the views of the author of the diaries with those of the presenter at the Calvaria Club because they were not one and the same. Piper had lied about everything, about traveling to Budapest, about writing the diaries, finding the cave, the skeleton, the Venus. All lies, pure and simple. He had taken the drawings, the detailed description of the project, and the skull, and claimed them as his own. And if Piper had lied, so had Károly Molnár. And if Károly had lied about this, he had lied about everything. In an instant my disappointment turned to rage. I was going to humiliate this man for deceiving me and everybody else. By the time I was finished with him, he would never hold down a decent job again.

I asked Hilary to direct me to a photocopier. I was going to make sure I kept a record of the damning evidence with me. That done, I asked her if I could use her computer to do an Internet search. It took about three minutes and only one search, to British Telecom, and I was ready to roll. I could see her looking at me wondering what was up. Perhaps I looked a little flushed.

Finally, I called the airline to change my flight, got a room at the hotel I'd stayed in the previous evening, and left a message for the Divas that I'd staying another night. I did not leave one for Károly.

I knew who had written the diaries. I still didn't know who had driven Anna Belmont to her death, although I knew why. And I didn't know who had killed Mihály Kovács. I did know that there was something lurking behind all this that was almost too horrible to contemplate.

CHAPTER ELEVEN

January 8

My hopes and dreams have been dashed. I am *told by those more skilled and knowledgeable than I, that what we have found is the skeleton of a man who died a mere 200 years ago. A gypsy, most likely, as these people wander through this region of the world. I am also told they are a bellicose people, much given to violence and other crimes, which would perhaps explain the blow this departed soul endured. I find this very difficult to accept, however well meaning and well schooled the individuals who espouse these opinions may be. I have seen these gypsies, do not consider them any more violent than the rest of society, but more to the point, I have never seen anything on their persons that would hark back to the beads buried with the man in the cave, nor, in my discussions with them—for I have tested this hypothesis with the gypsies themselves despite warnings not to do so—has there been any mention of a tradition of staining their dead with red dye.*

I had hoped that this discovery would enable me to join with others of like interests, and perhaps allow me to augment my allowance through some teaching opportunity or the like. Instead I find myself rejected by those whose approval I sought, and, worse still, almost penniless.

I believe I must also admit to myself that T will never join me. When I was busy and excited about my work, I did not notice as the months passed. My expectations were no doubt unreasonable, but still I am lost. I fear that the cold dark cloud will descend on me again. I am not certain I will survive it this time.

September 20/21

The next morning I was out at Gatwick and on to a flight to Edinburgh. I knew who had written the diaries. It was a simple process of elimination. They were, after all, written in English. The author of the diaries had described the excavation team as Zoltán Nádasdi, son of the landlord in Budapest and Lillafüred, Péter and Pál Fekete, sons of Fekete Néni. The diaries made it pretty clear none of these people spoke English, and even if they did, to write with such facility in a second, or maybe even third language was almost impossible to believe. That left, among the team members, S. B. Morison. S. B. Morison was not identified, no adjectives or descriptors were attached to the name. That was because there was no reason to do so. S. B. Morison was the author of the diaries.

Morison had written three letters to the Bramley Museum, one asking them to look at the skull, and theories as to its age, the other to tell them how it was to be delivered, and that drawings of the skeleton *in situ* were with the skull, so that Mr. Piper would see how it was found. There was no record of a reply. The diaries made it clear what that reply had been: the skeleton was a gypsy, dead for only two hundred years. A third, sad letter asked to be considered for employment at the Bramley, given the author's constrained circumstances. A job offer, I am sure, never came.

It was all relatively easy, once one was disabused of the notion that the author was Piper. The clues were there. Right at the start, for example, the author talked about coming down to London and on to Budapest. Piper was from London. He wouldn't have had to go to London first. There were several hints that I, and others, missed.

S. B. Morison's letters to Piper had given addresses in both Edinburgh and Budapest. I'd simply gone to the British Telecom online directory, keyed in the name and Edinburgh address and found there was an S. M. Morison living there. I called the number from my hotel in London, spoke to a very nice woman, told her I was doing research on Morisons with one *r*, that being an unusual spelling, and that I was particularly interested in an S. B. Morison who had traveled to Eastern Europe around 1900 to do some scientific research. Within five minutes, I had an appointment for tea the next afternoon.

From the airport, I took a taxi to a townhouse on Moray Place, a circle of lovely Georgian homes in a crescent surrounding a private park, in what is generally referred to as the New Town of Edinburgh, although there, new is a relative term. An elderly woman, well into her eighties, answered the door at my ring. Her hair, once red, had faded to a lovely soft beige. I rather thought she had just had it done, perhaps because of my visit. I handed her my card and was shown into a rather dark parlor. A man in a leg cast, his crutches propped up against a piano, was sitting in a chair by the window. "Sit doon, why don't ye," she said. "There's my young neighbor, Nigel," she said. "Nigel, this is . . . ooh I've forgotten your name already."

"Lara McClintoch," I said. "How do you do."

Young Nigel, who wasn't a day over fifty, got out of his chair with some difficulty and shook my hand.

"I got the scrapbook out last night," she said, pouring me some tea. "When you've had your tea and biscuits, I'll show you the pictures. There are letters, too. How did you hear about my aunt Selena?" she asked. "No one has asked about her before."

There it was, you see. Rereading the diaries the previous evening in light of what I now knew, I realized I should have known they were written by a woman. Károly had missed it, Frank had missed it, but I shouldn't have. It harkened back to that story Cybil had told the first time we got together only a few weeks ago, the one about the man and his son in an accident in which the man was killed, and the surgeon refusing to operate on his son. The surgeon, of course, was a woman. We just couldn't see that in 1900 an explorer and person of science could be a woman. But it was so obvious when, unfettered by that prejudice, you read them. T was her lover. It was as straightforward as that. I would hazard a guess that he was married. That's why she was never going to marry. She went to Budapest, not because it was the obvious place to find evidence of early man, but because she wanted to be with him. That there were limestone caves in the vicinity must have seemed a happy coincidence.

"I came across your Aunt Selena while I was doing some research in Budapest," I said, "It was on a different matter entirely." I was determined to come as close to the truth now as I could. There'd been enough lies told on this subject over the past hundred years. "I found her name on a list of people working on what I guess you'd call an archaeological dig in Hungary. I thought at first it was a man, you know, and of course the spelling was unusual and a Scottish name in Budapest at that, so I suppose I just became very curious about this woman and what she would be like. This is very good of you to talk to me about her."

"Oh, it's my pleasure, especially since you're interested in the Morisons. A 'dig' you say. I wouldn't have thought women would have been allowed on such things then."

"It was a bit unusual, I'm sure," I said. "A lot of people will be surprised to hear about her."

"There are Morisons in Canada you know, with one *r*, the same as us. No doubt one of the cousins emigrated. I'm the last of this particular branch of the family. My two older brothers died in the last war, as did my fiancé. One brother died at Dunkirk, the other in Holland somewhere. My Mick was shot down over France. They never found the body. For a long time I hoped he was taken prisoner, and I waited for him to come home for years after the war ended. It wasn't to be. I never met anyone after that I could love as much as him. That's them, my brothers and Mick, in their uniforms in that photograph on the mantelpiece. Go have a look."

"They were all very handsome," I said, taking the photo down for a close look.

"Ay," she said. "They were that. But you didn't come to talk about my troubles. You came to hear about my aunt. Selena Boswell Morison, that's her name. I'm Selena Mary. The Mary is for my mother. I never met her, you know, my aunt. She was long gone when I was born. My father talked about her a great deal, though, so I have a sense of her. She was his only sister, there was just the two of them, and with both parents dying when he and Selena were young, they were very close. He never understood why she left like that. Myself, I've often wondered if it was because of a man. We'll never know, I suppose.

"I think you're right about the man," I said. "His name started with a T. He may have been Hungarian, Tamás, perhaps."

"You have done your research, haven't you, hen? What did I tell you, Nigel? Nigel is here because when I told him yesterday I'd invited you to tea, he thought you might be planning to rob me, that it was a scam of some sort. I told him I didn't think he'd be much help when it came down to it, what with his broken leg, and anyways you sounded right nice on the telephone, but he insisted on being here."

Nigel laughed. "In truth, it was the shortbread I wanted. She always brings it out for company."

"It's delicious," I said. "May I have another?"

"Of course you can, hen," she said. "But to get back to my aunt. She must have been very brave to go off to the continent all by herself like that, and in 1900! I've read since about Victorian lady travelers, Mary Kingsley and the like, but still, I think my aunt must have been a very special person. I wish I'd known her. The sad thing is, she never came back. A terrible accident. Would you like to see the scrapbook? I got it out for you. It has the letter from someone in Hungary telling my father, her brother, that she'd died. In Hungarian, it was. He had quite a time finding someone in Edinburgh to translate it for him, and when he did, it was very bad news. There's a picture of her, there on the wall, a portrait. My father told me about her often. He told me she was very pretty and very smart but that she'd some funny ideas in her head, about science and also about marriage, which she insisted was not for her. Why she went to Europe my father never understood. She met some Hungarian boys who put crazy ideas in her head, according to my father, so maybe what you're telling me about this man, Tamás, is a fact. Here it is, the letter. It's dated as you can see. April 30, 1901. She was only twenty-four, poor thing."

I got up and walked over to the portrait as she spoke. Selena Morison had been more than very pretty. She was beautiful, with red hair and green eyes and pale, pale skin. It seemed to me that there was both a strength and yet a fragility to her. She had a strong mouth, a determined gaze, but there was something a bit tremulous, vulnerable, perhaps, about the eyes. I turned back to read the letter Selena held out to me.

Dear Sir:
I am writing to you with very bad news as to the health of your sister. There was a terrible accident. She was walking in the hills and lost her footing. It was a treacherous spot on Molnár Peak, and she fell a great distance. Despite all efforts by doctors, she was taken by the angels yesterday. She was a very fine lady, and not one to be taken lightly. I am sorry to be the bearer of such bad news. She was very brave at the end. My employer has seen to a Christian burial, so you can set your mind at rest on that score.

Perhaps when you are feeling more consoled, you will tell me what you would wish me to do with her belongings. There is not much, a few items of clothing and some unusual stones, some bones she found, and a carving, rather strange. If you would like me to send these items to you in Scotland, I would be most grateful if you could send me the postage as I am not a person of means. I have returned your letter, unopened. It is from this I have your address. She spoke of you often.

Your servant, Fekete Marika.

"He wrote back, of course," Selena said. "Here is his letter in English, and I suppose the same person who translated the first letter wrote back for him in Hungarian. That's why we have the English letter, not signed, you see. June 15, 1901, it was."

Madame—I thank you for your kindness in writing to me regarding my sister Selena's death. She was, as you say, a very fine lady. As to your question about her belongings, may I suggest that you keep for yourself what you would like, and distribute the rest to the poor of your city. It is, I'm sure, what my sister would wish. I have enclosed a bank draft payable to you which I hope will cover any outstanding expenses my sister might have incurred, and to cover the cost of the burial. With gratitude for your kindness once again, I remain, faithfully yours, etc.

"I don't know where this Molnár Peak is, do you?" Selena said.

"It's in the Bükk Mountains in Northern Hungary, near a little town called Lillafüred," I said, thinking what a perverse little cosmic joke that name was.

"What would she be doing there, do you suppose?"

"Your aunt Selena was a woman way ahead of her time, an amazing person. She was interested in science, particularly in finding evidence of ancient man. She explored the limestone caves in the Bükk Mountains, and she did, in fact, find a skeleton that dates back twenty-five thousand years."

"Nooo!" Selena Mary said.

"Yes. She also found an ivory carving just as old."

"Nooo!" she said again.

"You mean hunner, don't ye?" Nigel said.

"Thousand," I said. "Twenty-five thousand years old."

"That would be Neanderthals?"

"Not Neanderthals, *Homo sapiens*, ancestors of ours who lived in caves."

"I think this calls for a wee goldie, hen," Nigel said. "You're looking piqued." He hoisted himself up and hopped over to side table, returning with a bottle of Scotch and three glasses. He poured one and handed it to Selena, then at my nod, poured one for me, and for himself.

"How do you know these things?" Nigel said, suspiciously.

"I have her diaries," I said. "And I am going to give you a copy, Ms. Morison."

"Call me Selena, hen," she said. I'd decided by now that *hen* meant something like dear. "I'll have another, Nigel," she added, holding out her glass. It made me think of Lily Larrington, what seemed so long ago, passing out birdbath-sized glasses of sherry. I reached out for a wee bit more myself, seeing as I was no longer concerned about my drinking habits.

"I am going to leave you with this book," I said, taking *The Traveler and the Cave* out of my bag. "I have to warn you, though, that someone else took credit for finding the skeleton, a fellow by the name of Cyril Piper." Both of them looked at me as if I was a creature from outer space.

"She's away with the fairies, isn't she?" Selena said, turning to Nigel.

"Sorry," I said. "I know that this sounds implausible."

"It does," Nigel agreed. "Why should Selena here believe you?"

"I don't suppose you'd have something in her handwriting, would you?" I asked.

"I think I would," Selena said. "Here, further on in the

book. A letter to my father on his birthday. He was younger than she was."

Dear Robert, the letter said. *"I hope this letter reaches you in time for your nineteenth birthday, so that you know you are much in my thoughts on the day. You will have to think of marriage soon enough. Choose a girl with a pleasant disposition above all, and virtuous too. If she is comely and has a dowry of some value that would also be well. As always you are in my heart.*
Your loving sister, Selena
    P.S. Thank our uncle for me for sending the draft for my little inheritance so promptly. I will put it to good use. S

"He loved her very much, didn't he?" Selena said. "And she, her brother. You can tell from the words, can't you, the love that comes off the pen?"

"Yes, you can," I said. "Have a look at this letter. I had it copied at a museum in London. Does the writing look similar to yours to you?" I had, with some difficulty persuaded Hilary to let me copy just one. I chose the letter Selena sent asking for a job, perhaps because it rankled the most and I wanted to stay mad.

Both Selena and Nigel peered at the two letters. "I would say yes," Selena said at last. "And you, Nigel? You see better than I do."

"Looks like," Nigel said.

"Look, I know this is very presumptuous of me," I said. "But I would very much like to have a copy of your letter. I must have one. If you will permit me, and can direct me to a copy shop, I promise to bring it back in a few minutes. You see, the original diaries are now in Toronto. They are handwritten. I could arrange to have the handwriting on both compared. I am certain they will match, and I hope it will prove to you that what I say is true."

"You say my aunt found something important?" Selena said.

"Very important," I said.

"Nigel?" she said. "Your advice, please."

"Take my key, hen," Nigel said, handing a key chain to Selena. "You know where my fax machine is. It'll make you a copy, too."

Selena was a little breathless by the time we'd negotiated our way to the second floor of Nigel's place, but she was a determined little woman. She couldn't operate the fax, and neither could I, but between us we figured it out. In a few minutes I had the writing sample I needed, and we went back for another wee goldie.

"I know this next question is the worst yet," I said. "I'm going to ask it anyway. Was there an indication, anything you remember, about mental illness in your family?"

Nigel looked rather bothered.

"I'm asking because the diaries make reference—well, I'll read it to you. There are two: *madness does not always pass from generation to generation,* is the first. The second is *I must believe that madness is not an inevitable result of procreation of those who are stricken by it.* Perhaps I should say there are three references. The last written words say something to the effect that she fears the cold, dark cloud descending, and she may not survive it this time. I really don't think she wasn't referring to the weather, but rather to acute depression. Could I be right about this?"

"You don't have to answer that, hen," Nigel said.

"I don't mind," she said. "My father told me that his mother, my grandmother, suffered greatly from depression, and his sister did as well. He told me once that he feared his sister might not be in heaven because she had taken her own life, that it wasn't a fall, you understand. There was no way to bring the body back. The family she had been staying with had seen to it that she was buried properly, a Christian burial. But there was that reference that you've seen, about not worrying on that score. I think my father always wondered if they knew she had jumped, and not fallen. You go to the Bad Fire for that.

"He said many times when I was young that he was going to look for her grave, but he never did. He would have to have gone right away, wouldn't he? A few years after that, and there was a war, and then another. He lost two sons in the Second, and never really recovered. Perhaps he suffered from the curse of depression, too. I used to worry about that. Happily it seems to have passed me by. If I were going to lose my mind I would have when Mick and my brothers died."

"You're the sanest person I know," Nigel said. "Although perhaps a wee bit plootered by now."

"You're a bad boy, Nigel, for making mention of it. Nigel's from Glasgow," she said. "He has these quaint expressions."

Plootered? I suppose that meant plastered. I was having almost as much trouble following this conversation as I did Hungarian.

"I would like to go, to see if I could find her," Selena said. "Her grave, I mean. I am, after all, named for her. I suppose it will never happen, just like my father never got there. For years I couldn't, what with the Communists and everything. Now I'm just too old."

I spent at least an hour or so more with Selena and her young friend, Nigel. I told her about the Magyar Venus, about how I was trying to trace its provenance, and in so doing had happened upon her aunt. And I promised her I would make it right.

I left Edinburgh that afternoon with a box of Selena's shortbread cookies in my bag, and headed back to London, and on to Budapest. I should have been pretty happy. While I had uncovered the perfidy of C. J. Piper, a fact that could not help but be embarrassing to Károly, I was also very close to establishing the provenance of the Venus. What, after all, did it matter that Piper hadn't written the diaries, as long as I could prove that someone had, that the Venus had really been found in the Bükks?

It mattered, because Mihály Kovács had sold the Venus to Károly Molnár, and Mihály Kovács was dead.

The next afternoon I was on Falk Miksa with Laurie Barrett who had agreed, at my request, to come with me and translate. It was late in the day when we got to the address on Selena B's letters. The Divas had done well. It was one of the three they'd found. Laurie and I had met at a coffee house on Szent István körút, and as we walked past the flower stalls and turned toward Honvéd utca, I knew I'd found the right place. Honvéd út becomes Pannónia utca on the other side of the körút, and Pannónia was where, according to Károly, his mother had told him there had been a Russian tank during those terrible days in November 1956, when the Communists rolled back into Budapest.

I had terribly mixed feelings as we approached the building. I kept thinking how Laurie had told me the day I first met her at the Gerbeaud, that people in Budapest don't move houses the way we North Americans do, and I was hoping against hope that in this case, that would be true. Even if it wasn't, as long as someone here remembered the Nádasdi family, or for that matter, the Feketes, and knew what had happened to them, I might just have closed the loop on the Magyar Venus's provenance, or at the very least come close to doing so. If I could somehow prove that a descendent of the original Nádasdis had sold the Venus to Mihály Kovács, who had in turn sold it to Károly, then it would be not entirely, but almost, impossible to dispute the Venus's authenticity. Yes, Selena B. Morison could have made it all up, but somehow, I didn't think so. I was still feeling betrayed in some way by Károly, but I knew it was possible that his failing was one of poor scholarship, faulty research, rather than deliberate misrepresentation, or worse than that, a crime.

"Thanks for this," I said to Laurie as we rang the bell.

"My pleasure," she said. "I think it's fascinating to think it might be possible to trace the provenance of the Venus through a hundred years. There's no Nádasdi here, as you can see, nor Fekete. But I've buzzed the superintendent."

She spoke to the woman who came to the door for some time before finally turning to me. "I think we may be on to something here," Laurie said. "This woman is asking me why you want to know. I'm not entirely sure what I would say, so I told her I was only the translator and I would have to ask you. What do you want me to say?"

"I think you should tell her that I am doing research on a woman, a Scot, by the name of Selena B. Morison who was a tenant in this building at the turn of the last century, and who knew the Nádasdi family and their employees, Sándor and Marika Fekete. You can say that Selena stayed with the family both here and at their country estate, and that I was hoping I could speak to a descendant of the family. It's true, after all, even if certain details are missing."

"Okay," she said, and began speaking rapidly in Hungarian.

The woman said something, closed the door in our faces, and her footsteps faded away.

"I guess that was a no," I said.

"No, it wasn't," Laurie said. "She said she'd be back in a minute."

It was considerably more than a minute, but the door did open again, and we were beckoned in. We creaked and groaned our way up to the top floor in a tiny elevator where we were ushered through a door. We found ourselves standing in a rather austere hallway, a tiny kitchen visible to one side. Ahead of us was what I suppose we'd call a bed sitter, or a studio apartment. We just stood there for a moment wondering what to do, until a man of about sixty or so, poked his head around the corner and signaled us to come in.

The place was very small, but it had a little balcony where the last flowers of summer still bloomed. The room was in sore need of paint. You could see the spots where art had once been displayed on the walls, just a stain on the wallpaper, and an empty hook, witness to that now. There were books everywhere, and on the floor a threadbare, but once elegant carpet. I thought that this room, or one just like it, had been home for awhile to the author of the diaries.

Laurie did the talking. "This gentleman is János Varga and that," she said nodding in the direction of the bed where an elderly woman lay propped up against the pillows, is his mother Ágnes, also Varga. If I have this right, she is a Nádasdi."

"Ask her what her father's name was?" I said.

Laurie asked the question. "Zoltán," the woman said. Of course, I thought, one of the diggers at the site, son of the family that owned this building in Budapest, and the country estate.

"Ask her if she's always lived in this apartment," I said. Laurie did.

The man grunted, and then spoke rather angrily.

"He says if you are asking if this is the family home, then, yes it is," Laurie translated. "If you are asking if they have always lived here, then he says you don't know your Hungarian history."

"Tell him I'd like to learn," I said.

"He says that while the building is rightfully theirs, it was stolen from them. His mother has been given the opportunity—lovely phrase that!—to reacquire it. He says they can't afford to do that, but that he was able to move her back into the building in one of the tiny apartments. It is tiny, isn't it?"

"Her family would have lived on the first floor, the *piano nobile*," I said. "Apparently it was a really beautiful home."

Laurie told them what I'd said. "There was a particularly lovely painting, a landscape with mountains, the area where the family's country estate was located," I said.

Laurie translated. The man said nothing, but the old woman suddenly struggled to sit up.

"She wants to know how you know that," Laurie said. Through Laurie, I told her about the reference in the diaries. Then I took out a picture of the Magyar Venus and showed it to the old woman. She pulled it up close to her face and her son brought the lamp over so she could see it. She looked at it a very long time. "Yes," she said at last. "Yes, this was ours."

"Ask her if she sold it to an antique dealer on Falk Miksa by the name of Mihály Kovács," I said, holding my breath while I waited for the answer.

"She says she didn't have it to sell to anyone," Laurie said, finally. "She said it was taken with the rest."

"Ask her what happened—to the building and the art, everything. How she lost them, why she is now in this little apartment," I said.

And then, through Laurie Barrett's mouth, Ágnes Varga began to tell her story. "I have come back here for János," Ágnes Varga said. "My other boy, the younger, is in Baltimore where his father took him more than fifty years ago. He comes now to see me, once a year, and he's going to help me reclaim this place. I came back here for János. I want him to have it, to make a life for himself here in Budapest. This apartment was in ruins. Animals must have lived here, not people. But my son has worked hard. He remembers how it was when he was a little boy and he is trying to make even this little apartment like that. For me, I suppose. We do this for each other.

"We had some happy times here, when I was still with the boys' father. But then he left me, took up with another woman across the river in Buda. In 1950, he took our eldest son and his new wife and escaped across the border. These were terrible times, then, neighbor spying on neighbor, encouraged to report even the smallest of transgressions to the Communist authorities. I was suspect already because my husband had escaped with his new wife and our son to America. I don't blame him for that. Before the Russians came, my husband had been a very successful business person. Our home here was beautiful. But to be successful was, in those days, a curse. His business was taken over by the party, and instead of the fifteen workers András—that was his name, my husband, András—had employed, there were six times that, all lazy louts who felt entitled to a paycheck without having to work for it, accomplishing less, much less, than the original fifteen. And of course, my husband no longer owned the business. It belonged to the state.

"He was taken to that terrible place, you know, the secret police building at Andrássy út 60. It was a lovely place once, but not now. The National Socialist party, the people of the arrow cross, used it as a headquarters, and when the Russians came to replace them after the war, they just moved right in. There were basements and subbasements of terrible cells, and some say they had a giant meat grinder to get rid of their victims. I don't know if that is true, but a lot of people went in there and never came out. To this day, I have never walked on the sidewalk in front of Andrássy út 60. Always I crossed the street, so as not to walk too close. We all did. But they took András there, just because he had once been successful. He was one of the lucky ones. He got out, and when he did, he began to plan his escape. He said he would send someone back for us, for János and me, but it never happened. Perhaps that person was captured, perhaps he just never came. Or perhaps he never existed." The woman stopped for a moment and reached for her son's hand.

Laurie took a deep breath. "This is awful, isn't it?" she said to me. "I can hardly bear to translate it."

"Even though we were divorced, it didn't matter," the woman went on. "I was suspect, just because he had gone, and because we had a beautiful home. And they were right for suspecting me of incorrect thinking. Every day János would come home from school and he would tell me what he had learned. It wasn't true what they were teaching him. I tried to make sure he understood what the real truth was, not that version made up by the party cadre. I tried to undo, every day, the damage they had done. But I had to tell him to keep what I had told him in his heart and never to speak the words at school.

"I had a job, not a good one, but still a job, and I knew how to work the black market to see that my son was fed.

He wanted to be a dancer, was accepted into the ballet school where they trained the best dancers. It was across from the Opera House. The children took classes in the Opera House itself. János was a member of the Communist young people's organization. We tried to fit in while not forgetting who we really were. Our family was landed gentry, you know. We had owned land, and servants, and we treated them well.

"Maybe it was something János said. He was just a boy, and when his father sent him a photograph of his car in America, he wanted so badly to show it to his friends. Maybe that was it. Or perhaps it was simply that my former husband had escaped. Despite all the care I took, something happened. It was 1951. They came in the night, you know, always in the night in those dangerous hours just before dawn when sleep is its deepest and the pounding on the door brings only confusion and not resistance or flight. Although where to flee and for what purpose to resist? We were given two hours to get ready and allowed only 250 kilos to take with us. What to choose? What to leave behind?

"And then there was the journey to the countryside, to hardship and pain, death for many, loaded into trucks with others whose eyes were as confused or pained as yours. But that is not what you came to hear about, not what you want to know. You want to know about what was left behind? The art, the furniture, the once precious objects that suddenly, in those terrible circumstances, no longer held any value for those who were taken. They were given to people deemed more worthy by those who came in the night.

"So what happened to the lady you showed me? Someone deemed more worthy got her. I hope she was a curse," the woman hissed.

"Ask her if she has any idea who was deemed more worthy," I said. I waited a moment for the translation.

"She says she cannot say about the lady, but she did find out who moved into the apartment. It was a man and a woman and her family," Laurie said. "You'll understand that I'm not translating word for word. She called them rather more unpleasant things than a man and a woman, because she thinks there is a possibility that they betrayed them just to get the apartment. The couple's name was Molnár, Imre and Magdolna Molnár."

CHAPTER TWELVE

September 22

THE DANUBE WAS A DOVE-GRAY RIBBON BELOW ME, AS I sat, hands wrapped around a cup of coffee against the early morning chill. Behind me, Szent Mátyás Church towered over the Fisherman's Bastion where once again I sat to greet the dawn. The mist on the river, the stillness of early morning, would be like a painting etched on my memory forever.

They'd be here in a few minutes, all of them, the Divas, Károly, and Frank. The scene was set, the chairs in a little circle around the table on which Stalin, in his box, lay. I felt the cold of the stone floor beneath my feet edge its way up my body, heading, I was convinced, for my heart.

I heard the footsteps behind me. They were all on time. "Beautiful!" Cybil said. "How did you find this fabulous spot?"

"Frank brought me here," I said.

"What's that?" Frank said, pointing toward the box, and they all went over to look.

"Ew," Cybil said. "Is it real? Tell me it isn't."

Károly slid the cover off the better to see it and stared at it for several seconds before turning toward me. "It can't be, can it?" he said.

I shrugged. "It's possible," I said. "I found it in the right place."

"Does it have a name?" Morgan said, laughing.

"Stalin," I said.

"Oh, come now," Grace said. "Why have you brought us here? Surely not to see that grotesque thing. Tell us the truth!"

"Truth?" I said. "Now that's an interesting word for you to use, Grace. Or should I call you Dr. Thalia Lajeunesse?" Károly looked amused.

"What are you talking about?" Grace huffed.

"The author of that article that implies the Venus is a fake?" Morgan said. "Is that who you're talking about? You mean Grace wrote it?"

"Thalia," I said. "One of the three Graces, along with Aglaia and Euphrosyne, companions of the goddess of love. Lajeunesse, French word for youth. Grace Young, disappointed lover of Károly Molnár."

"Tsk, tsk," Morgan said. "Caught in a lie, are we, Grace?"

"You are in a rather vulnerable position on that score yourself, Morgan," I said, as Grace burst into tears. "You see, I believed your story, at least part of it, about how Károly was blackmailing you because you had had an affair with him. You knew I'd overheard a conversation that night at the Cottingham, didn't you? I assumed the woman Károly had broken up with that night was you. But in fact he never confirmed my assumption, when I thought back to the conversation. He was actually very discreet. It was Grace he had just given the old heave-ho to, wasn't it?"

"Twice," Grace blubbered. "He dumped me twice."

Morgan stared at me for a minute. "Okay," she said. "I propositioned him that night. I wanted to get back at my husband for screwing Courtney. A little tit for tat as it were. He turned me down, even when I wrote a generous check to the museum. It was unbearably humiliating for me, so I made up the story. Surely, though, you did not bring us up here to freeze our butts off while you individually chastise us for lies that are essentially face-saving and harmless."

"No, I brought you up here to tell you the story of two exceptional women over a century apart. One of them was named Selena B. Morison. She was a Scotswoman from Edinburgh who decided for some reason, very possibly because of a man she had fallen in love with, to travel to what was then the Austro-Hungarian empire, to Budapest, to wait for someone, again most likely this man, and to carry out some scientific research. She was self-taught in this area, but obviously exceptionally talented.

"While she waited for what I believe to be her lover—she referred to him only as T—she occupied her time in scientific pursuits. She traveled to the Bükk Mountains, explored caves, and in at least one, conducted what we would call an archaeological dig. She was talented, but also perhaps extraordinarily lucky, because she came upon a grave site containing a body adorned with thousands of shells, along with a beautiful mammoth-ivory carving."

I glanced in Károly's direction. Conflicting emotions—surprise, puzzlement, confusion—passed in succession across his face. "She was, by her own admittance, an amateur, so, conceding she could not do the research necessary, she packed up her account of the work, along with her exceptional drawings of the site, and the skull, and sent them to the Bramley Museum in London for further study. The chief curator of the Bramley at that time was a man by the name of Cyril James Piper."

"You're kidding," Frank said. Károly just stood there, hanging on my every word.

"I told you there was something the matter with those diaries," Diana said. "But are you saying the Venus is a fake?"

"Oh, get off that, Diana," Morgan said. "Just shut up."

"Piper took the materials Selena had sent to him, and gave a presentation to a group of anthropologists at a pub near Piccadilly in which he seemed to imply that it was he who had found the skull. The conclusion one is forced to make, on careful reading of the minutes of that meeting, is that he presented the drawings and the detailed explanation of the dig, as his own. Whether or not his fellow members of the Calvaria Club—I'll ask you to remember that name— were complicit in this deception, I do not know. They must have known their colleague had not spent a lot of time in Hungary in the recent past. But this was an old boys' club of the worst sort. Do you know what they used as a gavel at those little get-togethers? A real skull, from a real person. If they knew, they never said."

"That's the story of women everywhere," Grace said, bitterly.

"Not only did Cyril Piper not acknowledge Selena Morison's primary role in the discovery of both the grave and what we've come to know as the Magyar Venus," I continued, "he actively tried to discredit her. I found among his papers in the Bramley archives a letter he sent to colleagues who were considering hiring her, referring to her as difficult to deal with, unstable, and perhaps quite mad. In order to make sure she didn't come to work there, to find out about his deception and expose him to ridicule, he maligned her to his peers. You perhaps missed this letter, Károly, in your research there. You also perhaps overlooked the fact that Piper is listed in meeting minutes several times when you had placed him in Hungary."

Károly didn't say a word. I suppose he was quietly watching his career go down the drain.

"In any event, we don't know if T, the person she was waiting for, ever arrived, although it is highly improbable, and she seems to have reached that conclusion herself, nor do we know whether or not she found out about Piper's treachery. We do know that on April 29, 1901, she died, as a result of either falling, or jumping, off a cliff near Lillafüred." I didn't bother mentioning that the name of the cliff was Molnár.

"Well, Károly!" Diana said. "A little casual in our research, were we? Perhaps Thalia Lajeunesse will tell all."

"You're a little casual with the truth yourself, Diana," I said. "As I have recently discovered, if you look at something closely, without any hidden beliefs or prejudices, the truth usually comes shining through. In that regard, I have had another look at those files of yours, and I believe you were embezzling funds from the Cottingham, using Károly's expense claims to do it, were you not?" Diana paled, visibly. "Isn't that right, Károly?" I said, turning to him. He nodded. "You were trying to get back into the Cottingham that night to remove the evidence, Diana. I really wish you hadn't used my car to do it. What did you do? Shove me into the backseat and then go back and take a run at the window because your key didn't work in the

door, anymore? You must have been drunker than I was. As
for that claptrap about Károly being responsible for your
not getting tenure, I for one, would be interested some time
in what the truth there might be. I suspect you just didn't
cut it."

"But she got her PhD and everything," Cybil said.
"Didn't you, Diana?"

Diana shook her head. "No," she said.

"Forget tenure!" Frank said. "I want to know what you're
saying here. That Károly was wrong? Surely all this means
is that the diaries were misattributed, but the Venus is the
genuine article."

"The Venus may very well be genuine. As a matter of
fact, I'm almost certain it is. But you miss the point."

"I think I'm missing the point, too," Cybil said. "This all
sounds so unbelievable."

"It's completely unbelievable," Frank said. "Lara must be
mad."

"So now it's Lara that's being dissed, is it?" Morgan said.
"I'd be careful where you go with this, Frank. I smell a law-
suit in the air. What a sad, sad woman that Selena Morison
must have been. I mean, forget the Venus!"

"Very sad," I said. "Fast forward a hundred years or so, to
another sad woman. Because of a terrible and tragic accident, this woman became trapped in her own home. Her
illness was very specific. She couldn't go out, fearful as she
was that something terrible would happen if she did. She
lost her children to her ex-husband, her job, her life." They
all stood there, rooted to the ground, and silent at last.
Károly, unlike the others, wasn't looking at me. Instead he
was staring outward toward the river, the bridges, Margit
Island, to take comfort from it, perhaps.

"But she didn't give up entirely. She decided that she

would spend her time finishing her master's thesis, something she could do from home, thanks to the wonder that is the Internet. This thesis, as it turns out, was on Victorian travelers, and through that she happened on the name of Cyril James Piper and his discovery of ancient *Homo sapiens* in the Bükk Mountains of what is now Hungary. She regularly corresponded with a woman by the name of Hilary Edmonds, a librarian at the Bramley. I know that because I met Hilary while I was there, and because I phoned her last night to ask her one very simple question, a question that came to me as I thought about Selena's Morison's betrayal. Did the name Anna Belmont mean anything to her? As it turned out, it did. Hilary had regularly assisted Anna, who had told her she was a shut-in, with copies of documents in the Bramley archives. From her tiny bedroom office in Toronto, Anna was able to write her thesis on the group of anthropologists that called themselves the Calvaria Club. You will recall, Frank and Cybil, that we found that name on a slip of paper caught in her desk.

"Károly was wrong, yes, for more than one reason. He incorrectly named the discoverer of the Magyar Venus, and of the diaries. What really bothers me, though, is that he, you too, Frank, failed to credit Anna. She gave you her thesis, didn't she? That's why you visited her. She wanted your help to find a publisher. You took it, and you showed it to Károly. Maybe you were just asking him his opinion as to the quality of the scholarship, whether it was worth publishing or not. I expect that as soon as he saw it, he remembered the diaries that he had happened upon in Budapest. Without Anna, Károly would never had made the connection. As with Selena Morison, those who had benefitted unjustly from her work chose to malign her, calling her dishonest, mentally unbalanced, if not downright mad. We do know that, unlike Selena, Anna knew of the betrayal, and that she confronted those responsible.

"How could you think that she wouldn't know, that she wouldn't recognize her work? In this day and age! Did you really think she wouldn't put two and two together? That she would think that Károly found the diaries quite independently, which he quite possibly could have, when the publisher was you, Frank? Or did you just think if you kept telling everybody she was crazy, citing the fact that her children had been taken from her and she hadn't left the house in three years, that no matter what she said, no one would believe her?"

"You shouldn't have done that, Frank," Cybil said. "Did you chase her onto that bridge?"

"Don't be ridiculous," Frank said.

"I did not," Károly said, looking at me. "I would not, could not, do such a thing."

"Of course not," Frank said. "This is a simple case of failing to credit someone. It is unfortunate, but we will correct it in the next printing, won't we, Károly?" Károly said nothing.

"No, it isn't. But you did go to see her that night, didn't you? One of you? Maybe both of you?" I said. Károly turned back from his contemplation of the river.

"No," Frank said.

"For God's sake, Frank, tell the truth," Károly said.

Frank just stood there. "Let me help you, Frank," I said. "You were celebrating that night. You were on the prowl and you were looking for some action. Unfortunately you had to use the drugs you had planned for another purpose to keep me from going to see Anna. Later that night, you went looking for her, and you found her, where, out on the street somewhere?"

"She killed herself, okay? We did go to try to fix things up, but she was hysterical. We drove around in my car for awhile, Károly in the backseat trying to be charming and persuasive with an hysterical female, and then at the top of the street north of the bridge, she got out and started running. We went after her. Maybe she thought we meant her harm, but we didn't. She ran out onto the bridge. I drove my car into something at the end of the bridge, and then got out and tried to stop her. It was terrible," he said. "But I didn't push her over. Neither of us did. She did it all by herself. She was unbalanced. You can say she wasn't, but she was."

"Please believe me," Károly said, looking directly at me. "What he says is true. We, I, did not push her off that bridge."

"Poor Anna," Morgan said.

Cybil sobbed uncontrollably. "I think I knew," she said. "In my heart. She told me she'd been working on something and she asked me to find Frank to help her with it. I just couldn't bear to admit something like this could happen. I think maybe I felt if I just kept quiet, it wouldn't really have happened. I called you one night, Lara. I debated about whether to say anything. We were all such good friends back then, the Divas, and Frank and Károly. Those were the happiest days of my life. What happened to us?"

"Life is what happened," Morgan said. "Just life."

"It's over," Frank said. "We should have attributed Anna's work correctly. It had terrible consequences that we didn't anticipate. But this was unforeseen. If you insist, we will tell the authorities when we get back, but I don't see what we can be accused of. It was all most unfortunate, that's all."

"Perhaps you're forgetting Mihály Kovács," I said.

"What about him?" Károly said.

"He's dead, murdered," I said.

"That's impossible," Károly said. "I talked to him just a few days ago, before I came to Budapest. He was a little concerned about a business matter we were involved in, but otherwise perfectly fine."

"Not any more," I said. "I'm afraid he's dead, brutally murdered."

"How would you know Kovács?" Károly said to me.

"She found out from me," Diana said. "She's been helping us prove the Venus is a fake." A sound escaped from Károly's lips, something like a groan.

"I've been trying to prove it's real, Károly. And I did, except there were unexpected consequences," I said.

"Who the hell is Mihály Kovács?" Morgan said.

"The antique dealer who is supposed to have sold the Venus to Károly," I said. "Except that he didn't, because Károly had it already. His parents took it with them when they escaped from Hungary during the Revolution of 1956. Isn't that right, Károly? Isn't that the business matter he was a little concerned about? You didn't even know what you had until your parents died, and Anna's thesis almost miraculously fell into your hands. You would probably never have figured it out if you hadn't seen the drawings in her material." He bowed his head.

"And the real reason that you didn't want Anna to tell her tale, was that it would open up the question of the Venus's authenticity, and you really didn't want to do that, because you had essentially defrauded the Cottingham. You paid Kovács, and he in turn took his cut and paid you. You got a million dollars from Lily Larrington, supposedly paid $600,000 to Kovács but pocketed most of it, and then what? Gave a whole bunch of it to Frank to publish the book and save his firm? You've both done rather well, haven't you, from Anna's research? Frank gets paid twice to publish the catalog, in a sense, and Károly gets to take care of some of his debts and more."

"So what? That's the way business is done," Frank said. "Anyway, I'm not the one who had a twenty-five thousand-year-old carving in my garage."

"No, but you're probably the one who killed Mihály Kovács when he got cold feet and tried to tell me what he'd done," I said. "I went and scared him very badly by asking a lot of questions about the provenance. I expect he knew he would be in a bit of trouble if anyone found out his part in this. He followed me for a few days, right up the side of a cliff. I had a feeling someone was following me. I have no idea whether or not he knew you were following him. You hit him on the head with a stone, did you not, and then made it look as if he'd fallen and hit his head on it? What would you have done if I hadn't stayed in that cave? If I had come out and seen you? Would you have killed me, too?"

"No!" Károly said. "Tell me, Frank, that this isn't true."

"Are we talking murder, here?" Morgan said. Frank did not reply.

Károly took out his cell phone and started to dial. "I'm calling the police," he said, coming to stand beside me. "I will tell them everything. I cannot continue to live this lie. I did not kill anyone, Lara. You must believe that, no matter what else you may think of me."

Károly had the phone up to his ear when Frank made his move. He stepped forward, reached into the box containing

Stalin, and grabbed the gun. The Divas screamed as one. It had never occurred to me that the gun was loaded, nor that it would still work. He pointed it right at me. "Bitch!" he screamed. "You couldn't just let it be, could you?"

As Frank pulled the trigger, Károly stepped in front of me.

EPILOGUE

IF YOU LOOK CLOSELY AT THE SIDE WALL OF THE MUSTARD
yellow apartment building at Thököly út 61 in Budapest,
you will see a statue of a woman. The sculpture, rather
unsettling it must be said, is thought to have been put there
by a man as a memorial to his wife who stood on that balcony every day waiting for him to come home from the
Great War. If the story is true, she died in the terrible
influenza epidemic that swept through Europe at the end of
the war—one day before his return.

For me, that statue represents Selena Morison waiting for
her T, whoever he was, while the work she had done was
appropriated by others, who not only robbed her of the
credit her work was due, but of her good character. Most
especially it reminds me of Anna, a prisoner of her phobia
and unhappy life, waiting to hear from a man she thought
she knew and probably loved, like the rest of us, only to

learn hours before her death, just how untrustworthy a man he was.

There is another image of Budapest I carry with me. It is a simple marker on a grave in Városliget, the city park, put there many years ago to honor a city benefactor. At the benefactor's request, there is no name nor dates on it, only one word carved into the stone. That word is *Fuit,* Latin for *he was.* Károly Molnár was. He was a comet streaking across the sky shedding a light so dazzling it was almost painful to look at before it burned itself out. He was a proud, indeed arrogant man, whose drive to succeed blinded him to facts that did not support his unshakable faith in his own destiny.

He was a man I once loved. I have no idea whether he stepped in front of that bullet to save me or, perhaps more likely, because he'd rather be dead than publicly humiliated and possibly charged with fraud. I do not wish to delude myself on that score. There were more than enough illusions deserving to be shattered in those few days I spent in Hungary.

I doubt very much that the police will ever be able to do anything about Anna's death, nor that of Mihály Kovács. They have, however, had no difficulty charging Frank in the shooting death of Károly. He is claiming it was an accident, which I suppose it was, given I, and not Károly, was probably the target. It may be that he was as surprised as the rest of us that there was one bullet left in that gun, and that, old as it was, it would work at all. But there was, and it did. Heaven knows, there were enough witnesses.

I haven't seen much of the Divas since, although no doubt we'll all be together in court in Budapest in due course. Morgan, whom I have stayed in touch with, has left Woodward. She got enough money from the divorce settlement to open a very posh fitness club. She gave Cybil a year's membership absolutely free. She also offered one to Courtney Cottingham. Woodward, you see, doesn't give two hoots about how much money he had to pay Morgan, because about six months after the events in Hungary, Major Cottingham succumbed to Alzheimer's disease. Woodward and Courtney will marry as soon as his divorce becomes final. Morgan knows Courtney can afford the membership in her club. I expect she's trying to tell Courtney that if she gains a few pounds, her new beau Woodward won't be pleased.

The Cottingham has found a new publisher for the revised version of their catalog. They've told me that they're inviting Selena Mary Morison to the book launch in a month or two, and they're even paying her way. The new book credits both Selena B. and Anna Belmont. The museum has joined a number of other institutions and experts in arguing over Stalin, whose skull has still not been found. The Cottingham is also discussing restitution with Ágnes Varga's two sons. She may not be able to benefit much from it, at this stage of her life, but János is going to be able to take advantage of the "opportunity" to buy back the family home.

As for the remaining Divas, the Cottingham has declined to charge Diana with embezzlement, as long as she continues to make payments on her debt to them. I have no idea what Grace is doing. Furthermore, I couldn't care less. To her credit, it must be said, she did the best she could to save Károly, but even with all her medical training and experience, there was nothing that could be done.

Clive has gone back to being his usual unsympathetic self around me, after a week or two of rather tiresome concern, as has Diesel, the shop cat, who treats me with the disdain I clearly deserve.

*   *   *

A FEW DAYS after I got home from Budapest, I decided there
was something I needed to do. I waited until after midnight, turned off the motion detector, and then I carried a
stepladder to the back of my yard, propping it up against
the back wall. The neighbors on one side were away, I knew,
and I just hoped the others were sound sleepers. I knew I
was going to look like an idiot at best, up to no good more
likely, but I just didn't care.

I climbed up the ladder and peered cautiously over the
cemetery wall. The moon, almost full once again—had it
been that long since I'd been there?—cast shadows across
the gravestones. It was very, very quiet, just the occasional
creak of the branches of the old trees, and the low hum of
the city nearby.

"Hello, Anna," I said quietly, although the words
seemed to reverberate in the dark. "I've come to say goodbye. I've been thinking a lot about what I want to tell you.
A few days ago, our friend Cybil asked what had happened
to us all. The answer from Morgan was that life happened.
I suppose that sums it up, but the truth is, as you and I
both know, awful things happen in life. Relationships sour,
people's careers are thwarted through no fault of their own,
people steal from you, your friends kill themselves or die a
violent death, and worst of all, children die. So what do you
do? You keep going, Anna. That's what. You lost a child,
your beautiful little boy. That is a terrible, terrible thing to
happen to anyone. But you had two other children. Your
daughters are two of the sweetest little things I've ever
seen. They needed you. Shutting yourself up in a tiny
apartment with your poor old mother was not the answer."
I knew my voice was getting progressively louder and

louder, and I didn't seem to be able to stop myself. The Dea Muta was silent no more.

"Yes, you were betrayed by people you trusted," I said. It is possible I was shouting. "There were ways of dealing with that, too. I'll see to it, believe me, that you are given credit for the work you did. You could have done that yourself. You can't do it when you're dead. I do not understand why you did it, Anna. I don't believe I ever will. That's all I have to say."

I climbed down the ladder, watched as my neighbor's lights came on—one can only imagine what they thought was going on—went back into the house, called Rob, or at least his voice mail, and left a long, long message. That horrible digital voice cut me off several times. I told him everything, all the things I had done I thought he wouldn't approve of, the moral and ethical decisions I had made, how I felt about him, our relationship, and his daughter. I told him I thought that what had been wrong in our relationship was that we had never really talked about the things that mattered, that maybe I hadn't trusted him to trust in me. I told him about Anna, the Divas, and Frank. Finally, I told him about Károly. Not everything, maybe, but enough. Then, I put on my most comfortable, if ugliest, nightie, climbed into bed, and slept twelve hours straight.

It was afternoon when I came to. I peered at myself in the bathroom mirror. It was a terrible sight. My hair stood straight up, my face looked squished, and the ugly nightie hadn't improved any, overnight. I was starving. I went into the kitchen, and sitting there at the counter was Rob.

"You look nice," he said.

"I know," I said.

"No, really, you do, in some indefinable way. You got some

sleep," he said. "Maybe that's it. Shall I fix you some eggs?"

"How did you get in here?" I said. "You gave me back my key."

"I made a hugely dubious ethical decision, perhaps even illegal, and used some tools we law enforcement officers have to let myself in. People do that, you know, from time to time. Make dubious ethical decisions, I mean. I always think you have to look at the intentions behind them before you get too judgmental."

"And you had good intentions?"

"I didn't come to steal your toothpaste, if that's what you mean. I was worried about you. That was some message, or rather those were some messages, you left."

"Perhaps rather too much information, I'm thinking, in the cold light of dawn. Or is it the bright light of mid-afternoon?"

"Maybe a little bit more than I wanted to know, but on balance, better that than nothing at all. You were right. We didn't talk about what really mattered. Neither of us did."

"I know," I said.

"So do you want to get married?" he asked.

"No. I've done that already."

"Okay. Do you want to get a place together? I mean you sell your place, I sell mine, and we buy a place that's ours?"

"I'm not sure," I said.

"Okay. Do you want to get back together again?"

"I think maybe I do. Do you?"

"Yes, I do."

"Even after all that stuff I told you?"

"Yes."

"Okay, then."

"Good," he said. "As the song goes, one out of three ain't bad."

"Two," I said.

"Two? Okay, I'll call the real estate people."

"The song," I said. "The song says two out of three ain't bad."

He grinned at me. "I believe that's a gotcha," he said. "How do you want your eggs?

LYN HAMILTON

ARCHAEOLOGICAL MYSTERIES

"Hamilton's archaeological mysteries [are] sure to have
armchair travelers on the edge of their
settees. At once erudite and entertaining...
jaunty whodunits."
—*New York Times Book Review*